"When Mary Margaret Miller need: [ ] Amish community, she takes a vacation to Pinecraft, Florida, and is surprised to not only find true friends but also meet a handsome and charming Amish carpenter. *Her Heart's Desire* is a tender journey that explores friendship, heartbreak, second chances, forgiveness, and finding true love. Shelley Shepard Gray highlights that God's grace and mercy is with us even when we're certain we're alone and don't fit in with our community. Fans of Amish fiction will be hooked on page one and won't stop reading until they reach the end!"

Amy Clipston, bestselling author of *Building a Future*

"Childhood scars can stick around for a very long time. Healing those emotional wounds sets the tone in *Her Heart's Desire* by Shelley Shepard Gray. First in the A Season in Pinecraft series, *Her Heart's Desire* is full of endearing characters with insecurities and trust issues, each one lifted to a better place through hope, faith, and, of course, love. This entertaining tale of repaired friendships and kindled romances will delight readers."

Suzanne Woods Fisher, bestselling author
of *A Season on the Wind*

"*Her Heart's Desire*, Shelley Shepard Gray's latest novel, is destined to delight lovers of her sweet Amish romances. Set in beautiful Pinecraft, Florida, the story of three young Amish women who see themselves as wallflowers is a new take on the 'mean girls' theme popular in mainstream films and books. Watching these women blossom and gain confidence in their newfound friendships offers hope to any of us who have experienced the loneliness of being on the outside looking in. Gray gives her readers the additional gift of not one but two lovely romances. A sweet read!"

Kelly Irvin, bestselling author of *Love's Dwelling*

Her Heart's Desire

Her Heart's Desire

SHELLEY SHEPARD GRAY

Revell

a division of Baker Publishing Group
Grand Rapids, Michigan

Published by Revell
a division of Baker Publishing Group
PO Box 6287, Grand Rapids, MI 49516-6287
www.revellbooks.com

Printed in the United States of America

Library of Congress Cataloging-in-Publication Data
Names: Gray, Shelley Shepard, author.
Title: Her heart's desire / Shelley Shepard Gray.
Description: Grand Rapids, MI : Revell, a division of Baker Publishing Group,
   [2023] | Series: A season in pinecraft
Identifiers: LCCN 2022018325 | ISBN 9780800741679 (paperback) | ISBN
   9780800742683 (casebound) | ISBN 9781493439737 (ebook)
Subjects: LCGFT: Romance fiction. | Christian fiction. | Novels.
Classification: LCC PS3607.R3966 H464 2023 | DDC 813/.6—dc23/eng/20220420
LC record available at https://lccn.loc.gov/2022018325

Scripture used in this book, whether quoted or paraphrased by the characters, is taken from the *Holy Bible*, New Living Translation, copyright © 1996, 2004, 2007, 2013, 2015 by Tyndale House Foundation. Used by permission of Tyndale House Publishers, Inc., Carol Stream, Illinois 60188. All rights reserved.

The author is represented by The Seymour Agency.

Baker Publishing Group publications use paper produced from sustainable forestry practices and post-consumer waste whenever possible.

23 24 25 26 27 28 29   7 6 5 4 3 2 1

For my lovely friend Clara,
who gave me my first tour of Pinecraft.
Here's hoping that we'll get to meet
there again one day!

To those who use well what they are given,
even more will be given.

> Matthew 25:29

Do what you can, with what you have,
where you are.

> Amish proverb

1

There were only two beds in the motel room. Two beds for the three of them to share. Looking at the somewhat shabby space, Mary Margaret Miller felt her insides knot.

When the Pioneer Trails bus driver had announced they'd needed to make an emergency stop in Georgia because the storm was too fierce to drive through, it had almost sounded like a grand adventure. Mary had never traveled much farther than Sugarcreek or Berlin, Ohio. And though she did know quite a few Englischers, most everyone she knew was Amish, just like her.

She'd been so excited to see new things and meet new people, she hadn't even been too concerned when the bus pulled into the parking lot of a small, rather run-down motel just off the highway. But now, as she stood next to two girls she barely knew and studied the forlorn pair of beds, Mary realized that her spur-of-the-moment decision to travel to Pinecraft, Florida, by herself hadn't been the greatest idea.

Not at all.

Or perhaps her earlier prayers on the bus were to blame.

After all, she had suggested to the Lord that surely anything would be better than being on a large bus in the middle of an ice storm. Maybe He had decided to take her at her word.

Lilly broke the silence first. "Do either of you want to guess what that stain on the wall is from?"

All three of them turned to stare at the dark blob seeping down from the ceiling to rest near the light switch. "I-I've been trying to pretend it wasn't there," Betsy said. "Obviously, that plan isn't going too well."

"I would say that I've been trying to not think about the bedspreads, but I canna seem to think about anything besides who all has touched them previously," Lilly murmured.

Betsy wrinkled her nose. "M-maybe we should put them on the floor, jah? They m-might be infested."

"That would surely be best," Lilly said.

Straightening her slim shoulders, Betsy glanced Mary's way. "Are you all right?"

"Hmm? Oh, jah." Finding her voice at last, Mary attempted to sound optimistic. "Do you girls have any thoughts about how we should decide who gets to sleep alone tonight?"

"I don't mind sharing a bed with either of you," Betsy said. "I doubt I'll s-sleep much anyway."

"It doesn't matter to me either," Lilly said. "Betsy might be wide awake, but I'm exhausted. I've been so nervous about this trip, I haven't slept much for the last week. I could almost sleep on the floor." As they all looked at the threadbare carpet under their feet, Lilly wrinkled her nose. "Scratch that. I'm not going to put my head anywhere near that carpet."

Mary smiled at her. "I wouldn't let you even if you wanted to do such a thing. You'd likely get a skin rash or something."

After carefully pulling off the comforter and tossing it in the corner of the room, Betsy sat down on one of the beds. "That settles it, then. I'll share this bed with Lilly, and you may have the other one all to yourself, Mary."

Now Mary was embarrassed. Why had she even brought up their sleeping arrangements in the first place? No doubt the other girls thought she was the type of person who always needed her way, even at the expense of others. Tentatively, she said, "Sorry if I sounded pushy. I . . . well, I sometimes say all the wrong things."

Betsy shook her head. "There's nothing to forgive. If we're being honest, I-I'm so happy to be out of my little Kentucky town and doing something different, even staying in this motel feels exciting."

"I feel the same way," Lilly added as she carefully pulled the straight pins from her kapp, then set them on the dresser. "I can't even remember if I've ever had a sleepover with two friends."

"M-me neither," Betsy said with a smile before she seemed to realize what she'd just insinuated. "I mean, not that you two are my friends or anything."

Mary gaped at the other two women. All three of them were in their early twenties. Betsy, with her dark hair and matching eyes, was a true beauty, and Lilly looked like everyone's best friend. She was so chatty and smiley. How could they, too, have trouble making friends? It didn't seem possible.

Worried there was a private joke between them that she was unaware of, she frowned.

As soon as she did, Betsy said, "Did I offend you, Mary?"

"Nee."

"Are y-you sure?"

Seconds sped by as she debated what to say. It had been so

long since she'd felt like she could be completely honest. No, that wasn't right. It had been a long time since she'd been able to allow herself to be vulnerable. People could be cruel, and she'd learned that from personal experience. She'd been bullied and teased by so many kids when she was in school.

Almost everything inside her was protesting letting even the smallest bit of her guard down. Her heart wasn't eager to be bruised, especially not now, with these two new girls. If she said the wrong thing, it could ruin her whole vacation.

On the heels of that was the memory of her evening prayers a few weeks ago. She'd knelt at the side of her bed, praying and crying and asking the Lord to help her make a new start. And He had. In just a few weeks, she'd sold enough of her greeting cards to buy a bus ticket to Pinecraft for a long, much-needed vacation.

Her parents, well aware of how miserable she'd been for years, had been supportive. They'd even chipped in a little so she could stay at the Marigold Inn for two weeks. And her father refused to let her pay him back. All he asked was that she try to be positive while she was on vacation. Try to let other people see the *real* Mary Margaret that he and her mamm knew and loved.

Even Preacher Marlin had stopped by their house to offer encouragement. He'd brought over some of his favorite postcards from Pinecraft and told her about each one. While sipping his lukewarm coffee liberally laced with cream and sugar, Preacher Marlin even confided that he'd had one or two adventures on the beach in Siesta Key.

She'd giggled, thinking about their gentle, seventy-year-old preacher kicking up his heels in the sand and surf.

But most importantly, Mary's favorite preacher had reminded her that she was a person worth knowing. They'd prayed together about that too. By the time he'd left, her resolve had grown even stronger to experience as much as she possibly could on her vacation.

Now, sitting in the motel room, all those good feelings settled in her heart. She'd promised people who cared about her to try to come out of her shell. Was she really going to throw all those promises away and go back to the person she'd been in Trail, Ohio?

No. No, she was not.

After taking off her kapp and shoes, she sat down on the bed too. "Betsy, you didn't offend me at all. To tell you the truth, I was just thinking that both of you seemed like the type of women who have lots of friends and beaus. I was surprised." Realizing that neither had said a word about boyfriends, she cleared her throat. "Or do you have boyfriends?"

Betsy chuckled as if the question was mighty humorous. "N-nee."

"I don't either," Lilly said without even a flash of a smile. "What about you?"

Mary realized then that she could either keep all her bad experiences and disappointments to herself . . . or she could be completely honest. The decision was easy to make. She didn't want to lie and had the feeling that her lies wouldn't sound believable anyway.

Taking a deep, fortifying breath, she said, "The truth is . . . back in my hometown of Trail, I didn't really take."

Lilly's eyes widened. "What do you mean?"

"I wasn't popular," she replied, inwardly wincing because "not popular" was a big understatement. "I wasn't popular at all with the boys in my church district." Deciding she might as well admit the whole truth, she added, "Nor with the girls."

Comforted by Betsy's and Lilly's sympathetic looks, she added, "I've always kind of been on my own."

"Me too," Betsy said. "I have bad asthma and it's kept me from doing a lot of activities everyone else does. Plus, I used to stutter even more than I do now, so it was hard to even speak to the other kids." She shuddered. "E-every time I get upset or really excited, my mouth seems to freeze. I was teased a lot."

Teasing someone for stuttering was especially cruel. "I'm sorry."

"I am too, b-but I've learned to accept how things are." She smiled at Mary. "I only shared that so you'd know I mean it when I say I've spent a lot of time by myself as well."

Lilly joined them on the bed, leaning up against the fake wood headboard. "I've been a loner too. My parents adopted me and made sure everyone knew it."

When both Mary and Betsy gasped, Lilly chuckled softly. "Sorry, I guess that came out kind of bad. Was it too much to hear from a relative stranger?"

"Not at all," Mary said quickly. When Lilly gave her a knowing look, she smiled. "But it was a lot to hear so boldly."

After they shared another smile, Lilly looked down at her lap. "I don't usually confide so much. Actually, I never do. I guess I feel comfortable with the two of you. So comfortable I don't even think about how my words might sound. I'll try to be better."

"Don't," Betsy said. "I like that you're being so honest. B-be as honest as you want."

"Okay, then." Lilly took a deep breath. "I love my adoptive parents—I really do—but there's been times when I wish I wasn't a symbol of their good works. It's been hard to live down."

She rolled her eyes. "Here we are, all Amish. All in communities where living simply and being part of the group is valued. But instead of feeling like I was just one of the crowd, I was always known as 'poor Lilly, whose parents adopted her.'" She lowered her voice. "Or poor Lilly; there must have been something wrong with her because her real parents gave her up."

"Ouch," Betsy said.

"The label has stung. I'm not gonna lie."

The three of them regarded each other, and a new calm seemed to fill the air.

"You two are wallflowers like me," Mary blurted.

Betsy raised an eyebrow. "What's that?"

"It's, um, an old-fashioned term. It's a girl who kind of stands on the sidelines and watches while everyone else does things." Trying to think of a better example, she said, "Once, I checked a romance novel out at the library that was about wallflowers. See, in this book, all the girls were asked to dance except a pair of women. They were essentially ignored and had to spend most of the evening sitting in chairs and wishing for boys to ask them to dance."

"While everyone else lives, you mean," Lilly said. "If being a wallflower is the correct term for it, then that fits me perfectly. That's what I've been doing for years now—standing off to the side and waiting to be noticed."

Betsy nodded. "While everyone else just walks by."

Mary felt a lump form in her throat. The girls' comments were so close to how she often privately felt, it was stunning.

Betsy and Lilly seemed really nice. It was too bad that they also felt like they'd been overlooked.

Mary felt a little depressed . . . and maybe a little angry too. She wasn't perfect, but she wasn't a bad person.

It wasn't right. There was more to her than that. She was nice, was reasonably attractive, and had a really good heart. There was no reason every other girl in her hometown had a better chance than she did of finding a beau or making good friends. It was time people started seeing the person she always wished they'd see.

It was time to start anew.

"I don't know how you two feel, but I'm sick of being a wallflower," she blurted.

Betsy's eyes widened. "Well, of course you are. B-being a wallflower stinks."

Lilly giggled. "Indeed."

"Okay, no pun intended. However—"

Mary interrupted. "What I'm trying to say is that I don't want to just stand around and hope someone notices me or invites me to do things anymore."

"I don't either, but what can you do?" Lilly asked. "It's like our futures were determined when we were little girls."

"I can't do much at home, but I can be different in Pinecraft, right?" Though she was doing her best to sound confident, Mary realized she was really looking to them for guidance and support.

Betsy slowly nodded. "You're right. I can't exactly hide my stuttering, but no one here has to know that I'm an asthmatic with an overprotective mamm."

"No one is going to know I'm an adopted foster child except for you two," Lilly said. "What about you, Mary?"

"No one is going to bring up any embarrassing situations from my past because I'm not going to say a word about them. From this point on, all I'm going to be is Mary Margaret from Trail, Ohio."

16

Feeling cleansed by their confessions and almost buoyant, she added, "And you know what? I don't care if we make a ton of other friends anyway. If the three of us stick together, we can have our own fun, right?"

"Right." Betsy grinned. "Starting this minute, we are wall-flowers no more."

A knock on the door interrupted their conversation. After peeking through the peephole and seeing Anna, their English guide, and her husband Jerry, the bus driver, Mary opened the door. "Yes?"

Jerry held out a pizza box. "Here you go, girls. One pepperoni pizza and three sodas. Do you need anything else?"

Mary looked at the other two girls, then shook her head. "Danke, but nee. We have everything we need right here."

Anna smiled at the three of them. "I knew it. I told Jerry here that if there were three people on our bus who were going to take this setback in stride, it was you three pretty girls. I bet none of you has ever met a stranger."

Mary just smiled, but as she closed the door, she felt a surge of satisfaction. She might be in a run-down motel room in the middle of an ice storm . . . but already her future was looking a whole lot brighter.

2

Two days later, Mary was still getting the hang of life at the inn. She might be away from her parents, but she was absolutely still being supervised!

"I hope you aren't planning to get up from the table already, Mary Margaret," Nancy White, the proprietress of the Marigold Inn, said as she entered the dining room with yet another heaping platter of fresh fruit and blueberry muffins. "Breakfast is the most important part of the day, you know."

Mary felt her cheeks heat up in embarrassment, but she forced herself to answer the gregarious woman who acted as if they were old friends even though they'd arrived only yesterday. "I've already had a plate of eggs and bacon."

"Well, you're going to want one of my blueberry muffins, dear. I don't mean to brag, but they really are good." Nancy smiled at the dozen people sitting at various tables in the large dining area before disappearing through the swinging double doors.

"Nancy's so friendly. I can't get over how she seems to have memorized all of our names too," Lilly said as soon as the coast was clear.

"She is friendly, that is for sure." Mary thought she might be a little too outgoing to completely relax around. But that was likely because Mary was used to simply fading into the background. However, she couldn't deny that the inn was lovely. Each room had white wicker furniture, rocking chairs, lovely oak floors, and queen-size beds covered with crisp white sheets and bright quilts. Being in such surroundings simply made one feel happy.

Lilly stood up. "I'm going to get a muffin. Want me to grab you one too?"

"Nee, danke. I'll get my own in a minute."

"Suit yourself."

Mary sipped her coffee and covertly glanced around the room. To her relief, no one was staring at her plate. As soon as she thought that, she was tempted to shake her head in dismay. *Of course* no one was staring at her plate. They didn't know her. Not one of these people was from her childhood. None of them knew she'd been teased about her weight for almost a decade. Here, she was just a normal-size woman. One of many staying at the beautiful inn.

Shaking off her worries, she walked over to the large antique sideboard, picked up a small plate, and carefully chose five strawberries and one of Nancy's muffins.

"I'm glad she didn't scare you off," a man said as he walked to her side.

She turned to smile at him, then almost froze. The man looked about her age and was gorgeous. With his steel-blue eyes, shorter than average dark brown hair, and muscular build, he looked a bit like a model in a magazine. Caught off guard by both his looks and his comment, she sputtered, "I'm sorry?"

"I just meant that Nancy can be a little overbearing. I've

noticed that not everyone cares for her attention." He lowered his voice. "I'm pretty sure that she doesn't mean anything by it, though. It's just her way."

"I like Nancy. I imagine being outgoing and friendly is a necessary quality when one is an innkeeper. Besides, the blueberry muffins do look good."

"Trust me, they are. I've been here three days, and instead of sleeping late, I find myself waking up early just to make sure I get a plateful of her cooking." He grinned at her. "Just to let you know, if you don't get here in time, all the best choices will be gone."

"Danke. We only arrived last night, so I appreciate the tip."

"No worries. By the way, my name is Jayson. Jayson Raber."

Jayson seemed so nice, it was almost easy to let her guard down. "Nice to meet you. I'm Mary Margaret Miller."

His eyebrows rose. "That's a lot of *M*s."

She chuckled. "I've heard that before. Most everyone just calls me Mary, though."

"I bet." He looked amused but not in a mean way. "Will you be here long?"

"Two weeks. What about you?"

"A little longer. Sixteen days, I think it is."

"When I first planned my trip, I thought about only coming for a week, but that didn't seem long enough at all," she confided. "It's freezing up in Ohio."

"I hope you have a good time, Mary. Maybe we'll even see each other around town some. Pinecraft ain't all that big, you know."

She knew he was being kind, but there was a part of her that loved the thought of them chatting again. Just as she was about to walk away, the warm Southern twang in his voice registered.

"Where are you from, Jayson? Is it someplace in the south, by chance?"

Immediately, his expression turned guarded. "I'm from Kentucky."

"Ah. That's what I thought." She was about to explain that her new friend Betsy was from Kentucky too, but she realized he'd walked away.

Mary glanced his way as she walked back to her chair. He didn't even look up. Feeling a bit confused, she sat down and took a bite of the muffin without really tasting it.

Lilly leaned close. "Oh my stars! He's so cute! And he talked to you too. What did he say?"

There was no way she was going to admit that she'd already failed in her first conversation with him. "Hmm? Oh, nothing really. We talked about Nancy's breakfasts and how long we're staying."

"Probably so he can find you again!"

"Oh, he was only being polite."

"You think that's the only reason?"

"Lilly, you sound disappointed! How come?"

She shrugged. "Because he looked like he was anxious to meet you. He went over to the sideboard the moment you did. When I saw you two talking, I thought you had hit it off."

She thought they had too, but she must have misunderstood. Not sure what she'd done that had upset him, she felt some of her newfound confidence slip away. "I'm sure his walking to the sideboard then was just a coincidence," she said.

"Maybe. Maybe not." Lilly took a sip of coffee, then said, "I bet you two will have more to say to each other next time you talk."

Mary cleared her throat. "Lilly, don't you remember our pact in that motel room? We're not going to worry about impressing anyone. The three of us are just going to have a good time."

"I didn't forget, but I'm just saying if the opportunity arises, we shouldn't ignore it." Lowering her voice, she added, "You have a pretty smile, Mary. Next time he approaches, you should smile at him. I bet he'll warm up to you then."

She didn't really care if she and Jayson hit it off or not—but she sure didn't want to be uncomfortable around him. She'd had enough of that back in Trail. But Lilly was simply trying to help, so she said, "Thanks for the advice. I'll try to be as friendly as I can next time he and I are around each other."

"Hey, you two!" Betsy called out as she finally joined them. "How's breakfast?"

Mary couldn't help but giggle. She couldn't remember when she'd ever had so many conversations about a single breakfast. "It's good. You should go get a plate. Be sure to get a muffin too."

"Already on it."

Bemused by Betsy's eagerness, Mary leaned back and sipped her coffee. She was beginning to realize that Betsy was a joyous eater. She loved to try new foods and never failed to find enjoyment in a meal. It was adorable and a little envy-inducing, since Betsy was so slim and put together.

Everything from the perfectly placed pins on her dress to her neatly trimmed nails to her spotless white kapp was done with care. Mary couldn't help but admire the way Betsy always looked so fresh and pretty.

"She has biscuits!" Betsy announced as she joined them. "This Kentucky girl is mighty happy. Now, what do you want to do today?"

"How about we go to the market or rent bicycles?"

"I think going for a bike ride sounds like a lot of fun, but just not today," Lilly said. "I'm still so tired."

"What about you, Betsy?" Mary asked.

"Do you think it would be okay if I rent one of those three-wheeler bikes instead of the regular ones?"

"Sure. I mean, that's fine with me."

"Then I'll be happy to go for a bike ride too. I'm not very good at riding bikes."

"Betsy, does your church district not allow you to ride them?" Lilly asked. "A lot of them don't."

"No, we can. It's just real hilly near my house so mei eldras never allowed me to ride much in case I ran out of breath. It's my fault more than anything." She smiled more broadly. "Here, it's nice and flat. I'm going to become a great bicyclist."

Mary smiled. "Here's your opportunity then. I'll ride bikes with you if you'd like."

"Of course I'd like that."

Nancy came bustling in. "Ladies, how is everything? Do you have any questions I can answer?"

"We were just thinking it would be fun to rent bicycles," Betsy said. "Where could we do that?"

"There's a real nice place to do that just a few stops away on the SCAT—that's our bus line, the Sarasota County Area Transit. Be careful riding your bikes, though. Some folks don't like you riding too fast."

"Don't worry," Betsy replied. "We're going to take everything here real slow and easy."

The minute Nancy turned away, Lilly and Mary started laughing. "What did I say?" Betsy asked.

"Nothing. It's just the way you phrase things with that Kentucky accent of yours. It's really cute," Mary said.

Betsy rolled her eyes as she speared a strawberry from her plate.

Just as Mary giggled again, she caught the eye of the man she'd been talking to.

Though she thought about taking Lilly's advice and smiling at him, there was no way she was going to set herself up to be embarrassed again.

Quickly, she turned away, determined to pretend Jayson wasn't even there. Just like all the boys back in Trail used to do whenever she went to Sunday night singings.

It was too bad that being rude didn't make her feel any better. If anything, it made her feel a whole lot more confused.

3

As he walked next to his friend Danny on the sidewalk, Jayson Raber told himself to think about their upcoming golf game. Or the blue sky. Or even to listen to the group of women in front of them tease each other and chatter like magpies.

Instead, all he seemed to be able to do was think about what a jerk he'd been to Mary Margaret Miller. From the moment she'd entered the dining room, he'd been drawn to her. Maybe it was the way her dark blond hair looked kind of like spun gold under her kapp. Or that her light brown eyes were framed by dark lashes. Or that she seemed just a little shy and a little overwhelmed by the people, all the food set out, and Nancy.

Whatever the reason, she'd been the first woman in a while he'd wanted to get to know better. But then, of course, just as soon as he'd gotten up the nerve to talk to her, he'd gone and ruined it.

Yep, one could say that his conversation with her had gone as well as a bullfrog jumping into a cement swimming pool. Instead of simply answering her question about his hometown, he'd imagined she was looking down on his accent.

Now he realized that she'd been doing nothing of the sort. She'd simply been trying to make conversation.

To make matters worse, five minutes later when Mary was giggling with all her friends and caught him staring at her, she looked away like he wasn't even there. He probably deserved it, but it still kind of stung.

He should have handled things better. But maybe it was for the best. It wasn't like he was free to date anyway. He was practically promised to someone else—thanks to a deal he'd made with Ellen Schrock's father.

With effort, he pushed all thoughts of Ellen, her father, and the ugly reasons he'd been forced to even contemplate such a match to the back of his mind. He had a little over two weeks of freedom here in Florida, and he meant to enjoy it.

Real life would return soon enough.

"Jayson, did you hear me?"

Danny had just said something. "What?"

"*What?* What do you mean by 'what'? How about this: What's going on with you? Did you get up on the wrong side of the bed or something?"

"Maybe. Sorry."

His best friend rolled his eyes as they walked toward the Pinecraft Golf Shop. "Jayson, we've been planning this golf game for weeks. There's no chance of rain, and we've got two weeks to spend together. But instead of acting pleased, you look like you'd rather have a migraine."

Leave it to Danny to lay it on thick. "Oh, settle down. I'm fine and I know I don't look that bad."

"You do. No lie, ya look like I'm taking you out for a swim in the Everglades."

Jayson groaned. "Of course you had to bring that up. Again."

Danny grinned. "Give me some credit. I waited almost four days to tease you."

"I'm almost impressed," he joked.

Jayson had met Danny Troyer almost ten years ago. Like Jayson, Danny was also New Order Amish, but he had grown up in Pinecraft. His father and uncles were behind-the-scenes investors in several Amish-themed motels, rental properties, and restaurants in the area. Because of that, Danny had grown up around all sorts of folks. He seemed to have an easy acceptance of just about everyone, from the English and Amish from all over the country to the foreign tourists visiting America for the first time.

His family was wealthy, and the Lord had given him an ability to chat easily with just about anyone.

In contrast, Jayson grew up in a small house right outside of Marion, Kentucky. Most Amish families there were farmers or ran greenhouses. He was blessed to have learned his trade from a number of gifted carpenters. His skills enabled him to work all over the county—at least when his sister, Joy, wasn't in need of his help.

Because he sometimes felt as if all the weight of the world was on his shoulders, he was a little bit quiet and a little bit reserved.

Years ago, back when his mother was alive, his father worked more, and Joy hadn't been diagnosed with diabetes, they'd taken the bus down to Pinecraft for a short vacation. Jayson met Danny on the beach almost immediately, and they became friends. Danny didn't seem to care that Jayson's family didn't have much money or that sometimes even his Pennsylvania Dutch carried a bit of Kentucky twang. He liked Jayson for who he was—and promptly taught him how to play golf.

Soon after, Jayson began planning to visit Danny as often as he could. The Lord must have been in favor of that, because one of Jayson's mother's brothers had a house on Siesta Key. Once, they'd even invited him to stay there. Sometimes Danny's parents bought him a bus ticket too.

As the young men grew older, Jayson's father grew resentful of his friendship with Danny. He started accusing Danny's parents of being too fancy and often tried to stop Jayson from visiting him. Jayson knew none of that was true and that his father said such things only so Jayson would stay home.

By that time, Mamm had gone to heaven and Daed was struggling. Because of that, Joy got used to going to Jayson for just about everything, just as he got used to being the one person in her life she could completely depend on. He'd never resented the change in their relationship. Actually, it was his privilege to help her in any way he could, especially since she'd been diagnosed with juvenile diabetes when she was nine.

Joy's health was usually good. All she needed to stay healthy were checkups and insulin. Neither of those things was cheap, however, so almost everything Jayson earned went to help the family, especially since their father hated to accept any help from the other members in their church community.

Their church community was loving, but it was also small. Most members had enough on their plates without adding the Rabers' burdens to them. Only Wood Schrock, their neighbor down the way, had ever seemed willing to go out of his way for Jayson. Not only had he helped him buy tools from time to time, he'd also encouraged Jayson's small trips down South. Only recently did he realize that Wood never did anything without expecting something in return. The man he used to admire so much now made him feel slightly uncomfortable.

Over the years, he and Danny played dozens of rounds of golf at dozens of area public golf courses, swam for miles at the beach, and even toured the Everglades once with his family. Danny, being a native Floridian, took the appearance of the occasional alligator in stride. Jayson, on the other hand, had taken one look at the fierce, overgrown reptile and decided to always stay as far away from them as possible—which Danny loved to tease him about.

Returning to the present, Jayson shrugged. "Sorry about my bad mood. I let something get under my skin that I shouldn't have. I'll shake it off."

"What happened?"

He didn't want to talk about it, but he also knew that Danny was going to bug him until he did. "It's nothing. I . . . well, I saw this pretty girl at breakfast this morning and decided to talk to her."

"And?"

"And at first everything seemed to be going okay. We weren't talking about anything important, just introducing ourselves . . . when she asked me about my accent."

"What's wrong with that?"

"I got embarrassed and walked away. Then the rest of the time she wouldn't even look at me."

Danny slowed to a stop. "You've got to get over that."

"I know." He did too. Though it made no sense, he'd always considered his accent to be a reminder of just how poor he was.

"You canna change your family or your circumstances, Jayson. To be honest, no one really cares about what your house looks like or if you have money in the bank."

That was easy for Danny to say because he'd always had both a house and money. Yes, Danny was Plain, but his father and grandfather were also shrewd businessmen. Jayson's Amish community in the heart of Crittenden County was far different. It didn't matter if one was English or Amish—nearly everyone struggled there. Jayson was sure that Danny had no idea what it was like to have to scrimp and save to pay for Joy's medical tests and drugs—and put healthy food on the table.

Danny was right, though. To think value came only from a bank account was wrong.

"You have a mighty big chip on your shoulder for a small-town boy."

Jayson inwardly winced. "I know, but still . . ."

Danny raised his eyebrows. "I'm gonna say it. Your problem ain't that you grew up poor; it's that you are somehow still thinking that you have to spend the rest of your life as the sole support for your sister and father."

"They need me."

"Joy needs you right now—maybe your father will have to find someone else to give him a helping hand if you aren't there."

"It's a moot point since everything is about to change anyway."

Danny raised his eyebrows. "Because?"

"Because right before I left, I told Wood that I would seriously think about his offer."

Danny stopped in his tracks. "You told me that Wood Schrock wanted you to marry his daughter!"

"Yes, but nothing has been decided." When Danny continued to stare at him, Jayson added weakly, "Ellen is fine."

"She's not fine for you, though, right? Not if you don't love her."

"I'm going to love having a better paying carpentry job and

not having to worry about how I'm going to take care of Joy. Ellen won't mind Joy living with us."

"It's still not right." Lowering his voice, he added, "Jayson, you've lost your mind."

Danny's criticism hurt, but he pushed it away. "Nee, I think I finally found it. At long last, I've stopped wishing for things that can never happen."

"Like marrying for love?" Danny asked sarcastically.

"Like thinking that my father will go back to the man he used to be."

Danny's expression softened. "Look, I don't mean to joke or sound unfeeling about your daed. I'm sorry about your father. I really am. But marrying a woman as part of a business arrangement ain't good."

"Again, it's just an idea. Ellen doesn't even know about any of this yet. Besides, I'm sure I'll grow to love her."

"You hope you will."

"I have no choice. I'm twenty-five years old. Joy is fourteen. I have to stop thinking that something is going to change. It's not." He was determined to take care of Joy. Determined to do something to be proud of. Wood Schrock could give him a good job as a carpenter. Even though it wasn't his dream job, it would be fine.

After they walked another block, Danny said, "All right. I'll respect your choices."

"Danke."

"But how about this? You're here in Florida for two more weeks, right?"

"Right."

"Why don't you give yourself a vacation from your life?"

"What?"

"Just be Jayson. Stop worrying about jobs and money and medical bills and your future. Have fun."

"We're playing golf today, right? I'm already planning on that."

"That's a good start, but how about you push yourself a bit too? Make a few new friends, maybe even flirt with a couple of girls."

"I can't do that. I'm practically promised to Ellen."

"I'm not asking you to break vows . . . but you don't love her, and nothing is official yet." Danny lowered his voice. "Jayson, I've known you for years. In that time, you've always worked, always put yourself last, and always stressed about Joy and your future. If your plans for the rest of your life are to get a job for a man you don't admire and marry a woman you don't love, I think you owe it to yourself to live a little for fourteen days."

"You don't think that's wrong?"

"Compared to everything else in your life? Nee."

Danny sounded so certain. Maybe it was wrong, but his idea sounded wonderful. Pushing aside all his responsibilities for a handful of days was tempting.

"I'll think about it."

"Good. I'm going to hold you to it. Now, can we get you some clubs and go play golf?"

"Absolutely. I'm going to rent them for the whole week. That way if you lose today, you'll be able to have a rematch."

"Jayson, Jayson, Jayson, when will you ever learn? You might be a lot of things, but I'm the better golfer. It's a proven fact."

Jayson laughed but didn't argue.

It was only an hour later, when they were on the SCAT and heading toward the golf course, that he wondered if maybe the Lord didn't think Danny's idea was bad at all. Because there, on the other side of the aisle, was Mary. When their eyes met, she blushed and looked away.

And then, to his surprise, she seemed to gather her courage and she met his eyes directly. Practically daring him to acknowledge her.

Pulse racing, he looked right back. And then, because he was trying to turn over a new leaf, he smiled.

Surprise flared in her eyes, but then she smiled right back.

All right, then. Maybe it really was time to live a little bit and enjoy himself. What could possibly go wrong?

4

I saw him looking at you," Betsy said. "He wasn't looking at anyone else either, so don't try to deny it."

Mary knew she wouldn't since she'd just gotten the privilege of receiving the full extent of Jayson's near-blinding smile. "We had a bit of a misunderstanding. Maybe he was apologizing."

"Maybe. Or maybe he simply thinks you're someone he wants to know better."

All this talk of boys and flirting embarrassed her, especially since she didn't have any experience with either flirting or being the recipient of that attention. "Here's where we rent the bikes. Are you ready?"

"R-ready as I'll ever be." Betsy walked forward to the attendant. "I'd like to rent a b-bike, please."

"Two or three wheels?"

"Hmm . . ."

He pointed to a group of six bikes all in bright primary colors. They looked like overgrown tricycles and had baskets on the front. To his other side were four standard bicycles. They looked to be in good shape, but next to the large tricycles, Mary thought they looked a little sad.

Betsy seemed to be staging a war with herself between the two choices. "W-which do most people rent?"

"The trikes."

"Even people my age?"

He looked like he had to think about that. "Well, the older crowd is right fond of the trikes, that's for sure and for certain, but I'd say there's a fair amount of folks of all ages renting them. It's up to you."

Betsy turned to Mary. "What do you think?"

"I think they both look like fun."

"Do you have to wear a helmet with both kinds?"

Although Mary feared the man would roll his eyes at her question, he seemed to think about it before he answered. "You don't have to wear one at all, but most folks who choose the two-wheelers do choose to get a helmet. It's safer, you know."

"No helmets are needed for the tricycle?"

"Nope. You're more stable on three, you see."

Betsy turned back to Mary. "W-would you be upset if we took out the trikes?"

"Not at all."

"Are you sure?"

"Betsy, all we're going to do is ride around some of the nearby parks. I just want to have fun."

"I'm going to have more fun if my kapp isn't crushed."

"Then there's your answer."

Looking like she was about to make a monumental decision, she said, "I'd like to rent one of the bright blue trikes, please."

"It'll be twenty dollars, miss."

As he took Betsy's cash, he said, "And you?"

"I'll take a red one," Mary said.

"Same price, miss."

After they paid, they pulled out their trikes and adjusted the seats. At last they were on their way. Mary took the lead, smiling as she heard Betsy chatting to some children nearby. Then they pulled up to the park entrance.

It was a large park that backed up to a golf course on one side and a row of shops on the other. Palm trees dotted the area, as well as hundreds of multicolored flowers and shrubs, even Mary's favorites—white roses. Each bloom looked as delicate and perfect as the next. If she'd been walking, she would have been tempted to lean down to catch the scent.

Instead, she made do with simply appreciating the Lord's beauty. Spring was in full bloom in Florida and was a welcome change after the gray skies and snow-covered fields in Holmes County.

She couldn't help but slow her pedaling as she inhaled the fragrant scents.

"Mary, you're not getting tired already, are you?"

"Ah, no." She glanced back at Betsy. "Are you truly trying to get me to speed up?"

"Well, jah. There's a lot of ground to cover. Plus, this is so fun."

"Why don't you pass me? That way if I slow down again, you won't have to wait."

"I guess I'm acting like a child."

"No. You're acting like you're enjoying yourself, which is wonderful. I'm just wanting to look at the flowers. It's practically still winter back in Ohio."

"I understand. I'll be up ahead."

As Betsy pedaled ahead, Mary decided that their habits of being alone were something of a silver lining. She had no problem letting Betsy enjoy herself for a few minutes while she took her time to smell the roses—literally and maybe figuratively.

Hearing Betsy talking up ahead, she pedaled faster, curious as to whom she'd struck up a conversation with now. Then, when she caught sight of who it was, she wished she hadn't come upon them so quickly.

There was Betsy, chatting up a storm with Jayson and another man. Both had golf bags. When Jayson caught sight of her, he didn't look away. "Hey," he said when she came to a stop in front of them.

"Hiya. Long time no see." She smiled, hoping she sounded more confident than awkward.

He grinned. "I was just thinking the same thing."

"He's been complimenting me on my bike riding skills," Betsy said with a grin. "I told them that I'm a natural at tricycles."

"You are speedy, that's for sure," Mary teased. Looking at Jayson, she said, "So, you're golfing?"

"We're about to head onto the course." He pointed to a line of golfers just to his left. "Danny and me thought we'd better get in some time at the driving range."

Jayson's friend leaned forward, offering his hand. "I'm Danny Troyer, by the way."

"It's nice to meet you. My name is Mary Margaret."

"Good to meet you. Where are you from?"

"Ohio. Betsy here is from Kentucky."

"We learned," Danny said.

"A-as soon as they heard my accent, Jayson and I started talking about our home state," Betsy said.

"Are you from the same area?"

"Not really. I'm from southwest Kentucky. Crittenden County. Betsy's from Hart County, which is in the center of the state."

"It's all the same to me though," Danny said. "I grew up here in Florida."

"I like how we're all from different places but we're here together," Mary said. "Whenever I hear someone talk about his or her hometown, it feels like I get to visit there."

"Since we're here in your hometown, Danny," Betsy said, "tell me three things I should do."

"Okay. First thing is learn to ride one of the big tricycles around town," he said with a wink.

While the two of them continued to joke with each other, Jayson stepped closer. "Hey, Mary, before we part again, I just wanted to tell you that I was sorry about earlier."

She didn't pretend like she didn't know what he was taking about. "At breakfast?"

He nodded. "I . . . I guess I'm a little self-conscious about where I'm from. No, make that a *lot* self-conscious."

Mary wanted to ask him why he felt that way but didn't want to push him. If they got to know each other better, he'd tell her in his own time.

"I was worried that I said something wrong, but I couldn't figure out what I said. I liked your accent. I wasn't trying to be mean or anything."

"It wasn't you. It really was me."

"Thank you for bringing it up. I'm glad that I didn't hurt your feelings by mistake."

He blinked. "That's it? You don't want me to explain anything?"

She shook her head. "If you want to tell me more another time, I'll be glad to listen. But, ah, I don't think I want to be the type of person who needs explanations."

"Danke."

"Hey, Jayson, we better go!" Danny called out. "Our tee time is coming up."

"Just a sec!" Meeting her gaze, he said, "I'll see you back at the inn."

"Have a good round of golf."

He smiled. "Thanks. Enjoy your bike ride."

She watched them walk away, then got back on her trike. "Where to now?" she asked Betsy. Everything in her world suddenly seemed brighter.

"Want to keep riding on this trail?"

"Lead the way. I'll follow."

Betsy moaned. "Mary, are you still going to go as slow as a turtle and gaze at all the flowers?"

"Something like that," she said with a laugh.

As Betsy surged ahead, Mary kept the same steady pace. Sure, the flowers were pretty, but all she wanted to do was think about the way Jayson had looked at her. It was almost like he hadn't wanted to say goodbye.

She hadn't either.

5

The fifteenth hole was a par 5 and boasted both a pond and a meandering sand trap; therefore, there was any number of reasons Jayson was having such a hard time even getting to the green. The obstacles on the course weren't the complete reason for his problems, though. The main one was that he couldn't stop thinking about Mary and Betsy. The women fascinated him, for two very different reasons. Betsy, because she seemed to be so outgoing.

And Mary? Well, she was on his mind because he found everything about her compelling.

Setting himself up for his shot, he corrected himself. *Compelling* wasn't near the right descriptor. *Compelling* was what he'd call a good sermon or even a good book. It didn't come close to what he thought about that woman. No, the truth was that he found everything about her attractive.

Attractive. The word reverberated in his head as he swung, clipped the top of the ball, and knocked it directly into the center of the sand trap.

Danny groaned. "Jay, what's going on with you? At this rate, we're going to be riding the SCAT home in the dark."

"Sorry."

"Don't apologize; just get your act together."

A cough behind them made him realize that a foursome was waiting. Grabbing his wedge, he strode to the center of the sand trap, popped his ball out, and smiled when it almost magically rolled onto the putting green. It came to a stop mere inches from the hole. One more stroke sank it, then they were on their way again.

They'd elected not to rent golf carts. It wasn't that warm out, and the handcarts were easy to pull. As they pulled their golf bags behind them, Danny said, "Sorry about snapping at you."

"No reason to apologize. I think I needed to get a little kick in the rear to get my mind back in the game. Obviously, it helped."

Danny grinned. "I'll keep that in mind. When all else fails, I'll plan to bully ya in order to get you to play better."

"Noted."

When they reached the sixteenth hole, a group of women were just finishing up. Jayson was glad for the small break and sipped from his water bottle.

"Seriously, usually you play much better. Are you still dwelling on all your problems back home?"

"Nee. I've taken your advice and am trying to live in the moment."

Maybe he was doing it too well. What a mess he was. Barely four hours after telling Danny about his plans, which included Ellen Schrock, all he seemed to be able to think about was Mary Margaret Miller—the woman he'd hardly exchanged more than two dozen words with.

"Sure?"

"Of course." Seeing that the women had moved on to the next hole, he said, "Come on. We can tee off."

He barely got through those two holes but seemed to be back to normal by the seventeenth and birdied the eighteenth—all by putting his thoughts regarding Mary to one side.

Heading back to the pro shop to return their pull carts, Danny clapped him on his back. "You sure proved me wrong. Obviously you were fine."

"I only beat you by two strokes."

Danny chuckled. "That's what I get for asking you all those questions about where your mind was. You got back your game."

"There's always next time," Jayson said.

"Yep. I'm sure I'll beat you then." Giving him a fist bump, he said, "Not that it matters all that much, right?"

"Right. Bad day at golf is better than the best day at work." It was tempting to simply ignore the subject, but Jayson couldn't do it. Danny had been too good a friend for too long to push away his concern.

"Just for the record, you were right. I was thinking of something else."

"Let me guess . . . that woman we just met. Mary Margaret."

"Was it that obvious?"

"Maybe. Maybe not. I've seen you interact with a lot of people, but I've never seen you so focused on a woman."

"I don't know why. I mean, sure she's pretty and sweet, but a lot of women are like that."

"You're on vacation, remember? I don't think you need to worry too much about why she's struck your fancy. She just has."

"What about Ellen?"

"Jayson, if you end up marrying her and come down here to vacation, I'll be nothing but kind to Ellen. I promise. I'll respect your vows and wish you well. But that hasn't happened yet."

Though it didn't exactly sit well with him, Jayson had to admit that Danny had a point. "You're right, Dan. Yet again."

Looking slightly embarrassed, Danny shrugged. "I do have a talent for giving unwanted advice. It's my gift."

"It's something," Jayson said with a laugh. "Come on. I'll buy you a piece of pizza."

Jayson thought a lot about Danny's words the rest of the afternoon. After a quick slice of pizza, they took the SCAT to Danny's house and stored their clubs. Then they hopped on the SCAT again, this time heading west to Siesta Key.

When they got to their favorite beach, they bought sandwiches at a beach shack and sat on a grouping of rocks.

Jayson had gotten an Italian sub. After taking the first bite, he smiled with contentment. "How come everything tastes better on the beach?"

"Because it's the beach."

"You're probably right. Everything is better here."

"I am so blessed," Danny said. "I love living in Florida. Life is so good here."

"It is. I'd move here in a second if I could."

"Are you sure you have to stay back in Kentucky?"

"Jah. It's where the job is. And Joy."

"What if you found a good job here?"

"I can't. I promised Wood that I'd marry Ellen."

"Or did you promise to consider it? And couldn't you find a job here and both of you move out? Or would everyone get mad at you? Was that part of Wood's plan? Do you have to work for him, marry his daughter, and stay in Crittenden County?"

"I don't know. I doubt it. I know I'm making Wood sound

awful, but he's really not. He just feels bad for me and wants his daughter settled."

"So you possibly could."

"I guess . . . if that's what I wanted to do."

Danny rested his arms on his knees and stared out at the ocean. "Oh, okay."

Jayson was surprised. All day long Danny had been pushing him to think about things a different way. Now it felt like he was backing off rather suddenly. "That's it?" he asked. "You're not going to try to convince me otherwise?"

"Nee. I want you to be happy and all, but you are right. You need to do what you think is best. I started thinking that I should've kept my mouth shut a whole lot more today."

Though Jayson had been a little irritated with his best friend, he realized that there was a part of him that was glad Danny was forcing him to think about the consequences of his choices. Back in Crittenden County, he didn't share much with anyone. He needed to be pushed a bit, even if it was only to feel better about the decisions he had made.

"Do you really think that there's a chance I could find another job and move out here?" Maybe he could even take Joy with him.

Slowly, Danny nodded. "Stranger things have happened, right? I mean, think of the story the preacher told the other day in church, about Abraham leaving home. No one saw that coming."

Jayson thought that was a pretty bold comparison, but he simply nodded and stared at the ocean. Looking out across the horizon, he spied a ship in the distance. He tried to watch it sail, but no matter how long he stared, it never seemed to move. He wondered if it was anchored there for some reason.

After just a few seconds, the vessel seemed to have jumped

miles out to sea. Far, too. Almost twice as far as he could imagine it going. That ship was like his life, he decided. For so long, he had felt anchored to a tether. Rocking and rolling in the same spot, unable to get away no matter how much he tried.

Now, at long last, he was thinking about breaking free. He didn't know if it was even possible, but he was starting to feel like it could be.

The thought was taking him off guard, though. Instead of gliding forward easily, Jayson felt as if he were rushing into a current on the heels of a fierce storm. He wasn't sure if he was going to stay upright or eventually capsize. He certainly hoped it would be the former and not the latter.

He took another bite of his sandwich and absentmindedly chewed as he watched the waves crash onto the shore, leaving a film of white foam each time they retreated.

"Hey, Jayson, I never asked. What does your father say about your plans to work for Wood and marry Ellen?"

"I haven't told him."

"Why not?" Danny finished the last of his sandwich, then crumpled the wrapper in his hands.

"He's not going to be pleased." That was putting it mildly.

Danny raised his eyebrow. "Because?"

"Because while my father doesn't do much right anymore, he's not a bad person. If he finds out that I'm going to marry Ellen just to ensure that Joy is taken care of? Well, he's going to feel pretty guilty."

"Maybe he needs to feel a little guilty. Ain't so?"

Jayson shook his head. "My father don't work like that. If things become too much, he'll just shut down. That will only make my life harder—and make me feel bad for hurting his feelings."

"You're too kind."

"I'm not. It's . . . well, it's my reality." He sighed. "Then there's also the possibility that Daed will somehow let the news slip to Joy and she'll be mad at me."

"That don't make sense. I mean, you'd be doing all of this for her."

"That's why she'd be mad." Jayson smiled. "Joy is an independent girl. Bossy too."

"Maybe everyone will take the news better than you think."

"Maybe. Or maybe not."

Danny gave him a sideways look but didn't say another word. Instead, they simply sat side by side watching the tide come in, lost in their own thoughts.

No doubt his best friend was wondering what in the world had gotten into Jayson.

That was certainly what was on his mind.

6

The sun was just starting to set when Mary and Betsy arrived back at the inn. Stopping on the front stoop to rearrange their shopping bags, Mary smiled at Betsy. "I can't remember the last time I've been so wonderfully tired. My legs feel like they're about to fall off."

"Mine feel the same way." Betsy added, "I can't believe how many stores we visited—or how many souvenirs I bought. What was I thinking?"

"I don't know. That we're on vacation?"

"That must be it." Chuckling, she held out her arms. "At least I have a nice tan to show for our day outdoors. I was feeling like my arms and legs looked like pale sticks against this green dress."

"They never looked like that . . . but you did get some color. I think I got too much sun. My nose feels sunburned."

"It looks sunburned too," Betsy said. "Just as I'm sure mine is."

"At least it looks like we've been in Florida," Mary said as she opened the door.

The inn's living room was filled with guests. A family of

five was playing cards at a table, a pair of elderly ladies were looking through travel brochures on the couch, a middle-aged man was on a laptop in a chair by the fireplace, and Lilly was writing in a journal.

When she spied them, she motioned them over. "You're back!"

"At last," Mary said. "How was your day?"

"It was great. After we ate breakfast, I took a long nap, then I took a long walk. I also bought a book and thought about reading it."

"It sounds delightfully lazy," Betsy said.

"Oh, it was. It might not sound all that exciting, but since I feel like I never have a moment to myself at home, it was delicious. Tomorrow I'll probably be up at dawn, ready to be productive again."

"I hope not. I might be of a mind to laze about with you," Mary said.

Setting her journal on a nearby table, Lilly asked, "Did you two have a good time?"

"We did."

"W-we rode bikes," Betsy added. "Which was wonderful fun. And . . . we just happened to run into that man Mary met at breakfast this morning."

"Oh? Was he any nicer?"

Looking mischievous, Betsy said, "What did you think, Mary?"

Feeling a little on the spot, she nodded. "Jayson was a lot nicer. He even apologized for the way he acted, which he didn't have to do."

"He and Mary talked a lot." Eyes sparkling, Betsy added, "I even think there might have been a spark or two between them."

"Betsy's making more of a five-minute conversation than it was. We had a bit of a miscommunication this morning, but it's all worked out now."

"Hmm," Lilly said, sharing a smile with Betsy.

"Mary, you are just the person I was looking for!" Nancy called out. "I have something for you."

"Yes?" she asked as she hurried across the room.

Pulling a packet of slips from the front pocket in her brightly patterned apron, Nancy thumbed through them. "Ah, here we go. You have a message."

Surprised, Mary scanned the note. There in Nancy's cramped handwriting was a short and simple statement: "Call home."

"Nancy, did you speak to my mother?"

"I did. She was adamant that you call home as soon as you can."

Imagining everything from a buggy accident to her father catching a cold, she gripped the paper tight. "Did she say anything? Do you know what happened?"

"I'm sorry, dear. I don't."

"May I use your phone?"

"Of course." Nancy pointed to the white swinging doors. "Go on through. You'll see a phone on the desk. Just pick it up and dial out."

"What about payment?"

"Oh dear, don't worry about that. All you have to do is write down your name and the time you're using the phone, just in case we get a surprise in the billing."

"I'll do that." She hurried into the kitchen, found the desk Nancy mentioned, and dutifully wrote down her name in the call log. Then, with shaking hands, she called home. Two years ago, when her grandmother was ill, her father had received permission to use a cell phone so they could hear from the hospital. After she passed, they put it in a drawer and didn't use it—unless something came up that they perceived as an emergency.

At first, Mary had been shocked by this. Her parents were the type of people who did everything by the book. She'd even gotten up the nerve to ask her father why he hadn't gotten rid of the phone. He'd simply shrugged. "I figure I'm a grown man and I've loved the Lord all my life. I canna help but believe that He ain't gonna get too put out with me if I need to use a cell phone for an emergency every once in a blue moon."

"But the bishop might think differently."

"The bishop don't need to be worrying about me, child." His voice had been final.

The ringing on the line brought her back to the present.

"Jah?"

Never had her father's gruff voice sounded so good. She breathed a sigh of relief. "Daed, it's Mary. Nancy, the owner of the Marigold Inn, gave me a message that Mamm called."

"She did. Mamm and I called you four hours ago."

Stung by how critical he sounded, she winced. "I'm sorry, I just got home. We rode three-wheeled bicycles and looked at all the shops."

"I see."

Well, she didn't, because she still didn't know why they'd called. "Daed, what did you want to tell me?"

"We were just wondering how you were doing. Are you having fun?"

"I am, but we only just arrived last night, Daed."

"And the weather? How is it?"

Feeling more confused, she pulled out the wooden chair next to the desk and sat down. "It's just as sunny as we had hoped it would be."

"I'm glad. We had snow today." His voice petered out.

Mary shifted uncomfortably. Her father was not the type of man to ask about the weather. Honestly, he'd never been one to even ask about her day. It was time to get some answers, and the sooner the better. "Daed, where's Mamm?"

"She's right here."

"May I talk to her, please?"

His voice brightened. "Of course. Here you go, Mary. Good-bye."

Mary shifted and crossed her legs while she heard her parents whisper to each other. Thirty seconds passed, then a minute. She tapped her foot, already contemplating the letter she was going to receive from Nancy asking for another amount for her very lengthy long-distance phone call.

At last her mother got on the phone. "Hello, dear. How is the weather? Is it warm there?"

Oh, for heaven's sake. She was not going to do this again. "Mamm, why are you two calling? Tell me now, because Nancy is going to charge us for this long-distance bill."

Her mother took a deep breath. "Mary, I thought I better prepare you . . . Esther Lapp is on her way down to Pinecraft."

Her mouth went dry. "Are you sure?"

"Very much so. I spoke to her mother this morning when I went over to the Super Walmart."

The van took a group of them to the supercenter every other Wednesday. "Why did she tell you that?"

"I can only assume she told me about the trip because Esther was excited."

"Oh, Mamm." Surely her mother wasn't that naive? Practically everyone in Trail knew that Esther and Mary weren't friends.

"I think she also told me about Esther going because Esther had told her parents that you were going to be there."

"I can't believe she's going to be here the same time that I am. Where's she staying?" Wherever it was, Mary was going to stay far, far away.

When her mother didn't answer immediately, her stomach sank. "Esther is staying here, isn't she?"

"I'm afraid so, dear."

She felt like crying. She literally felt like throwing something across the room and bursting into tears. "So, my vacation is over."

"Don't say that, Mary! Her going there doesn't mean that. It's just a coincidence, that's all."

"Who is she traveling with?" When her mother hesitated again, Mary braced herself for more bad news. With her luck, Violet and Abbie would be on that bus as well.

"She's traveling alone."

"That doesn't sound right. Are you sure?"

"I am. Naomi made a point of telling me that she wasn't going to be able to stop praying until Esther let her know that she had arrived." She paused, then added, "I am very sorry, dear. I know this is difficult news to hear."

It was more than that. All she'd been doing since she arrived was thanking the Lord for her blessings. She'd been so thankful that He had given her this *wonderful-gut* opportunity to start over again.

Now He'd taken it away. Just like it had been a joke for Him.

"Daughter, I know this is difficult news to hear, but don't

forget that the Lord never gives us burdens that we canna bear. I'm sure there's a very *gut* reason He put Esther there with you."

"I think there is. He obviously doesn't want me to ever move forward, have friends, or find a boyfriend."

"Surely you don't mean those things. You must try to be positive, jah?"

No. No, she didn't think she should.

She couldn't have this conversation any longer. It felt impossible to pretend that everything was going to be all right and that she wasn't upset. She was upset, and nothing was going to be all right.

"I need to get off the phone."

"Nee. Dear, let's talk about this. I'll mail a check for the charges. You won't need to worry about that."

"No, Mamm. You and Daed knew that I would be distressed by this news. That's why you called—and why you had out your cell phone. You were right too. I'm very upset, and I don't feel like talking."

"Will you call back in a couple of days? We'll be worried."

"Nee. I went on this trip to have some independence. I wanted to prove to myself that I could do things on my own. That I could be the person I always wanted to be. I canna do that if I'm sitting in a back corner of the kitchen talking to you both. I'll see you when I return."

"I understand."

"I'm glad. I love you, Mamm. Goodbye."

"I love you too. Goodbye."

When she finally hung up the phone, she sat in the quiet and stared at the empty space. Nancy kept a clean kitchen, but there were still some things in disarray, as one would expect. A few dishes in the sink, a few ingredients on the counter, obviously waiting to be used. A few crumbs on the floor, waiting to be swept away.

It was life, she supposed. Even under the best of circumstances and under the most exacting watch, nothing was ever completely perfect.

Maybe the Lord was trying to tell her that nothing ever would be.

That thought continued to play in her head as she exited the kitchen. And then right there in front of her were Lilly and Betsy, sitting across the table from none other than Jayson and two men she'd never met. All three of them looked up as she stepped into the dining room.

"Is everything okay?" Lilly asked.

"Jah." She wasn't about to spill her troubles in front of the men.

"Come over and join us then," Betsy called out with a bright smile. "We're thinking about playing a board game or Uno. We need you to even up the numbers."

This, in a nutshell, was everything she'd always wanted. Girlfriends, a handsome man, a group of people in which she was included. It was all here, and she'd finally gotten to experience it. For the moment, she was a wallflower no more.

Though it was tempting to go hide in her room and have a good cry, she didn't dare. She needed—deserved—this one special moment. Tonight she was going to live exactly like she'd always wanted to. "Danke," she said.

When Jayson smiled in her direction, she smiled back.

"I'll deal," said Betsy.

Everything was going to be great. She'd make sure it was.

Well, she would until Esther arrived tomorrow.

7

One hour to Pinecraft!" Toby, the bus driver, called out. "Everyone needs to start thinking about packing up their belongings."

Esther looked up from her book as everyone began doing as Toby bid. She watched Lavina, the robust woman sitting next to her, open three ziplock bags and start sorting her needlework into each one.

"Isn't an hour kind of early to start packing?" she asked.

"Oh, nee, dear. Look around you. Some of these folks are real messy. They practically use every spare space within spitting distance for themselves. If the driver doesn't encourage everyone to get started early, people leave without half their belongings."

Esther was even more pleased that she'd kept herself as neat as she had. Her mother had taught her from an early age to always be neat and never be messy. She'd never questioned the directives, though now she realized that the words *always* and *never* were difficult directions to follow. She shouldn't have to live her life constantly thinking about being neat and organized, should she?

Unless, she supposed, she was traveling on a Pioneer Trails bus for more than fifteen hours.

While Lavina continued to fold her quilt and fuss over her extra pair of socks, her sweater, and her books, Esther looked at her book and pretended to read. Really, though, she was attempting to convince herself not to regret her decision to travel to Florida on her own.

Or maybe she was actually trying to convince herself that she hadn't been wrong to choose to stay at the same inn where Mary Margaret Miller was residing. What must Mary think of her?

You know, that same voice uttered. *She hates you. And you'd hate yourself too if your situations were reversed.* She'd been so awful to that girl.

For years.

Her stomach knotted as she recalled the many things she'd said, both directly to Mary and behind her back. She couldn't even blame her age or naivete for all of it either. No, she'd been a mean girl simply because she could, and her callousness had given Mary years of unhappiness.

Oh, she knew she hadn't been nice, but she never imagined the damage she'd done until her two best friends turned the tables on her, all because Micah had stopped by after she broke up with Xavier and she'd dared to be nice to him.

"Where are you staying again, Esther?" Lavina asked.

"At the Marigold Inn. Have you heard of it?"

"Jah, I certainly have. It's a nice place. Big and bustling. Nancy White runs it, and she runs a tight ship." Looking Esther over, she sniffed. "I'm sure you'll appreciate that."

Esther was fairly positive there was a criticism in there somewhere, though she wasn't sure why. Was that the type of woman she seemed to be? The sort who needed everything to be run in a smooth manner?

"Where are you staying?" she asked, mainly as a way to keep talking instead of dwelling on her own faults.

"Me? Oh, me and Freida, Sylvia, and Ruth rented us a house within walking distance to Pinecraft Park. We've been renting the same place during the same week for years now. Why, we've been going there so long, it practically feels like home. We know where every fork and dish is located."

"How wonderful that you are able to always get the same place."

"There's no chance to it, dear. We take care to always book our stay a year in advance." Looking across the aisle, she smiled at her friend Sylvia. "We'd be devastated if that had to change."

"Indeed," Sylvia said with a chuckle. "We are creatures of habit."

"I suppose we all are," Esther murmured.

Lavina, who had begun inspecting all her snacks and reorganizing them in her quilted tote bag, paused. "Perhaps not you, though."

"Why would you say that?"

"Because you are traveling by yourself, which is something new, jah? You're also going to Pinecraft for the first time, so that's not your habit either."

"Both of these things are new," Esther said.

Sylvia leaned closer. "Why are you going?"

They'd already had this discussion when they first got on the bus. "Like I said earlier, I wanted to try something new."

"Jah. But why?"

While everything inside her was screaming to tell the nosy women that it was none of their business, Esther was enough of a realist to know that no good would come from keeping everything inside. "I had a falling-out with my two best friends. It's been bad. We're not really speaking anymore," she admitted. "Because of that, I felt like I needed to do something on my own."

"Because they've shunned you," Freida murmured from behind her.

Esther felt her cheeks heat. These women were not only forcing her to speak the truth, but they were unabashedly listening as well. She drew back her shoulders. "I have not been shunned."

"Oh, don't get your panties in a pinch," Lavina said. "You know Freida ain't being serious."

"Mei muddah says that there are some things one shouldn't joke about." And yes, Esther knew she sounded both mighty prim and rather like a stick-in-the-mud.

Obviously not intimidated by either Esther's tone or her mother's words of wisdom, Freida waved off the criticism. "I'm sure your mother is a good and just woman, but I happen to disagree."

Feeling some sort of strange need to clarify her situation, Esther added, "I really have not been shunned by my friends. I . . . I simply realized that it was time I tried some new things. Vacationing in sunny Florida was one of those."

"How did you afford it? Or did your mother buy your bus ticket?"

"I have been working at a hotel, cleaning rooms. My parents allowed me to keep the money to use for my expenses."

Lavina whistled low. "Well now. Ain't you a surprise? I would've never imagined you to be a maid."

"Why not?"

"Look at you, dear. So pretty. So proper. So contained. Honestly, you are a fitting tribute to your namesake. Queen Esther was many of those things, jah?"

She honestly could not wait to get off this bus. "I am far from being a queen."

"Oh dear," Lavina said as she reached out and patted Esther's knee. "Aren't we all?"

With a screech, Toby's microphone turned on again. "Thirty minutes away from Pinecraft, everyone. If you aren't packed up, do so now. Also, Andrew is going to come around for your trash. Don't even think about sticking anything in the seat in front of you. We ain't got no time to be cleaning up your old tissues."

Chuckles rang through the full bus, but sure enough, more people started unzipping their backpacks and totes and securing their belongings.

Just as Esther carefully placed the two granola bar wrappers inside a paper towel to dispose of later, Lavina leaned closer. "I know you are worried, dear, but keep your chin up, jah? The Lord is in charge. He must be wanting you to be going on this journey. Have faith in His will."

Her journey. Yes, that's what this was. Her journey to try to be someone new. To make amends. And maybe to learn something about herself in the process.

All were grand ideas, but they weren't going to be easy. Nothing worth doing ever was. "I will try," she finally replied.

Lavina shook her head. "Don't you go around and just say that you'll try, Esther dear. Simply *trying* won't get you anywhere."

"No?"

"This is what you do, child. You say to yourself, *I will*. Take it from someone who reserves a vacation spot a year in advance. One needs to be confident in order to get things done."

"I'll remember that." Esther smiled at Lavina but felt weak inside.

She currently felt anything but confident about this trip. In fact, she was starting to think that coming to Pinecraft had been the worst idea she'd ever had.

8

The morning was glorious. Jayson rose just before sunrise, filled a to-go cup with coffee, and went for an hourlong walk. He told himself that walk had a purpose—to look for signs advertising both construction jobs and available rental units. Just in case he really did want to think about living here with Joy and eventually Ellen.

But that was just an excuse.

The real reason for his walk was that he'd been restless. Restless and unable to stop thinking about Mary. He couldn't deny it any longer. There was something about her that had taken hold of him. She was special, and he wanted to know her better.

He was also a bit worried about her.

She'd acted so differently last night when they were all playing cards. Her laugh was a little bit louder, her smiles quicker, and her eyes a little bit sadder.

It was obvious that something was very wrong.

They all knew that she'd been asked to call home. She never discussed what the phone call had been about. Well, not beyond saying that her parents were fine and no one was ill.

But he couldn't help but reflect that, as they played Rook,

there had been a slight tinge of panic in her manner, as if she'd been trying to have as much fun as she could in one evening.

After the game, when they were all about to head to their rooms, he'd pulled her aside and asked if she was all right.

"Of course," she'd said—right before she hurried to her room.

He'd worried about her all night, much to his chagrin.

"Ellen," he murmured to himself. "Don't forget Ellen. And Joy. And your responsibilities."

By the time he walked another three blocks, Jayson felt like he'd gotten himself back in the right mindset. He might be worried about Mary, but he needed to remember that she could only ever be his friend. Besides, he had a fourteen-year-old sister to take care of—even when she was miles away.

He used his calling card at a pay phone and called home. Because his family was New Order, they had a phone in the kitchen. Though keeping the line was expensive, his daed had always made sure the bill was paid on time. If Joy ever got sick, they needed a way to get her to the hospital fast.

The phone rang three times before his sister picked up. "Hello?"

"Joy, it's me."

"Jayson, hi!"

She sounded good—like her regular, happy self. He relaxed. "How are you? How are you feeling?"

"Fine and gut. What about you?"

"The same," he said. "Where is Daed?"

"Daed is outside shoveling the sidewalk."

"We had snow?"

"Jah. Not a lot—just enough to make a mess of things. Daed was worried about it icing up later."

"I'm glad he's taking care of that. What about you? What are you doing?"

"I'm washing dishes because . . . guess who came over?"

Pleased that she sounded so good, he leaned against the side of the booth and grinned. "I couldn't begin to guess. Who came over?"

"Ellen."

Taken aback, Jayson coughed. "Oh?" Realizing he sounded less than thrilled, he attempted to inject a bit of enthusiasm into his voice. "That's a surprise. Why was she there?"

"I don't know, but she was being her usual self, Jayson." She lowered her voice. "You know how Ellen gets. I swear, you're the only person she likes in our family."

"I'm sure that isn't true. You shouldn't talk like that, Joy."

"I canna help but speak the truth, *bruder*. And I'm pretty sure it is true. Her eyes never look pleased when she comes over."

"No one's eyes look pleased or displeased."

"Oh yes they do, and hers were squinty. You're not thinking of courting her, are ya?"

Not wanting to lie, he said, "Why would you ask that?"

"She kept talking about you and things that you two might do together in the future."

"Hmm."

"Jayson, sorry, but she acted like she knew something that I didn't. It was weird. Plus, I know she wanted to boss me around."

"Joy."

"I'm serious. Ellen had the nerve to ask if I was keeping up with laundry since you weren't there to help. As if you ever pinned clothes on the basement line."

"No need to be so sarcastic, Joy."

"Sure there is. Jayson, please don't say that you like her, because Ellen would be a horrible sister."

"I'm sure she's better than you think," he said quickly.

"I'm sure she isn't." Lowering her voice, she added, "Ellen even asked why I was wearing my old blue dress. She acted like I should've been wearing a new one while I cleaned the house. Can you even imagine?"

He wasn't sure if she was referring to cleaning in new clothes or Ellen's rudeness, but maybe it didn't even matter. He was starting to feel a ball of dread lodge in his stomach. "I hope you were polite, Joy."

"I was." Sounding a little guilty, she added, "Just barely, though."

"If you see her again, be nice," he warned, though he was starting to think that maybe Joy was right. Ellen could be rather snobby when she wanted to be. "I better get off the phone. I only called to check on you."

"I'm fine. All my numbers are good."

"I'm glad. I'll call in a few days. I love you, Joy. Don't forget, okay?"

"I never do."

He ended the call feeling melancholy. He intended to do whatever it took to make sure Joy was happy and settled, but it was beginning to seem like achieving that goal wasn't going to be as easy as he'd hoped.

After that, almost against his will, he ended up touring two places that had apartments for rent: one was a three-room apartment in a garage on the back of an Amish-run house, and the other was a tiny efficiency unit in the heart of downtown Sarasota. That condo community had a pool and lots of other amenities. He noticed a young Amish couple walking out of one of the units. His family back in Crittenden County wouldn't be pleased with him living in such a fancy place, but the idea of having air-conditioning in his home after working construction all day did have its appeal.

Not that he was actually going to move, he firmly told himself.

After washing up, he joined the group of people sitting at the large community table. Mary's friend Betsy was there. She smiled when he sat down next to her with his plate of fruit and cup of coffee.

"Gut matin, Jayson."

"Good morning to you. How are you?"

"I'm g-good, danke. Happy to be in sunny Florida today."

The other people at the table nodded. "We're going to Siesta Key this morning," a lady said. "What are you two young'uns planning?"

"I've already been on a walk," Jayson replied. "I might be lazy the rest of the day."

"Don't you want to sightsee?"

"Nee, I've been to Pinecraft several times before."

"Is that right? You must really like it here."

"I do. I'd live here if I could," he joked. Well, he kind of joked.

While the woman frowned, Betsy seemed to understand. "I've often wondered where the Lord intends for me to live. Sometimes I think it's near my big family in Hart County. Now that I've gotten to meet Mary and Lilly, I'm starting to think that there might be other places where I could be happy as well."

"You will have to live where your future husband lives, miss," the woman said.

"To be sure." Betsy raised her chin. "However, I don't know if my future husband lives in Hart C-County."

Eager to stop the woman from being so free with her two cents, Jayson interrupted. "Hey, Betsy, have you seen Mary or Lilly this morning?"

Betsy shook her head. "My room is on the third floor, and their rooms are on the first and second floors."

"Ah yes. I keep forgetting that you three aren't rooming together."

"I wish we were—I know we'd have a grand time."

"It seems like y'all were meant to know each other."

"I think so too. When the bus had to stop at a motel outside of Atlanta on the way here because of a bad ice storm, the three of us were put in a room together. Within two hours, we all knew that we'd be friends forever."

Thinking of how he and Danny had clicked almost immediately, Jayson murmured, "Sometimes you just know when you like someone."

Betsy smiled. "I think so."

He was getting ready to ask about her plans for the day when the front door opened and a blond Amish girl entered. Her dress was slightly rumpled, and her eyes looked sleepy. She was pulling a large navy blue suitcase on wheels. Though it was obvious that she'd been on the bus, Jayson could honestly say that he'd seen few other women who were so classically beautiful.

As if she'd been on the lookout, Nancy zipped out of the kitchen. "Hallo! Are you Esther from Trail?"

"I am."

"Well, bless your heart. That trip takes longer and longer every time, don'tcha know?"

"This was my first bus trip."

"Was it? My, then I know you're exhausted. I'm sure you are ready for a hot bath and a warm bed." Nancy motioned her over. "Come have something to eat and some juice if you'd like. I'll go get your key and registration."

"Danke." She looked around hesitantly.

Jayson met her eyes, then looked away. No doubt the gal was having a hard enough time without everyone staring at her.

Betsy went to her side. "Hi. My name is B-Betsy," she said slowly. "I haven't been here long either."

"Hi," Esther said with a smile. "I'm—well, I guess you know my name already."

Looking more comfortable, Betsy continued. "Esther, it's nice to meet you. Believe it or not, I just met another girl about our age from Trail. Her name is Mary Margaret. Do you know each other?"

"Jah."

"That's gut! Now you won't worry about traveling by yourself. Ain't so?"

Still off to the side watching, Jayson noticed that Esther seemed uncomfortable. All she did was nod before she walked to the sideboard, filled up a bowl with strawberries, and selected a poppy-seed muffin before returning to her chair.

"Here you go, dear," Nancy said as she blew in again. She set a small clipboard to Esther's right. "Whenever you are ready, fill out the paperwork and give me the deposit. I'll take care of it while you eat. You'll be in your room and ready to go to bed in no time."

"This is so kind of you. I was so tired, I wasn't sure what to do."

"Oh, honey. I do this all the time! If there's one thing I've learned in my thirteen years of running this inn, it's that weary travelers like to get something to eat and drink and go to their room for some peace and quiet, fast."

Esther smiled as she speared a strawberry. Then, just before she took a bite, she stopped.

Jayson turned to see who she was staring at.

Mary and Lilly were chatting in the entryway. Actually, Mary was telling a story and laughing when she caught sight of everyone. When her attention settled on Esther, she froze.

Concerned, Jayson got to his feet. "Mary, are you okay?" When he got to her side, he realized that she had gone white.

"I'm not hungry anymore," she murmured. Without another word, she turned and walked out the front door of the inn.

The entire room fell silent as the door clicked behind her.

"What just happened?" Lilly asked.

"I don't know," Betsy said. "It was as if she saw a ghost." She looked at Jayson. "Do you think I should go after her? We've become friends, but we haven't known each other very long."

He didn't know what to say. Then he realized that Esther had both of her hands over her face. "Esther, do you know what happened?"

With obvious reluctance, she nodded. "I'm afraid I do."

"Well?" Jayson prodded. He was really worried.

"Mary Margaret saw me."

Betsy frowned. "But I thought you two were friends. You said you were."

"Nee, I said we knew each other. There's a difference, I'm afraid."

Lilly joined them at the table. "So, you and Mary actually aren't friends?"

Looking miserable, Esther shook her head. "Nee, we aren't. I hate to admit it, but we aren't even close to being friends."

Both Lilly and Betsy looked at Esther in confusion. Then Betsy said, "One of us needs to go after her. Do you care if I do, Lilly?"

"Nee, though I can. Maybe we—"

Already on his feet, Jayson said, "I'm going after Mary." He headed to the door before anyone else could try to intervene. When the door closed behind him and the warm, humid air enveloped his skin, he looked left and right. There was no sign of Mary.

She was a grown woman and likely didn't want anyone looking after her, but something told him that maybe what she wanted wasn't important at this moment. What was important was that she needed to be with her friends. She needed to know that she wasn't alone. She needed to know that someone cared.

Even if it was just him.

9

ary! Mary Margaret, stop!"

She turned to see Jayson striding down the side-walk toward her. His expression was so intense, worry for him replaced all the ugly emotions that had been churning inside her body. "Jayson, are you all right? What is wrong?"

"I'm fine. It's you I'm worried about. Come on." Without another word, he took her arm and led her toward the parking lot of a nearby church. She allowed him to redirect her, mainly because she was too stressed to do anything but give him that leeway.

When he continued walking, still silent, she'd had enough. "Where exactly are you leading me to?"

"Someplace where we can talk in private."

That surely wasn't anywhere exact. Feeling more peevish, she slowed their pace. "I don't want to talk, Jayson."

"That's too bad."

"Excuse me?"

"Oh, stop. We both know I don't mean you no harm. In

70

this instance, you're going to have to simply do as I ask. Take a deep breath and look around. This place is pretty, ain't so?"

Mary dutifully exhaled and took a better look at the Mennonite church they were circling. It was a stucco building with an arched entryway and Mexican terra-cotta tile leading to the side door and a garden. Riotous blooms decorated the area, along with a number of palm trees. It was a pretty place. Very picturesque.

But the visit was not in her plans. Just as she was about to tell him that, he pointed to a small, pale green iron bistro table. Three chairs surrounded it, and a fountain and birdbath were nearby. The fountain was simple, merely a cascade of water flowing down a slate panel. It was lovely, though. Soothing.

"How did you know this was here?"

"I've been to Pinecraft a lot. Before this was a Mennonite church, it was a Catholic mission. I've always loved how this church has retained its Spanish roots all this time." He sat down. "Have a seat, okay?"

"I'll sit, but I don't want to be questioned," she said.

"I understand."

He looked far too confident. She didn't believe him. But she did sit. After all, what else was she going to do? Keep walking all over the city of Sarasota until she felt brave enough to go back to the Marigold Inn? She didn't even have her sunglasses or money with her.

"I'm glad I found you," he said. "By the time I ran out to see where you'd gone, I couldn't find a trace of you. I kept standing in the middle of the sidewalk looking right and left."

She didn't want to tell him that she'd been practically running. "How did you decide which way to go?"

"I decided to go three blocks one way. If I didn't see you, I was going to go in the other direction." When she stared at him, he shrugged. "I know. It wasn't a very good plan."

"I'm glad you found me."

"Really?"

She nodded. "I thought I wanted to be alone, but I'm starting to think that would've been the worst thing for me." That was the truth too. For too long she'd kept all her worries and fears deep inside her. For too long she'd tried to pretend to both herself and her parents that the constant teasing hadn't scarred her like it had.

But she was starting to believe that she'd been lying to herself. It was all crashing down on her now.

Jayson studied her. Folded his hands in his lap. Waited another half a minute. "I don't mean to sound dramatic, but you're kind of starting to freak me out. Are you okay?"

She nodded, then stopped, angry with herself. Hadn't she just decided she was going to stop lying? When tears filled her eyes, she knew it was time to be completely honest. "No. No, I am not okay."

Looking even more concerned, he leaned closer. "Tell me what's wrong then. Has someone hurt you?"

"Yes. But not in the way you are probably thinking. I . . . Esther and I aren't friends," she admitted at last. "I . . . well, there was an incident years ago. I made a fool of myself one day, and it's haunted me ever since."

"How long ago?"

"I was eleven."

Much of the concern that was in his eyes faded into amusement. "Are you trying to tell me that you're still upset about something that happened over a decade ago?"

He didn't understand. She hated that he was making it sound

as if she were being silly. But then, she reminded herself, he really had no idea what she was referring to. It was time to get braver.

"Yes, but also no."

He raised his eyebrows. "Well?"

"Jayson, I don't want to tell you about it."

"I won't think less of you, Mary. Come on. You're acting like I'm going to find fault with you over something that you did when you were a child! I would never do that."

"I realize it doesn't make sense, but you see, from my point of view, this is the first time in more than a decade that I haven't felt like that incident has been following me around. I've felt free."

"Sorry, but I think you should let it go."

"It isn't easy."

"I have a fourteen-year-old sister. Joy is always bringing up old stories and things that happened when she was younger. I don't know how many times my mother had to tell her that forgiveness is a virtue."

Whistling low, he added, "She can sure hold a grudge, though. I think she's still upset with me from when I accidentally threw out one of her favorite stuffed animals."

She knew Jayson was trying hard, but his story about his little sister told her everything she needed to know. He wasn't going to understand just how awful everything had been.

He wasn't going to be sympathetic or understanding. Not for either her silly, stupid eleven-year-old self or the pain she'd been experiencing ever since. She stood up. "Danke for coming out to find me. I'm glad you were concerned. But I would rather not discuss this with you."

He got to his feet as well. "Really? That's all you're going to say? That's all you're going to do?"

"Jah."

"Come on, don't be so sensitive."

"If you only knew how many times people have told me that!"

"Sorry, but maybe they have a point."

She shook her head. "They might, but not in this instance. You have no idea what you are talking about. You have no idea how Esther treated me."

"She seemed upset that you left."

It wasn't fair to Jayson, but she felt especially hurt by his concern for one of the three people who'd caused her years of misery. "At the moment, I don't care."

"What are you going to do next then?"

What was she going to do? The answer was obvious, though it felt like she was swallowing a bitter pill. "I'm going to do what I've always done. I'm going to go back to the inn, pretend that Esther's criticism, jokes, and sly remarks don't bother me, and then I'm going to pray that one day I'll finally be free of her cruelty."

He inhaled sharply. "Mary, I'm sorry that you're so upset. What can I do to help?"

What could he do? What, really? "I don't expect you to take sides or even want to get embroiled in any of this mess. But, if you wanted, maybe you could try to believe me."

"I already do. I'm sorry that I sounded judgmental. I shouldn't ever tell you not to feel what you do."

Mary felt as if her heart had just started beating again. He had just done what most of the people in her life had never done—he'd given her feelings credence. "Thank you."

"Want to go back now? Everyone is concerned about you."

His voice was so gentle, she yearned to cling to it like a lifeline.

"I guess I'll have to." Though she was pretty sure that Lilly and Betsy wouldn't have anything to do with her now—surely Esther had taken great pains to tell both of them all about her embarrassing past. Mary knew she didn't have a choice. Life continued, even when it wasn't all that good.

Since there wasn't much else to say, they began walking back to the inn. The early morning clouds had burned off, and the sky was a hazy blue. The faint scent of salt water tinged the air, mixing with fragrant florals. The streets had started to fill up with cars, and the sidewalk was filling with a number of Amish families, the parents wearing flip-flops, straw hats, and short sleeves over pale skin and holding hands with their children, who were wearing happy smiles.

Life had continued.

"Maybe things will go all right," Jayson said.

"I pray that they will, but I'm afraid that the likelihood of that happening is fairly slim."

"You need to think positive. Remember that the Lord is always with us. If He's by our sides, then there's always a chance that things are going to go better than expected."

"There's a chance that pigs will start flying too," she said.

He laughed. "It can happen, ain't so? After all, God performs miracles every day."

Looking up at him fondly, Mary knew he was right. "Thanks for coming to find me. I feel a lot better."

"Anytime. Anytime at all."

10

In the end, there wasn't a big showdown when Jayson and Mary returned to the inn. Nancy was back in the kitchen, all the guests that had been sitting at the tables were gone, and even Lilly and Betsy were out of sight. Jayson breathed a sigh of relief.

Looking exhausted, Mary poured herself a cup of coffee and sat down.

Jayson said, "I'm going to go back to the kitchen and see if Nancy will let me make some eggs. Do you want some?"

"That's not necessary. I'll go out later and get something to eat."

"I'd like something. Don't go anywhere—I'll be right back."

To his relief, she didn't put up a fight. She merely took another sip of her coffee.

Nancy was zesting a lemon when Jayson entered. "Did you find Mary Margaret?" she asked in a kind voice.

"I did. She's in the dining room now."

Wiping her hands on a dishcloth, she said, "Poor thing. She looked like she'd seen a ghost."

"I was worried about her, but I think she's going to be okay."

"I hope so. What do you need?"

"I hate to ask since the kitchen's so clean, but we're both hungry. Would you mind if we had some eggs and toast?"

"I don't usually make meals to order, you know."

Stung, he said, "I'm happy to make them. I'll clean up after myself too."

"Oh, go on with you." She playfully wagged a finger at him. "I'm just joshing ya. Go sit down with Mary. I'll bring ya out some breakfasts in a few."

"I appreciate it."

"Of course. I'm glad you could stay here for a spell."

"I'm enjoying it."

Nancy looked delighted. "See? It's like we're old friends now. Go on with ya and sit with that sweet girl. I'll be right out."

After sending another grateful look her way, he went back to the dining area. Mary was exactly where he'd left her.

"What did she say?"

"To sit tight and she'll be right out with our food."

"That is so kind of her."

"She's a kind woman." When she looked like she was about to stand up, obviously intent on going to the kitchen, he said, "I don't know Nancy well, but my friend Danny does. His mother and her are longtime friends. When he came over yesterday, we chatted with Nancy for a while. If I learned anything from that conversation, it's that you shouldn't make a big deal out of Nancy making you a plate of eggs. It's pretty obvious that she isn't going to do anything she doesn't want to do."

"All right."

He got himself a cup of coffee and sat down. Looking up at the clock, he noticed that some of the woodwork in the hallway had come off. More to give himself something to do than anything, he walked over and examined the area better.

"Ain't that a shame?" Nancy said as she strode in with a glass of orange juice for Mary. "It fell, then somehow cracked. Now I've got to find someone to cut a new piece of molding and fix it."

"I can do that while I'm in town."

Nancy smiled. "Could you really?"

"Of course. I'll take care of it soon."

"I would say you shouldn't, but I pride myself on keeping a well-kept inn. That missing piece of wood has been driving me crazy."

"It won't take me but an hour or two."

"You just made my day, Jayson," she said as she hurried back to the kitchen.

Mary said, "I know you do construction, but what do you do, exactly?"

"I'm a finish carpenter."

"Which is?"

"I do some of the trim work on houses and buildings. Baseboards, doorframes. Whenever you see fancy molding around a room or doorway, it's likely a finish carpenter is responsible for it."

Her brown eyes lit up. "You do all the things that add character to a house."

"Exactly."

"That can't be easy to do."

"It's not, but I enjoy the work. I've been a carpenter for years now. I started apprenticing when I was fourteen."

"Who taught you your trade?"

"One of my uncles helped me with the basics, then a friend

of the family let me work with him. Now I do some contract work around my town." He knew he should add that he would be working for a company real soon, but he wasn't ready to share that.

"There's that much work in your town?"

"There is in our county. Not as much as would be here, of course . . . but enough."

"I see." But her expression said quite the opposite. He didn't blame her for her confusion, but he didn't want to explain why he'd mentioned Pinecraft just now either.

Just in time, Nancy entered with two plates heaping full of eggs, sausage, and toast. "Here you two go."

"I appreciate you going to so much trouble," Mary said. "It's so kind of you."

"I reckon you're worth it," Nancy teased. Softening her voice, she added, "Besides, I think everyone needs a hand now and then. This is your day. Now, eat up and bring your plates to the kitchen when you're finished." She turned and walked through the swinging door without a backward glance.

"I wonder if her kinner move at the same fast pace," Mary mused.

"I couldn't guess, but I kind of hope so. If they don't, they're likely always out of breath. Nancy is practically a whirling dervish."

She giggled. "Indeed."

They bowed their heads in silent prayer, then dug in. Jayson was pleased to see that Mary hadn't lost her appetite.

"Everything tastes better here in sunny Florida, doesn't it?" she asked.

"I've always thought so," he replied with a smile.

11

⌒

It might not have been the right decision, but Esther knew she had no choice. She'd come to Pinecraft for a reason, and it wasn't just to escape Violet and Abbie. After what she'd witnessed that morning, Esther realized that it didn't even matter any longer what she hoped to accomplish or gain from her vacation. What did matter was that she simply wasn't going to be able to live with herself if she didn't try to make amends as soon as possible.

She was scared, though. All kinds of horrible thoughts spun through her head like some sort of spiderweb gone wrong. What if she made things worse? What if Mary told everyone at the inn that she was a horrible person? What if she did her best to apologize, and it still wasn't enough to feel better?

That is the problem, Esther, her conscience murmured. *You keep thinking about yourself and about how you feel. You need to put yourself second and put Mary's needs first.*

She nodded to herself. She needed to put Mary Margaret Miller first for a change.

Taking a deep breath, Esther knocked on Mary's door. After

a few seconds passed, the lock on the door clicked and Mary peeked out.

Their eyes met.

"Hi," Esther said.

A mixture of pain and irritation filled Mary's features. Her feelings were so bare, so honest, it almost made Esther want to take a step back. If looks could kill, she really would be a pile of ashes lying in the middle of the hallway.

One second passed. Then two.

"What do you want?" Mary finally asked. Her tone practically shouted that Esther was not welcome.

That hurt, but she shouldn't have been surprised.

"May I come in?" When Mary's eyebrows shot up to her hairline, Esther started talking fast. "Please don't say no. I have something I need to tell you. It's important."

"I don't know what you could possibly say that I want to hear."

"I bet I deserve that, but please let me come in anyway." When Mary looked like she was still going to ignore her pleas, Esther added, "I promise I won't stay long, and I really, really don't want to make you cry."

"Fine." She stepped back and pulled the door wide open, almost as if she didn't even want to risk the skirts of their dresses brushing against each other.

Her nerves feeling singed, Esther walked in. Unable to help herself, she scanned the area. It was lovely and neat as a pin. "Your room looks so different than mine."

"How so?"

"My room is decorated in a bunch of bright colors. Your room looks so peaceful."

After a slight pause, Mary said, "I heard every room is decorated a little differently."

Esther nodded. "I guess that makes sense. It's a nice bed-and-breakfast." Her voice drifted off. Now that she couldn't delay her speech, her mouth felt like sandpaper. She clenched her hands so tightly together, she was sure her nails were making marks in her skin.

"Are you here in Pinecraft alone?" Mary asked.

"Jah."

"Why?"

"I needed to get away." Realizing she couldn't simply spout a few apologies and walk out, Esther forced herself to open up a bit more. "Things back in Trail have become mighty hard. Suffocating."

"What do you mean?"

Esther weighed her response but finally gave up trying to choose her words with care and simply blurted out the truth. "I had a falling-out with Violet and Abbie. It was very bad. I . . . I doubt we'll ever make up."

"Oh." Mary exhaled. "Is that what was so important that you had to tell me?"

"Not exactly." Ach, but this was so hard. But then again, why had she ever thought this moment would be easy?

"What is it then?"

Realizing she was running out of time, Esther said, "Look, I know nothing I've been going through with them compares to what you've been through, but I wanted to apologize. I'm sorry for the things I've done." Glad that she'd said her piece at last, she met Mary's eyes. Surely now she would thaw a little bit. It had to have been obvious how hard it was to share all that.

Mary didn't warm in the slightest. In fact, after she studied Esther for a long moment, she turned her head away. "Did you come to the Marigold Inn because you knew I was here?"

"Not exactly."

Mary turned back to face her. "What does that mean?"

"It means that I chose to come here because it's freezing in Ohio, and I want to be someplace warm while I figure out my life. That's why I came to Pinecraft."

"I asked you about being here at this inn."

"The truth is that I didn't know where to go and someone had told me about this inn. How the owner was nice and that single women would feel safe here. I'd be lying if I said that I didn't know you were going to be here, though. I knew we'd see each other." Knowing that it was better to own the truth than to hide behind vague phrases, she lifted her chin. "I was planning on it."

Pure pain filled Mary's features. "Why would you do this to me? Do you really hate me so much?"

Every single word hurt. "What? Nee! I don't hate you at all."

If anything, her declaration seemed to make Mary even more upset.

"Esther, from the time I vomited on the school's playground when I was eleven, you gossiped, teased, exaggerated what I did, and generally made sure no one ever forgot it. You made me a laughingstock—even after we all graduated and grew up. You, Abbie, and Violet took hold of one stupid thing I did when I was just a child and ruined me."

Esther could hardly swallow. "I'm—"

Mary kept talking. "I've been lonely, ashamed, and stuck. I've been *stuck* in Trail, Esther! I had nowhere to go to get away from the snide looks and tiny jabs." Tears filled her eyes, and she swiped them away with the side of her hand. "Now, the first time that I've been able to get away—to finally get away from you—you follow me here." She inhaled sharply. "Esther,

I knew you were cruel, but this seems even crueler than I knew you could be."

Crueler than Mary knew she could be. Feeling like she was in an awful dream, Esther shook her head. "Nee! It wasn't like that."

"Are you sure? Because from my point of view, it feels like you not only can't help but make sure I'm alone and sad, you've now gone out of your way to do it. Why would you do all that if you didn't actually hate me?"

Tears filled Esther's eyes as she finally realized just how much her actions had affected Mary. "I don't have an excuse for my behavior. I . . . I don't know what to say except that I'm sorry for the hurt that I've caused you."

Mary merely glared like everything that Esther had just said didn't matter. "I still don't understand what you want."

"What do you mean?"

"Are you expecting something from me? Is this some kind of blackmail? Like I better forget how horrible you've been or else you'll be even worse when we get back to Trail?"

Esther was flabbergasted. "Of course not. I can't believe you would think that."

"Why wouldn't I?"

"Whatever you might think of me, I promise I would never blackmail you or . . . or any of the things you're thinking of."

At last, something Esther said seemed to have resonated with her. Mary closed her eyes. "Listen, I don't even care anymore if you hate me or not. The fact is that I don't know you, and you don't know me. I'll do my best to stay out of your way. Please stay out of mine. If we do that, then there's a chance that we'll be able to get through this."

That was it. Mary Margaret Miller wasn't going to forgive

her or be her friend or even trust her to behave in a normal manner. Esther supposed it was no less than she deserved.

"Thank you for listening to me."

All Mary did was open the door.

Esther walked out, realizing right then and there that making amends was going to be far harder than she'd imagined. Maybe even impossible. She was tempted to go into her room and hide but couldn't do it. Instead, she got her purse and sunglasses, and then walked out the Marigold's front entrance into the warm air and bright sunshine.

Yes, her insides felt hollow, but Pinecraft was filled with laughter and sunshine and flowers. It might be a difficult week, but she was going to do her best to enjoy every moment. She'd gone through too much not to do that.

An hour later, she was sitting on the beach, eating a vanilla soft-serve cone, and watching waves lap the shore. To her surprise and relief, she wasn't the only person by herself on the beach. Lots of people were. She was in the minority as far as the way she was dressed. She had on her kapp and dress. Her only concession to being in Pinecraft was the rubber flip-flops she was wearing.

In contrast, there were a lot of other Amish girls wearing shorts, bathing suits, and their long hair in braids or ponytails.

Esther couldn't stop watching the group of teenagers. Their laughter was exuberant, and they all looked so carefree. She couldn't remember ever being that way, not even when she was little and content to simply be home with her parents.

No, she'd always been the type of person to worry and plan and wonder and doubt. Maybe that was why she'd embraced

Violet and Abbie's friendship so much. They'd made her feel like she was prettier, smarter—no, *better*—than everyone else.

For a time, you believed it too, she reminded herself.

"If you're not careful, most of your ice cream is going to drip on the sand," a voice said quietly.

She looked up, and standing beside her was one of the boys who had been part of the group of teenagers. He was as blond as she was, and he was wearing long board shorts and a T-shirt. His feet were bare. And he had a tan.

Esther wasn't sure what to say. But since he was right—her cone was dripping something awful—she swiped the ice cream with her tongue. Then swiped it again. "Danke," she said at last.

"No problem." His eyes lit up. "I'm great at making sure my ice cream doesn't drip too much."

It was such a silly comment, she giggled. "Is that your talent?"

"Pretty much, though I'm also good at drinking hot coffee without burning my tongue and eating chocolate-covered donuts without getting frosting all over my hands." He held out a palm. "People ask all the time how I manage it."

"I'm impressed. If I ever need help eating or drinking, I'll come find you."

"Michael."

"Pardon?"

"My name is Michael."

"Ah."

Still standing over her, he murmured, "It seems I'm also better than you at making friends. You're supposed to tell me your name now."

"That's assuming I want you to know it. Maybe I don't."

"Why wouldn't you?" He crouched down. He was still about two feet away. Close enough for her to now see that his eyes were almost the color of the sea but far enough that she didn't feel crowded. "Aren't you just an Amish girl from up north, hanging out in Siesta Key on your first day here?"

She was a little embarrassed by his spot-on description. "It seems like you have some wonderful-gut detective skills too."

"Not so much. Your skin looks like cream. That's a dead giveaway for tourists every time."

In spite of her intentions to eventually give him the cold shoulder—after all, her mother would scold her for being so open with a man she didn't know anything about—she couldn't help but continue. "Do you live here year-round, Michael?"

An even more mischievous look filled his eyes. "Tell me your name and I'll answer."

Oh, but he was cheeky! Suddenly, it seemed ridiculous to withhold her name. What did it matter anyway? "My name is Esther."

"Esther," he murmured, seeming to try out her name on his tongue. "It suits you."

She wondered why. To be honest, even though her parents had often teased her about being named after the beautiful queen in the Bible, she'd always considered her name to be rather awkward. No Englischer girl had such an old-fashioned name. Or, perhaps it all went back to learning to read and struggling with spelling, but there had been more than a few days in her life when she would have happily changed her name to Tina.

"I meant that as a compliment, by the by," Michael said.

She shook her head. "It wasn't you. I . . . well, I guess my mind did drift off. Sorry." She licked the last of her ice cream, then folded the cone in the napkin. She wasn't hungry anymore, and it felt awkward to eat that cone in front of Michael.

"Are your fingers sticky? We can walk down to the water if you'd like."

"That sounds like a good idea."

"Leave your flip-flops on until you get close," he said. "That sand gets hot."

"What about your feet?"

"Mine are used to it." He looked amused again, like she was silly to be concerned about him. "When you grow up here, you soon learn that this ain't nothing. Not compared to the middle of July, anyway."

This boy really was full of himself. He probably knew more about walking on hot sand than she did, though, so she kept her flip-flops on as she walked to the water's edge. The white sand was so fine and soft, it kept brushing against her toes and the tops of her feet. Even its warmth felt wonderful—she wanted to savor it after experiencing so many cold days in Trail.

The water, though? It was just chilly enough to feel refreshing but not so cold that it made her wince. No, to sum it up, it felt like heaven.

Bending down, she hastily picked up the flip-flops with one hand and gathered the edges of her dress with the other, pulling it up so it lingered about her calves. Then Esther simply stood in place and wiggled her toes. She loved the way her feet sank into the sand underneath the water. That sensation, together with the unmistakable scent of salt water and the warm sun on her face, made almost all her worries lift from her shoulders.

She didn't want to move.

"Want me to hold your shoes for ya?"

Michael was standing next to her in the water. For a second, she'd completely forgotten about him. "Why?" she asked.

"Didn't you come into the water to wash your hands? It's

kind of hard to hold up the hem of your dress, hold your shoes, and do that at the same time."

He was right. And that was why she'd stepped into the water. How could she have forgotten? "Danke," she murmured, handing him her flip-flops.

He reached for them like he carried other people's dirty shoes all the time. "Not a problem."

Still holding the edge of her dress, she crouched down and first washed one hand and then the other. It was harder than she thought. The current was at times stronger than she'd imagined. She'd be so embarrassed if she fell.

When at last she was standing upright again, she held out her hand. "I can hold them now."

"No need. Just tell me when you're ready to start walking on the hot sand again."

"You'd really stand here for ten more minutes, just holding my flip-flops?"

"I really would."

"Michael! Ya coming?" one of his friends called out.

Looking irritated, he turned. "In a minute!"

"I guess you'd better go," Esther said. "They sound like they're getting mad."

"They're fine. And they can wait a little while longer."

She looked at him curiously. "Are they used to waiting? Do you help hapless women on the beach all the time?"

"Never." He flashed a smile. "You're the first."

"Yeah, right." He acted too smooth and too confident for her to believe that.

He looked upset that she didn't believe him. "I mean it. I don't."

"Why me, then?"

His eyes widened before he visibly regained his composure. "Come on. You have to know why."

"Uh, no, I really don't. Why did you?"

"Because you're beautiful."

She laughed. "Come on. Why?"

All traces of humor had left. "I mean it. You're the prettiest girl I've ever seen. Plus, you were sitting alone, eating that ice cream like it was the best treat you'd ever had in your life. It was adorable. Of course I had to come over to talk to you. How could I not?"

Esther wasn't sure what to think about what he was saying. It was flattering, of course, but it also took her off guard. Her mother had always found fault with the slightest imperfection. She'd grown up trying to make sure her hair was neatly arranged under her kapp, her clothes were neat and orderly, and her nails were carefully filed down. That she never gained too much weight.

"You're sweet to say all that, but of course it's not true."

"You can't tell me that I don't know my own mind."

"How old are you?"

Michael lifted his chin. "Nineteen."

"I'm twenty-four."

He smiled. "Only five years older."

"What does that mean?"

He shrugged. "Where are you staying?"

"Why?"

"Why do you think? I want to see you again."

He was so . . . so direct, he made her feel like she was the teenager. "Michael, I'm on vacation. And I'm older than you."

"So? We just determined that I already know both of those things."

90

"Michael! Come on."

He frowned. "I really do have to go. Where are you staying? Please tell me."

"Marigold Inn," she replied before she chickened out.

"In Pinecraft, right?" After she nodded, he smiled again. "I'll see you soon then. Gut day."

Esther gaped at him as she watched him lope back to his friends, laugh at something one of them said, and then head down the beach. Even in the midst of all those boys, Michael seemed to stand out. He was a little taller, his shoulders were a little broader, his whole appearance a little more confident. He never looked back once, though two of the girls in their crowd did turn and peek at Esther.

Only when they were far down the beach did she realize that she'd been standing there motionless for at least five minutes. Maybe longer.

He'd taken her off guard. Definitely a surprise, but maybe not a bad one.

Then reality set in. She was staying alone, and the woman she'd hoped to make amends with not only hated her but thought she was cruel. Esther realized that she was actually glad that she'd told this boy where she was staying. If things continued the way they were, he might be the only person who would want to talk to her during the entire trip.

12

The house was quiet when he entered. Breathing a sigh of relief, Michael locked the door behind him and took off his shoes. If he was careful, he'd be able to get to his attic room without anyone being the wiser.

Just as he was about to climb the creaky wooden stairs to the attic, his aunt appeared in the hallway.

"You are home late, Michael," Aunt Vera said. "I expected you two hours ago."

"I'm sorry, Aunt, but it couldn't be helped."

"What were you doing?" Uncle Paul asked as he joined Vera.

They always asked the same questions, and they never failed to spark his temper. "You know what I was doing. I went to the beach, then went to work at On the Boardwalk."

"Until this late?"

He stifled a harsh retort with effort. Though their complaints were nothing new, tonight their questioning felt even more like an invasion into his privacy.

"The restaurant takes reservations until eight o'clock. Some of my customers stay until after ten. Then I had to help clean, just like I always do. It's not even midnight. I'm not h—I mean, back that late." There was no way he'd ever call this place his home.

"Did you get paid?" Paul asked.

"Not today. You know I get my paycheck only once a week."

"Don't forget to pay your rent when you do," Paul said before he headed back to their bedroom. "I'll be waiting for it, boy."

"Are you planning to come back downstairs after your shower?" Vera asked.

"Jah." He'd learned over time to be direct with her. Whenever he wavered or was hesitant, she was quick to take advantage. "I'll want something to drink and likely something else to eat too."

"Don't forget to clean up after yourself. We'll be attempting to go back to sleep, you know."

"I understand."

Vera let out a long sigh before turning away. Michael knew within minutes both his aunt and uncle would be in their bedroom with the door tightly shut.

Relieved that the questioning had ended, he headed upstairs once again. Once he got to his room, he closed his door and locked it. Only then did he open his small closet, carefully pull out the piece of trim that covered up his coffee can, and then at last pull down the can from its hidden spot.

Four years ago, when his parents died and his father's sister Vera had been obligated to take him in, Michael learned a great many things about life with Vera and Paul. The first was the most important—that his aunt and uncle were not like his parents. Not at all. They were rigid, childless, and unhappy. They found fault with most everything—with him, with their lives, and with each other.

His being there had not improved their demeanors or their outlook on life.

Michael had also learned that since his parents had been rather free-spirited, they hadn't saved a lot. That meant that even after the sale of their small house and all their belongings, there hadn't been much left over to give to him.

At least, that was what Paul and Vera had always said.

That, of course, led to Michael learning what might not have been the most important but had surely been the most sobering lesson from life with them. His aunt and uncle didn't always tell the truth.

They also saw no harm in charging him room and board—or asking him to help them pay for their bills. Not that anyone else knew that. To all their friends, they were wonderful-gut folks, taking in Vera's poor, orphaned nephew.

Since nothing would change if Michael told the truth, he bided his time. He worked hard not only to pay the money they expected but also so he could afford his own place. Now that he was nineteen, he would be able to lease an apartment soon. He wanted a good cushion, which meant he needed both the first and last months' rent but also enough to allow him to buy a bed and a few pieces of furniture and to be able to pay his bills.

He was close. So close, thank the good Lord. Maybe only two more months if the tips continued to be as good as they'd been. Maybe even sooner if he had more evenings like this one. He'd had a really good night.

Sitting on his bed, he carefully emptied his pockets and put the day's tips into the can. It was true his paycheck came once a week. But the tips—those he needed to save. Every time he opened the coffee can, he breathed a sigh of relief that his relatives hadn't discovered his stash. He knew it would be gone within seconds if they found it.

After putting two twenties in his wallet, he replaced the lid, slid the can into the secret cubby in the closet, put back the trim, and put the twenty-pound weight back in front of it. His money was now as secure as he could make it.

Pleased, he pulled out a clean T-shirt and pants and got ready to take a shower. Having his own private bathroom was one of the unexpected good things about his life. The shower was roomy, the water was hot, and his aunt and uncle never complained about him taking so many showers.

Only when he finally stood under the hot spray did Michael allow himself to think about Esther. What a girl.

He'd told her that she was beautiful, and that was true. But there had been something more than just her good looks that had drawn him to her. She'd looked so content to be sitting on the beach alone. It had been something of a surprise too, given that she didn't look like the type of woman who had ever lacked for companions.

She certainly hadn't been impressed with him! She'd seemed to chat with him only with the greatest reluctance. He hadn't cared, though. As long as she kept talking to him, he would count that as a win. He wanted to know her. No, it was as if the Lord had put her in his life but would take her away if he didn't appreciate her.

He certainly did.

His infatuation didn't make sense. Not really. Esther was older, it was obvious that she was preoccupied with something important, and she lived someplace else. Michael knew he shouldn't be thinking about her much at all. But it was as if the Lord was keeping her on his mind for some reason.

After going downstairs to get a glass of water and a package of graham crackers, he went upstairs, ate a few crackers, then eventually crawled into bed. The sheets smelled fresh and vaguely like the ocean. For some reason Vera still washed his sheets and hung them on the line outside. That was a blessing.

But he had more than one blessing to be thankful for this evening. In the morning, he'd do his chores and visit lovely Esther at the Marigold Inn. He couldn't wait.

He didn't know how he was going to get her to take him seriously, but he was going to do his best.

"Lord, I'm gonna need Your help with that one," he prayed. "After all, it's Your fault that I canna stop thinking about Esther. I figure that means that You have to follow through a bit, right?"

He went to sleep imagining the Lord biting back a sigh but agreeing to help him. Michael liked that idea a lot.

13

After spending most of the day feeling sorry for herself, Mary had taken a walk, visited a few shops, and joined her friends at the Shrimp Shack. They'd sat at a picnic table and ate french fries and fried shrimp and drank cold lemonade. The food had been wonderful, and Betsy's and Lilly's stories about their trip to the Ringling Brothers museum had been entertaining.

She was feeling almost like herself when Lilly and Betsy knocked on her door near ten that evening. Mary felt torn but let them in. To her relief, they were wearing pajamas and robes just like she was.

"What's going on?"

"Oh, nothing much," Lilly said. "We just decided to stay up and bother you. You know, since you seem to be in the middle of a personal crisis."

She winced. "I thought I was better at supper."

"Y-you were, but it's still obvious that something terrible has happened," Betsy said.

"It's terrible for me, but it's not a crisis or anything."

"It's definitely something," Lilly said. "Mary, why don't you like Esther?"

That question stung. She didn't want her new friends to think she was an awful person. "It's not a one-sided thing," she said in a rush. "I promise, Esther doesn't like me either."

Of course, as soon as she said the words, she remembered Esther's devastated expression when they first saw each other. Her stomach started to hurt.

Lilly sat down on the side of the bed. "How come?"

"I'd rather not say." She held her breath, ready for the girls to leave her to her pity party.

Betsy shook her head. "Nee. Y-you don't get to do that."

"Do what?"

"You don't get to pretend that the three of us aren't friends. Friends share things that are important to each other. Or have y-you changed your mind about Lilly and me?"

"I haven't. Of course I haven't," Mary said quickly. "It's just, well, it's a stupid story from my childhood. I really didn't want you two to know about it."

"How come?"

"Because you two girls are the first friends I've had in a long time who don't know about something I did ages ago."

Lilly tilted her head to one side. "Are you really afraid that if we know something about your past, we're not going to want to be friends with you?"

Okay, that did sound kind of paranoid, but she'd learned the hard way that it could happen. "Maybe?"

Lilly and Betsy exchanged glances. Then Lilly cleared her throat. "Sorry, but I don't think that you keeping your secrets here is going to help you much."

If it was any other situation, Mary knew she'd think the

same thing. But all she could think about was how awful it was going to be if the first real girlfriends she'd made in years turned against her.

But . . . maybe she could share just a little bit. "I'm not going to tell you the whole story, but I could tell you a little." When both girls leaned forward slightly, she continued. "I should first tell you that I used to be pretty chubby. One day, I made a fool of myself with, ah, some food, and it's haunted me all this time."

"Where does Esther come in?" Betsy asked.

"There were three girls who were best friends. Not only did they make it their goal to make sure that no one ever forgot what I did, but they took a lot of pleasure in reminding me about it."

Remembering all the snubs, the jokes, and the lunches when she sat alone, the same tight ball that used to live in the pit of her stomach returned. "They made me miserable for a long time. For years," she added, just in case the girls were thinking she was holding a grudge for something small.

Lilly asked, "Why on earth is Esther here? Was it just a co-incidence?"

"Nee. Esther told me that she had a falling-out with the other two and needed to get away too."

"So she chose to come here?" Lilly looked as incredulous as Mary had felt.

"Jah," she replied. Shaking her head, she murmured, "I still can hardly believe it. Esther acted like it was the perfect opportunity for us to be friends. Like I would ever believe her."

"Y-you think she's lying?"

"I don't know, Betsy, but I wouldn't put it past her." Of course, as soon as she said that, Mary wanted to take back her words. She was making Esther out to be some kind of villain in a book. She wasn't that—just a mean girl.

"Did you tell Jayson all of this when he ran after you?" Lilly asked.

Boy, she was in the middle of such a drama. It was so embarrassing. She nodded. "I did, but I don't think I did too good a job of describing everything that's happened. I'm pretty sure he thinks that I'm being too hard on Esther."

Both girls exchanged glances. "Esther did seem awfully upset after both you and Jayson left," Lilly said.

"She was crying too," Betsy added.

Knowing that Esther had been crying didn't make her feel good, but it didn't exactly make her feel all warm and fuzzy toward her either. "If you knew how many tears I shed because of the way Esther treated me, you'd understand why I don't care all that much about her crying." She cleared her throat. "I promise, I'm not vindictive by nature. It's just that I came to Pinecraft to get a break from her."

"All right," Betsy said. "Now we know."

"That's it?"

"We didn't come in here to change you, Mary. All we wanted to do was understand what happened," Lilly explained. "Now we do."

For some reason, that easy acceptance made her feel worse. "I'm sorry if I've made things uncomfortable between you all and Esther."

Betsy shook her head. "You haven't. I'm still going to be kind to her, especially since I now know that the four of us can't do things together."

It felt like she was free-falling off a cliff. "Betsy, you're actually going to take her side after everything I just told you?"

"I don't see why I need to take anyone's side. All I do know is that I lived most of my life being surrounded by people who didn't think I should be their friend for a number of reasons. I-I promised myself that if I ever had the chance, I wasn't going to treat someone the way I've been treated if I could help it."

Even though Betsy's words made sense, Mary still felt betrayed. "What about you, Lilly?"

"I feel for you, but I can't exactly say that I disagree with Betsy. Making the decision to travel alone was a big one for me. If the three of us hadn't become fast friends, I'd be so lonely now."

"I see."

Betsy smiled. "What should we do tomorrow? Want to go to the beach?"

So glad that the discussion was done, Mary smiled. "Jah. I'd love that."

"Gut. We'll leave soon after we eat breakfast."

"That sounds like fun. Danke."

Betsy hugged her. "No need to say thanks for that. I want to go. I'm sure we'll have a great time."

"The best," Lilly agreed as she hugged Mary too. "Now don't stay up too late!"

"I won't," she said as she walked them to the door. "Night."

"Gut nacht," Lilly said. "Don't worry, okay? Everything will be all right."

Mary smiled in response, but after she got back in bed she wondered if that was really going to be the case. Somehow she doubted it.

Early the next morning, soon after she awoke, Mary got on her knees at the side of her bed. Resting her elbows on the edge of the mattress, she prayed with all her might. She prayed for her family and Lilly and Betsy. She prayed for Jayson and asked the Lord to give her insight on how to act around him. Finally, she prayed for Esther and then for herself.

"Lord, I can only guess what Your plans are for me and Esther. Maybe You put the two of us here together for Esther to grow and change, or maybe it's for me. I can't say I'm glad You've done this, but Betsy and Lilly brought up some good points last night. I can't expect the world to feel sorry for me, and I don't want that either. Please help me, if not to mend fences with Esther, then at least to not break apart my new, fragile friendships with Jayson, Lilly, and Betsy."

When she stood up, Mary couldn't rightly say that she felt better—but she didn't think she felt worse. That was something, she decided.

She dressed with care, putting on her new turquoise dress. She wasn't trying to compete with Esther—but she did want to feel better about herself. Of course, the moment she looked at herself in the mirror, an inner voice reminded her that good looks weren't what mattered. She firmly turned away. That adage might be true, but not all the time.

At last, with a heavy heart, she exited her room. Happy chatter floated from the dining room. Not wanting to put a damper on the conversation for the second day in a row, she smiled as she entered. "Gut matin."

"Good morning, Mary!" Nancy called out. She was entering the room as well, holding a glass casserole dish filled with cinnamon rolls. Their heavenly smell wafted through the entire room.

"Those smell and look amazing," an older lady said. "Nancy, I don't know how you do everything! You must get up before the sun."

Nancy laughed. "I do, but these rolls weren't this morning's reason. I made them last night. All I had to do was pop them in the oven." After she set them down carefully on the sideboard, she said, "Everyone, don't be shy. Come eat while they're hot."

Though a few of the other diners got to their feet immediately, Esther, Lilly, and Betsy stayed behind. There were only two empty seats. One was at another couple's table and the other was next to the girls.

Mary had only one choice, especially when she noticed that Esther was looking at her warily. Mary felt that pensive stare in the pit of her stomach. She knew it well—she'd certainly peeked at Esther and her girlfriends that way a time or two.

Or a hundred.

Propelled by both her prayers and Betsy and Lilly's visit the night before, she sat down in the empty seat. "I'm so hungry. I hope there will still be a couple of those cinnamon rolls by the time we get there."

She felt rather than heard a collective sigh. "I hope so too," Betsy said. "They smell too good to pass up."

"I agree," Lilly said.

Esther smiled tightly but didn't say a word.

Mary wondered if she was thinking that Mary shouldn't be eating baked goods at all.

Five minutes later, almost everyone who'd surged to their feet was heading back to their chairs. "Come on, girls, don't be shy. Go get yourself a roll while they're warm," Nancy said. "Who wants coffee?"

"I do," Mary said.

"Me as well," Esther said softly.

The four of them stood up and walked to the sideboard. Mary went last. There were two rolls left. She took one, along with some fruit, eggs, and sausage. When she returned to the table, she was relieved to see that the other girls had gotten practically the same thing.

"I learned the first day not to be embarrassed about getting a big breakfast," Lilly told Esther. "This is paid for. Lunch around town is not."

"I was thinking the same thing," Esther said. "So, what are your plans for today?"

"We're going to the b-beach," Betsy said. "Siesta Key."

"I went there yesterday," Esther said.

"Did you enjoy yourself?"

"I think so."

Lilly looked at her curiously. "You aren't sure?"

"I know I loved the water and the white sand. It's just . . . well, a boy started talking to me."

"What happened? Did he bother you?" Lilly asked.

Looking bemused, Esther shook her head. "Nee. At first I wasn't sure what to think of him, but I eventually told him that I was staying here. I still can't believe I did that."

"Do you want to see him again?" Betsy asked.

Esther shrugged. "I'm not sure. He was nice and chatty. He didn't let me just sit quietly. There was something about him that I liked. When he said goodbye, he was pretty adamant about wanting to see me again. So I told him."

"Do you think he'll show up here?" Mary asked before she could help herself.

Esther blinked. She looked taken aback, though whether it was because of the question itself or the fact that Mary had actually asked her a direct question, she didn't know. "I think he will," she said. "I didn't lead him on—coming over was his idea."

"That's romantic, don't you think?" Lilly asked.

Esther looked even more flustered. "I don't know. I mean, I don't really know what to think." She lowered her voice. "He's nineteen!"

Betsy giggled. "Nineteen is young but not that young, Esther."

"Do you really think so?"

"Jah. Though my opinion likely doesn't count for much. I-it's not like I've had much experience in love or romance."

"I'm surprised. You're so sweet and awfully pretty," Esther said.

Mary bit her lip to keep from smiling. If any other girl she knew was saying such things, she would have teased her, saying that age shouldn't matter when it comes to love.

But this was Esther, whom she'd half feared and half hated for more than a decade. Shouldn't she continue to distrust everything about her?

Obviously spurred by Lilly's and Betsy's interest, Esther continued. "I went from thinking Michael's chattiness was because he was just a teenager to realizing that he was older than I'd first imagined, to finally wondering how I'd feel if I never heard from him again."

"How would you feel?" Lilly asked.

"I think I'd feel disappointed!" Esther covered her mouth, almost like she was trying to take back everything she'd said.

"Maybe you shouldn't worry about how you feel, then. I mean, unless there's another reason for you not to want to see him," Betsy said. "Do you have a beau at home?"

Esther cast a worried glance at Mary before answering. "Nee."

Mary shifted uncomfortably. Why was she getting the feeling that somehow Esther felt she had something to do with her lack of suitors? Then all of a sudden she remembered that Xavier had been courting Esther seriously. Mary hadn't followed the romance carefully, of course, but she had seen Esther and Xavier walking together around town. They'd seemed very close. A couple of people had even hinted that an engagement was imminent.

"What happened to Xavier?" Mary asked before she realized how rude the question was. Feeling her cheeks heat, she added, "I'm sorry. Please forgive me for intruding."

"You didn't intrude." Obviously searching for the right words, Esther added, "One of my friends started flirting with him and he flirted right back! When I got upset about that, he said some hard truths about my character. We decided we didn't suit."

"Oh." She wished she had something else to say, but she couldn't think of anything that sounded both thoughtful and kind.

Betsy looked far more sympathetic. "I'm sorry, Esther. That must have been really hard."

"It was, but now I realize that it was probably for the best. I don't want a man who flirts with other women. And, well, I don't think I'll ever be able to forget all the things he told me. It was obvious that there were some things about my character that he didn't care for."

That was telling—and it was enough of a mystery that it was on the tip of Mary's tongue to ask what, exactly, Xavier hadn't found appealing.

Luckily, Nancy broke through the tension-filled moment as she rushed forward, holding an insulated carafe. "Who's ready for a refill?"

When all of them raised their hands, she chuckled. "You four girls are a full set, I think." Refilling each of their cups, she said, "Do any of you need help with directions for your outings today?"

"I wrote down everything you told me about getting on and off the SCAT, Nancy," Lilly said. "We should be okay."

"Esther, what about you? Do you need anything, dear?"

"No, thank you. I think I might stick around for a little while this morning."

Nancy's expression turned concerned. "The second day is always hard, ain't so? The excitement of arriving has faded, but one's body is still recovering from the long bus trip."

"I'm not too tired. I'm choosing to relax here. I don't get to simply sit on the front porch at home."

"If you choose to sit in a rocking chair all day, I won't tell a soul, dear," Nancy teased. "Enjoy the rest of your breakfast, girls," she said before she moved on to the next table.

"She is the perfect innkeeper," Betsy declared. "I want to be her when I grow up."

Mary chuckled. "Maybe you should be the person to stay here all day. Nancy could give you some lessons about running an inn."

"I might do it," Betsy said. "Just not today."

Lilly got to her feet. "I don't think I can eat another bite. I'll see you girls in thirty minutes."

"I'll meet you at the door," Mary said as she stood up. "Esther, I hope you enjoy your day as well."

"Danke."

"I'm already ready," Betsy said. "I think I'll stay here a little while longer."

Mary nodded before heading back to her room.

As she walked down the hall, Mary fought back a feeling of guilt. There really was no reason that she should feel guilty for not inviting Esther to go with them. However, she was realizing that living guilt-free wasn't as easy as she'd thought.

Lost in those thoughts, she practically ran straight into Jayson, who was coming out of his room.

"Whoa," he said, taking hold of her shoulders.

She stumbled. "Oh! I'm so sorry. Did I step on your toe?"

"Nee, but since I've got my boots on today, I wouldn't have noticed if you did." His hands lingered on her shoulders—probably to make sure she was steady. After another long second, they returned to his sides.

She noticed then that he was definitely not dressed for a day in the sun. "What are your plans for today?"

"Danny's busy, so I'm going to try to help out Nancy with that piece of molding and maybe explore Pinecraft some more."

"You're going to play tourist after all?"

"Not exactly. I feel like the Lord is encouraging me to think about getting a job and a place to live here."

"That's exciting!"

"Well, it's a long shot." Looking worried, he added, "I have some responsibilities at home I can't ignore . . . but Danny reminded me that I might not have to be in Kentucky in order to take care of, um, things. So I'm going to look around at a couple of places. Both employers and places to live."

"Good luck."

"Danke. I'm going to need it." Still looking apprehensive, he added, "There's a part of me that can't even believe that I'm doing this."

"There must be a reason, though, right?" Thinking of her own prayers that very morning, she added, "Someone once told me that one shouldn't be surprised when the Lord actually does answer prayers."

"That is something good to remember." His gaze warmed. "So, I'm sorry I missed you at breakfast. What are your plans for the day?"

"We're going to Siesta Key. I can't wait to sit on the beach!"

He smiled. "I'm glad. Wear sunscreen."

"I will."

"Gut." Nancy's voice carried down the hall, and he frowned. "I'd best go, or Nancy will run out of food."

"You missed the best cinnamon rolls."

"Did I? Rats," he teased. "Bye now. I'll look for you this evening to see how you enjoyed the beach."

"Okay." She smiled, then felt herself blush. Honestly, she was acting like a giggly schoolgirl.

Jayson grinned again before continuing down the hall. Mary walked into her room and took a deep breath. What was happening to her? She had a crush on Jayson and was actually thinking about not hating Esther.

God, what are You doing to me? What is happening to my heart? she silently asked.

Almost instantly, she felt His will. Her heart was opening up at long last. She was making new friends, trying new things, and discovering new stuff about herself. Yes, it felt painful and awkward, but she couldn't say it was terrible.

In many ways, it even felt freeing.

14

Jayson had told Mary the truth. He really was feeling as if a force stronger than himself was guiding him in Pinecraft. Ever since Danny suggested that he think about living in Pinecraft, he could hardly stop thinking about the possibilities. He could totally see Joy and him in their own apartment in this area.

What he couldn't imagine was living there with Ellen as his wife.

Pushing all his worries about Ellen out of the way, he took the piece of molding from Nancy's dining room to the hardware store, found a close match, then asked around for a local carpentry shop.

It took a little bit of persuading, but Larry, the owner of Pinecraft Construction, allowed him to work on the piece of molding during the crew's lunch break.

Jayson, long used to working with others, didn't mind one bit. Before long, he'd added some more cuts to the piece so it would easily match the existing woodwork, sanded it, and finally painted it white with the small can of paint he'd also bought at the store.

Larry ate a large sandwich and a bag of chips while Jayson worked. At first he seemed skeptical of Jayson's skills, then mildly interested, then very interested.

By the time Jayson was finished, the other workers had returned. Jayson pulled out a ten-dollar bill and handed it to Larry. "This ain't much, but I figure it might help pay for your lunch tomorrow. Thank you for letting me use your workshop."

"Hold on now." Larry lumbered to his feet. "What did you say this was for again?"

"A broken piece of molding at the Marigold Inn. I'm staying there while on vacation."

"You made those cuts easily."

"It wasn't hard. I've been working with wood for a long time back home in Kentucky."

"How long did you say?"

Jayson hadn't told Larry the length of time. "I started working with my uncle when I was around eleven but started apprenticing when I was fourteen," he replied. Still feeling Larry's stare, Jayson added, "I'm twenty-five now."

"What else can you do? Do you have experience with hardwoods, windows, and cabinetry?"

"Jah. I have experience with all of it." He was proud of the years he'd spent apprenticing. He'd worked hard and learned a lot.

One of the workers, a man who looked to be about five years younger than Jayson, chuckled. "You better be careful with Larry. He's gonna have you working here with him if you're not careful."

Jayson grinned. "I wouldn't say being here would be a hardship."

Larry zeroed in on his comment like a dog with a bone. "Are you looking to get a job here in Florida?"

There it was again. The Lord was with him. Giving him opportunities. "I'm not sure if I am or not . . . but I might be," he said slowly.

"You know, I've always considered vacationing to be expensive. Food and such adds up, fast. Any chance you want to work today?" Larry asked. "I'll pay twenty dollars an hour."

"Doing what?"

"My best finish carpenter retired. My men are good, don't get me wrong, but they canna do finish work easily. It takes double the time. I thought maybe you might be able to help me out for four or five hours." Larry shrugged. "Or not. Don't make no difference to me."

Jayson could practically feel the other men's amusement behind his back. Larry seemed to be a master of manipulation—but Jayson didn't mind it one bit. The truth was, as much as he enjoyed a lazy day in the sun, the smell of a carpentry shop beckoned him like catnip.

So did the possibility of making his elusive dream a reality.

Besides, Larry's comment about vacationing being expensive wasn't a lie. An extra hundred dollars would be welcome. "I could do some work for you today. I'd be pleased to make some extra money."

Larry grinned. "I can't tell you how glad I am to hear that. I need the help, and it would be good to get to know you . . . just in case you do end up looking for work around here."

"I haven't made up my mind yet," Jayson warned. "I'm still just thinking about making a move."

"Well, you've got to start somewhere, right?" Before Jayson could answer that, Larry walked to the back office. "Come with me, son. Let's get you some gloves and such, and then I'll show you what I've got in mind for today."

Feeling like he was being pulled on a conveyor belt he hadn't even realized was turned on, Jayson followed.

"I told ya," the guy who'd called out to him earlier said. "Where there's a will, Larry *will* find a way to get you here."

"Looks like you were right," Jayson said.

After receiving his gloves, safety goggles, and instructions, Jayson started working on spindles for a staircase. Pinecraft Construction had been hired to refurbish an old Victorian, so the spindles were ornate and took a delicate hand to fashion. The project excited Jayson. It was just the thing he loved to do—he had discovered several years ago that he enjoyed carving intricate designs. On the best days, he could practically feel the wood talking to him, guiding his hands and tools. It was soon apparent that this was one of those days.

Eventually, two of the workers, Doug and Aaron, invited him to take a coffee break at a corner sandwich shop. The coffee was fresh, and Jayson enjoyed their company.

When they returned and he was back at work, Jayson knew that something huge had just happened in his life. He felt at home here. He felt comfortable and like his efforts were appreciated.

All he had to figure out now was what that meant.

15

Just as she'd promised, Esther had written her parents a letter soon after she arrived in Pinecraft. It had been tempting to simply call and leave a message for them, but she didn't dare. Before she left Trail, she'd bought a phone card in case she needed to call home in an emergency. But if she called, the first thing her mother would ask is how she'd come to have such a thing. Esther knew that she'd then spend the balance of the time on the card attempting to explain her reasoning.

So she'd written a long and chatty letter, describing the white sand on the beach at Siesta Key and her pretty room at the Marigold Inn.

When she'd put the letter in the mailbox, she felt a pinch of sadness. It really was strange not to be writing to Violet and Abbie too.

Esther supposed she should simply admit the truth, at least to herself. She missed them. She missed them a lot.

There was no harm in admitting that, she reasoned. After all, there wasn't anything she could do about the state of those relationships.

From the time she'd been six or seven, they'd been in her life.

When they were little girls, the three of them had been friends with everyone. All the mothers in the Amish school used to host little parties at each other's houses for holidays and birthdays. Gifts were never exchanged, but they usually had cupcakes or cookies and played tag or some game outside.

By the time they reached nine or ten, however, all the kids had started to find their own "best" friends. Esther had been delighted when Violet and Abbie asked if she wanted to be best friends with them.

Then everything changed. Soon, when other girls asked if she wanted to play with them, Esther found herself refusing, citing that she already had friends to play with. All that was before poor Mary had gotten so sick and become everyone's favorite scapegoat.

No, not *everyone's*. She, Abbie, and Violet had been the worst. They'd teased her, then acted as if she weren't even there. Other girls began to follow their lead. Eventually, even most of the boys kept their distance from Mary. It was almost as if Esther, Violet, and Abbie had created an environment where it was okay to be mean.

She'd been awful for years.

Now that Esther had some distance from it all, even thinking about her words and actions made her feel sick.

Only getting a taste of her own medicine had been able to bring about a change in her. She'd needed to be reminded how much words could hurt. She'd needed to experience a little bit of what Mary had lived with for years.

Sitting on the front porch in a pale pink dress and the brand-new pink rubber flip-flops she'd purchased at the dollar store that morning, Esther looked at the little pile of items she'd brought with her outside. Just to keep herself occupied. She had a book, a magazine, a cross-stich project that she hated but was too stubborn to conveniently lose, and a notebook and pen.

Esther had started writing herself lists and such—trite, fluffy things as well as strong, empowering phrases. All were things intended to boost herself up. So no one would know how insecure and anxious she'd become. She'd be so embarrassed if anyone read even a page of the notebook's contents, but perhaps that was the point. It was better to get it all out in private so she didn't inadvertently share her weaknesses out loud.

She had plenty of things to do . . . but for once she wasn't trying to be the picture of Amish goodness and productivity. Instead, she needed to simply be Esther. This Esther didn't want to do anything but kick her legs out so the sun could shine on her feet and ankles and watch a pair of bumblebees hover over Nancy's flower beds.

"You do know that you're gonna have tan feet and white legs if you sit that way, right?"

She turned to the right and came face-to-face with Michael. He was striding forward, looking far too handsome and far too full of himself. He was also smiling. Not like she was part of a secret joke—but like he was genuinely pleased to see her.

She pulled her feet in. "This seems to be your habit, Michael. Walking along and calling out unnecessary statements to virtual strangers."

He chuckled. "I don't think my comment is unnecessary at all. Your skin is as pale as soft cream. If you're not careful, your ankles are going to get torched."

She wasn't sure, but she kind of thought his comment about her skin was not a criticism. "Did you just happen to be walking by?"

He walked up the porch steps and stopped in front of her.

"You know that ain't the case. I walked over here to see you." He lifted the sunglasses from his eyes. "Were you here waiting for me?"

"Of course not. I simply felt like sitting outside." That was kind of the truth. It wasn't like she'd known for certain that he would stop by. Taking care to keep her voice cool, she added, "You're welcome to join me if you'd like."

He sat down in the chair next to hers. "Danke."

"Would you like some iced tea or lemonade?"

"If you do a half-and-half, I'd love it."

"Half lemonade, half iced tea?" she asked, just to be sure.

"Jah." Looking unsure for the first time, he added, "Or I can go get a glass of water for myself. You don't need to wait on me."

"Getting you a drink isn't waiting on you," she said as she stood up. "I'll be right back."

Still looking unsure, he nodded. "Thank you."

Something about his hesitancy struck a chord with her. She felt a little warmer as she hurried inside to the dining room. She'd learned yesterday that Nancy put out cups, drinks, and trays of cookies every day. Finding two plastic cups, she filled them with ice, tea, and lemonade. Then, as an afterthought, she picked up a few of the lemon-chip cookies and folded them in a napkin.

Michael opened the door for her when she returned and took one of the cups from her. When their fingers brushed, she felt herself blush, which was really too silly. It wasn't like she'd never had a suitor before.

Though, had her body ever reacted so intensely to Xavier? She didn't think it had.

Whether Michael noticed her silliness or not, she didn't know. All he did was drink half the liquid in his cup before sitting back down.

"I guess you were thirsty?"

"I was. The half-and-half tastes good. Danke."

"Of course." She sipped her drink, then realized she was still clutching the trio of cookies. After taking the top one, she handed the napkin with the other two his way. "Do you like cookies? These are very good." When he didn't move to take them, she added, "They're lemon and white chocolate."

At last he took them and set them on the napkin next to his drink. "That is kind of you."

She shrugged. She didn't want to point out the obvious—she hadn't made them. "Do you live far away from here?"

"Not far at all. Only a couple of blocks."

"Do you live with your parents?"

"Hmm? Oh, no." Everything in his expression changed. "I live with my aunt and uncle."

"Oh?"

"My parents died about four years ago. My aunt and uncle took me in."

He didn't sound all that grateful or pleased about their kindness. She wondered why. "I'm sorry about your parents. That must have been hard."

Looking her directly in the eye, he nodded. "It was. It was very hard. But they're in a better place, right?"

His tone was slightly mocking. She was a bit shocked until she remembered that he would have been only about fifteen when his parents passed. That was very young. "What do you do? Are you a farmer?"

"Nee. Not a lot of farming here, though there are some Amish farmers when you head toward the central part of the state. I work at a restaurant in downtown Sarasota."

She was intrigued. "What do you do?"

"I'm a waiter."

"Really? Do you like it?"

His easy smile returned. "Jah. It's a gut job and my manager is nice."

"Do a lot of Amish go there?"

"Hardly any at all. The restaurant is fancy. It caters to Englischers. Most probably don't even realize that I'm Amish." Before she could ask another question, he said, "What about you? What do you do back in Trail?"

"I'm a maid."

He blinked. "Truly?"

"Oh, jah. I work at a hotel in Sugarcreek. It's a good job too."

"It's likely a hard job, ain't so?"

"Only on my hands, though I wear gloves most of the time."

"It still doesn't sound like much fun."

She smiled at him. "Cleaning bathrooms all day isn't exactly fun, but it's not that bad. The manager likes two of us to clean rooms together—he feels it's safer that way. I always try to work with one of the same two ladies. They're usually hard workers, and they like to talk. It makes the time go by fast."

"I guess it would."

He was looking at her like she had something on her face or nose. "Why are you looking at me so funny?"

"I didn't mean to. You took me by surprise, that's all."

She was still confused. "Why?"

"Because you look so perfect. I imagined you were a coddled girl on a fancy vacation."

His inaccurate description made her giggle, but perhaps she'd done the same thing to him. "I guess the two of us are proof that first impressions aren't always right. Why, yesterday I was sure you were a silly teenager having a bit of fun with me."

He smiled slowly. "What did you think I was doing, Esther? Did you think I was flirting with you because no one else was around?"

"Jah."

"We both know there were other girls around. I wasn't interested in them, though."

"Maybe next time you will be?"

A line formed between his brows as he shook his head. "Esther, I'm not like that. I don't go to the beach every day and flirt with girls."

"It's okay if you do. I'm not here to judge."

"Nee, you don't understand. Yesterday was the first day in weeks that I took most of the day off and hung out with my friends. Usually I am working or doing chores for my aunt and uncle."

"I'm sorry if I offended you," she said in a rush. "I was only teasing you."

He closed his eyes. "Nee, I am the one who's sorry. I overreacted. I . . . I guess there's something about you I want to impress."

Feminine chatter caused them both to look down the street. Esther smiled at the group—just as she caught Mary's eye.

Mary barely looked at her or Michael when she climbed up the inn's front steps.

Betsy and Lilly stopped.

"H-hello," Betsy said. "That lemonade looks perfect. I'm going to have to go in and get some."

"You should. It's great," Michael said.

"What happened?" Esther asked. "I thought you three were going to the beach today."

"We still are, but we decided to go to a few shops first," Lilly said. Holding up her bag, she added, "I asked if we could drop off our stuff first."

"What beach are you wanting to visit?" Michael asked.

Betsy turned to Mary. "What was the name?"

"I don't recall. One of the ones on Siesta Key. Nancy told me that any of them will do."

"I can help you there. When the SCAT arrives on the key, take care not to get off at the first stop. That's the most crowded one."

"Which one should we take?"

"The second," Michael said patiently. "If you get off at the second stop instead of the first, there's a small beach that is usually half empty. There's a good snack shop there too."

Mary turned to join them. "Thank you. We'll keep that in mind."

"I hope you have a good time. I'm Michael, by the way," he added with a smile.

Esther felt herself flush. "Forgive my manners. Michael, this is Lilly, Betsy, and Mary Margaret. Girls, this is Michael. We met on the beach yesterday."

After murmuring that it was nice to meet him, the girls disappeared through the front door.

When the door closed again, Michael said, "You didn't want to go to the beach with them today?"

"Nee. I went yesterday."

"You went by yourself, right?"

"Right."

"Today, you're sitting by yourself too."

"I was. Now I'm sitting with you," she teased.

"Why?" He studied her like she was a new puzzle he was attempting to solve.

She was in no hurry for him to learn about her treatment of Mary. "Sorry, but how I spend my days on vacation isn't any of your business."

"I know . . . but why aren't you doing things with them?"

She was becoming flustered. Too flustered, considering she was only being nice to him because he stopped by. "If you are going to continue to be so nosy, I think you should leave."

Instead of standing up, he had the gall to lean forward and grin. He waved his right hand like she'd singed the tips of his fingers. "Ouch. You got me good."

He . . . he was exasperating. And for some mysterious reason, completely attractive. She'd never met anyone like him. She'd sure never met any man who couldn't care less about following proper protocol.

"Honestly, Michael." Stung by both his questioning and the fact that she knew she was being secretive, she folded her arms across her chest. Unbidden, tears sprang to her eyes. She was frustrated with herself, embarrassed about her past, and unsure of what to tell him.

Though it was no less than she deserved, she really, really didn't want to give him a reason to never see her again.

Which didn't make a bit of sense. Not at all.

He immediately stood up and crouched in front of her. "Hey. I'm sorry. I didn't mean to make you cry."

"Nee. It's not you. And I'm not crying."

He swiped the tear that had just escaped her eye. "You're right. This must have been something else. Are you sweating, Esther?" he said.

Just the idea of her dripping with sweat in front of Michael and his perfection made her wince. "I am not!"

Still crouched in front of her, he smiled. "I knew that would get you in a dither."

She opened her mouth. Shut it again. "I hardly know what to say to you."

"I don't blame you. I was being a jerk and you were right to be upset. I'll try to be better in the future." He stayed there another second, seeming to take in every single freckle on her nose, then sat down again.

Her body shivered. Not from fear or from cold, but because he affected her. "We don't even know each other."

"That's not true. We know each other now."

"You know what I mean. We just met. I'm leaving next week."

"I'm aware of both of those things too. But I still want to see you every day."

"I won't be camped out on this porch tomorrow."

He grinned. "I have to work most evenings, but I can take you out to brunch. Do you eat brunch?"

"Yes."

"What do you think about ten? Is that too early? Too late? I don't want to ruin your day."

"Ten is fine." She wasn't going to touch the fact that they both knew she didn't have plans with other people.

"I'll be going then . . . unless you'd care to take a walk with me."

She did want that. She wanted to walk by his side and feel his gaze on her and feel like he thought she was special. But the lessons her mother taught her about being modest and proper were too well-ingrained for her to accept his offer. "I don't think a walk today would be appropriate."

"Then I'll see you tomorrow, Esther." He lifted the cup, drained it, and picked up the two cookies. "Thank you for the

drink and the lemon–white chocolate chip cookies." He nodded, then walked down the steps before she could come to terms
with the fact that she'd just watched him swallow his drink.

Quickly, she stood up. "You're welcome."

He turned around, smiled, then continued walking.

Feeling slightly dizzy, Esther watched him until he was out
of sight.

When she sat down again, she sipped her own drink, then
placed the sweating cup on her face. She felt warm all of a
sudden.

So strange.

16

They were headed back to Siesta Key on the SCAT. While the bus maneuvered through traffic, Mary passed the time by watching all the passengers get on and off and thinking about their day.

Mary was still a little hesitant to ask Betsy and Lilly things that they might take exception to, which was why she hadn't dared put on the bathing suit she'd brought. If she'd known them better, she would've asked what they were going to wear and confided that she'd brought a suit just in case she was brave enough to wear it.

Instead, she'd opted for a pale-yellow dress in a lightweight fabric. She had brought a beach towel, sunscreen, water, snacks, and a book to read. Everything was nestled neatly in the canvas tote bag she'd brought on the bus. She noticed that Lilly was also carrying a tote bag, but Betsy was carrying a flowered pink-and-orange beach bag. The bag, combined with her short-sleeved, tangerine-colored dress, made her look like a ray of sunshine.

After exiting the bus, they followed the other visitors through the parking lot to a set of stairs that led to the beach. Walking down the steps felt a bit like entering Narnia. Within seconds, all thoughts of the bus, the parking lot, and Ohio faded away. In their place was the glorious expanse of beach and the faded blue water lapping at the shores.

The three of them stood still, in awe of the sight.

"I love it here," said Lilly.

"I was thinking the same thing," Mary said. "Where do you two want to sit?"

The beach wasn't close to being crowded, but there were several groups of people scattered in the area. Some of them were obviously English; others were wearing traditional Amish clothes and coverings.

Then there were other groups who looked to be Amish but were wearing shorts or bathing suits. Some of the men had beards and the women had their prayer coverings off and their long hair either hanging down their backs or fastened in ponytails.

"I wish I would've worn my bathing suit," murmured Betsy. "Going into the ocean would be so wonderful."

"You brought a bathing suit?" Lilly asked.

"I did." Suddenly looking worried, Betsy said, "I hope you two don't think I'm awful."

"I brought one too," Mary confided. "I almost wore mine under my dress."

"I wish you would've," Betsy said. "One of us needed to be brave."

Mary was so excited. "We're here for several more days. We should come again in our bathing suits!"

"I agree!" Betsy exclaimed. "It will be the best memory— doing something we would never do back in our hometowns."

Suddenly realizing that Lilly had been very quiet, Mary turned to her. "Uh-oh. Have we shocked you?"

"A little. It never occurred to me to bring a bathing suit. I don't know how I would've gotten one anyway."

"An English friend took me to the supercenter, and I got one there," Betsy said.

Lilly didn't exactly act as if she wanted to get a suit. "Lilly, it doesn't matter to me if you want to wear a bathing suit or not," Mary said. "We don't all have to want to do the same things."

"I agree," Betsy said. "We should be supportive, not forcing each other to do things we don't want to do."

"I'm not sure if I want to wear a bathing suit. My parents would be disappointed in me."

The worried expression on Lilly's face brought forth a bunch of questions, but Mary didn't want to pry. "If you don't feel comfortable, then you shouldn't," she said. "What matters is we're here at the beach instead of in the cold."

Looking relieved, Lilly smiled. "I agree." Pointing to a spot close to the water, she said, "How does that spot look?"

"Perfect," Betsy said. "Y-you lead the way."

In no time at all they were seated in a row, each settled on a colorful beach towel, with the skirts of their dresses pushed up to their knees. The air around them smelled of tropical-scented suntan lotion. "This is exactly what I used to dream about when I was saving up for this trip," Mary said.

"Me too. I never thought it would actually come true, though," Betsy said. "My parents were so worried about me. I kept expecting them to change their minds about me being here."

Lilly's eyebrows lifted. "Even at your age?"

"Jah. See, I was really sick with lung ailments when I was young. I was in the hospital a lot." She shrugged. "Their over-protectiveness was bothersome, but my brother keeps telling me to try to see things from their perspective. They almost lost me once; they're afraid it could happen again."

"I can't believe I didn't know that," Mary said before realizing that it would've been surprising if she had known more about Betsy's past. It wasn't like they'd known each other very long. "I guess we don't really know each other very well," she murmured.

"I was just thinking the same thing," Lilly said. "It's funny because I kind of started thinking that we've been friends forever."

"H-how about we each share something about ourselves?" Betsy said.

"Does it have to be a secret?" Lilly asked.

"I don't think so. After all, pretty much everyone in Hart County knows about my bad lungs," Betsy said. "I say let's share whatever we want to share."

Since Lilly looked petrified and Betsy looked embarrassed, Mary decided to do her best to help them both out. "I'll share," she said as she shifted to wrap her arms around her legs. "I really like ice cream and don't like most meat all that much. Sometimes I even think about being a vegetarian."

"My mamm would call you picky," Betsy teased.

Mary giggled. "I guess she would be right. Since I'm now completely embarrassed, it's time for one of you to go."

"I love vanilla ice cream and hate to weed my mother's garden," Lilly said.

"I like ice cream too, but rocky road or chocolate almond or something like that. Not vanilla," Betsy said. "And . . . I'm not sure if I'm going to be baptized."

Mary couldn't help but gape at her. It wasn't the news that shocked her as much as the fact that Betsy was sharing it with them. Deciding whether to be baptized or not was a serious decision and usually something no one talked about. "Oh my stars, Betsy!"

Doubt filled Betsy's eyes. "Was that too much to say too soon?"

"Nee," Lilly said in a rush. "I'm glad you told us."

Betsy's eyebrows rose as if she wasn't quite sure that she agreed.

"What do your parents say?" Lilly asked. "Or have you kept it a secret?"

"Oh, I told them. I couldn't keep something like that from them." She folded her arms around her knees. "As for how they reacted . . . well, they weren't happy about it. They also want me to pray about it some more." She took a deep breath. "B-but they also said that they understood on account of me being around so many Englischers when I've been in the hospital."

"Your parents must be really nice," Lilly said.

"They are. I love them dearly. I love my brother, Bobby too."

"Wait, your bruder's name is Bobby?" Mary asked.

"It's Barnabas—a gut, solid Bible name. He's always hated it, though. He said he was going to be called Bobby when he was about five."

"What did your parents say?"

"About what you'd imagine. Something about, they gave him a good name and he should be proud of it." Betsy giggled. "But the story goes that my brother started crying and said it was their fault that everyone called him 'barn and a bus.' I guess my p-parents didn't argue about 'Bobby' ever again."

Mary started laughing so hard she could barely stop. "I'm sorry," she said. "I just keep thinking about little boys calling him that and him being so aggrieved that he told your parents."

Betsy giggled too. "If you saw mei bruder, you would think it was really laughable. He is a big man—over six feet tall and real strong. Every time we read about Barnabas in the Bible, I teased my brother."

And so it continued. They shared childhood stories that weren't too serious or too painful. They talked about likes and dislikes. They went into the water up to their knees and held Lilly's hand when she squealed because she thought she'd stepped on a crab.

When a couple of men their age, obviously also Amish, smiled their way, they smiled back.

The day was everything Mary had always wanted—nee, everything she'd always dreamed of having but never imagined would happen.

Her secret truth was that she hadn't had great aspirations for a long time now. She didn't need to be the most popular or the prettiest girl around. She'd never hoped to be really smart or even a really good person.

All she'd ever yearned for was to be with a couple of friends. Good friends, close enough to giggle with over things that didn't matter and who didn't try to hurt her with cruel words or gossip.

For these few hours, she was one of the girls she used to look at during singings or in the public middle school she'd attended. For a little while, she felt confident, the kind of confidence one gets only when she's accepted wholeheartedly. It was lovely.

It felt just as wonderful as she'd always dreamed it could be—if she ever had that chance.

After several more hours passed and the crowds started to lessen, they slowly started picking up their things. Mary felt melancholy, but she held tight to the knowledge that their trip wasn't over. She didn't have to say goodbye, either to her new friends or to moments like she'd shared with these two friends. "I guess it's time," she said. "We need to get cleaned up and find some dinner."

Lilly glanced up at the sky. "We've got hours until sundown, but I think you're right. I forgot how long the SCAT bus runs too."

"C-come on, then," Betsy said as she picked up her bag and started walking across the beach.

They found the bus stop easily enough. After asking a few of the teenagers there when it was scheduled to arrive, they learned that it stopped there every hour.

"It's good we headed back when we did," Mary said as they joined the line of passengers.

"I agree," Lilly said.

After another couple of minutes passed, Betsy and Lilly exchanged meaningful glances.

"What's going on?" Mary asked.

"Well, Betsy and I have been thinking about something but haven't been sure what to say."

"If you two want to go out for hamburgers, we can go. I'll just ask for something else when we're there."

"It's not that," Betsy said. In a small voice, she added, "No offense, Mary, but I couldn't help but think about Esther today."

"Why?"

"Well, she was all alone."

The girls had a point, but she pushed any sympathetic feelings she had about that to one side. "Esther was here yesterday. It isn't like she would've wanted to come back here today."

"I guess not," Lilly said.

"I suppose she probably wouldn't have wanted to spend two

days in a row at the beach." Betsy looked like she wanted to say something else, but she refrained.

Both of their expressions made Mary feel bad, especially because deep inside she knew Lilly and Betsy's concern about Esther being all alone was natural. Half of their conversations today had been about how they'd missed out on so many experiences in their teens because they'd been excluded.

And here they'd done some excluding of their own.

Feeling that pinch of guilt, she tried to justify it. Esther probably deserved getting a taste of her own medicine. Maybe?

Or maybe not. Putting Esther in her place didn't make Mary feel all that good. Actually, it made her feel like maybe she wasn't any better than Esther, Abbie, and Violet had been.

Or maybe she was actually a whole lot worse because she knew how it felt to be left behind. She knew that feeling all too well.

"Maybe when we get back, we should see if she wants to join us for supper." Mary felt like the words were being clawed out of her, but she didn't want to take them back. As much as she'd like to keep pretending that this glorious day could continue forever, it couldn't. The Lord was giving her a chance to make a difference in her life—and maybe help someone else too. It would be wrong to pass that up.

Lilly brightened. "Really? I'm so glad. Danke, Mary."

"Whew!" Betsy smiled. "I'm so glad that conversation is over with. I was really worried."

Now she felt even worse. "I'm sorry you were worried about bringing her up. And that you didn't think I'd be very nice."

"I didn't think that," Lilly said. "It's just . . ."

"I know," Mary said softly. "It's hard to know what to do, especially when it involves making a change."

"I'm glad the three of us talked," Lilly said.

"Me too." And Mary meant it.

She realized that not only was this trip becoming a chance to try new things, it was giving her the opportunity to grow a little more. She didn't have a lot of experience having two close friends. She wasn't used to compromising or looking at situations from other people's perspectives. Obviously it was time she started doing that.

17

The SCAT wasn't difficult to take home, though they couldn't decide which stop to take when they neared Pinecraft. They decided to get off near the post office bulletin board. There were several Mennonite and Amish people milling around that spot—it was the main place to discover where people from different areas got together and who was hosting coffees. One of the ladies knew how to get to the Marigold Inn and pointed them in the right direction.

That detour took an extra thirty minutes, leaving them feeling rather exhausted when they finally arrived at the inn's front porch.

"I've never been more excited that we aren't sharing a room," Lilly said. "Now we won't have to take turns to use the shower."

"Want to meet here in thirty minutes for supper?" Betsy asked.

Seeing Esther sitting by herself in a corner of the living room, Mary knew it was time to make things right. "Could we make it forty-five?" she asked. "I want to speak with Esther."

Lilly gave her a sympathetic look. "Would you like us to come with you? I don't mind."

"I don't either," said Betsy.

"Danke, but nee. You two were right to bring Esther up and to remind me about how she might be feeling, but I'm the one who needs to do this, I think."

"I pray you'll find the right words," Lilly said before she started up the stairs.

"Danke." Mary smiled at them both before peeking Esther's way again. For just a second, she caught sight of Esther looking her way before quickly looking back down at the magazine she was reading.

That small action was all she needed to see to know that she was doing the right thing. Even if Esther responded to her invitation by being mean, Mary knew she couldn't ignore the way Esther was feeling any longer. She was human, but Mary liked to think that she was also kind. *Please, Lord*, she silently prayed. *Help me be the person I want to be.*

Decision made, she entered the living room. Esther glanced up and seemed to still as Mary headed in her direction.

"Hiya," she said.

"Hello, Mary."

"Did you have a nice day?"

Esther shrugged. "I think I did. What about you? Did you enjoy the beach?"

"Oh, jah. The sand feels like sugar and the water wasn't even very cold. We had a great time. I didn't want to leave."

Esther raised her eyebrows. "I'm glad you enjoyed it."

Their conversation was just as stilted and awkward as Mary had feared it would be. It was time to get to the point.

"I came over to see if you would like to join Lilly, Betsy, and me for supper. We're going to leave in about forty minutes or so."

"Why?"

"Why forty minutes?"

"Nee." Esther still wasn't smiling. "Mary, why are you asking me to supper? It's just the two of us here, you know. You don't have to pretend that we're friends or that you like me."

Esther's words were honest and bare. They were also so direct Mary felt a bundle of nerves take hold of her. Old habits kicked in. It was so tempting to simply walk away and ignore Esther for the rest of the trip—Esther would likely be fine with that too. After all, they'd certainly had lots of experience ignoring each other during the last twelve years.

But that wasn't the right thing to do. It was time to grow and push aside old habits. "May I sit down?" she asked.

"Help yourself." Esther gestured to the chair next to her but didn't look very happy about it.

"Esther, I . . . I've thought a lot about the things you said when you visited my room. I've felt guilty for not responding in a better way."

"I've thought about our conversation too," Esther said. "I realized that I shouldn't have acted like one small apology would change years of abuse."

"It doesn't," Mary admitted. "But I don't think we need to keep track of the good and the bad." When a line formed between Esther's brows, she added, "To be honest, there's a part of me that wants you to hurt too. I want you to know how it feels to be left out, but that isn't right." She lowered her voice. "Besides, I know what it's like to be the target of Abbie's and Violet's cruelty."

"It's not pleasant, but it's not your fault, Mary. Like I said before, I want things to be different between us, but I don't expect you to automatically trust me."

As vulnerable as it made her feel, Mary pushed herself to

open her heart a little more. "The truth is, there's a part of me that's afraid when we see each other in Trail, you'll pretend that we never talked here in Florida. You'll be mean to me again."

"I hate that you think that's what I'm like, but I suppose I don't blame you." Taking a deep breath, Esther added, "I don't know if you'll believe me, but I won't ever act that way to you again."

A small voice inside Mary's head wanted Esther to promise those words. To practically make a blood vow. But Mary knew that only Esther's will and the Lord's intervention could make the way they treated each other in the future different. That had to be enough.

"Okay," she said.

Esther blinked. "Okay? That's it?"

"That's all I needed to hear. So, would you like to join us for supper? I'm not sure where we're going, but all three of us would like you to be with us."

After the briefest pause, Esther nodded. "All right."

"Meet us in the entryway in about half an hour or so." As Mary stood up, she glanced at the large clock on the living room wall. "At six."

"See you then."

Mary smiled slightly, then headed to her room. To her amazement, she didn't feel as tired as she had when they'd entered the house. Actually, she felt rather refreshed.

Almost exactly thirty minutes later, Mary was standing in the entryway with Betsy and Esther, waiting for Lilly to appear, when Jayson opened the door.

Though she could hardly look away from him, Betsy and Esther continued to discuss restaurant options. Betsy was even double-checking that she had the code for the inn's front door in case it was locked when they returned.

Jayson walked to Mary's side. "Hi."

"Hello, Jayson," she said.

After the other girls smiled in his direction, they went back to looking at the restaurant list that Nancy had given them.

"What's going on?" he asked.

"We're about to go out to eat."

"Are you trying to decide where to go or waiting on someone?"

She chuckled. "Both. I guess Lilly needed a bit more time than the rest of us."

He lowered his voice. "So, four of you are going out to supper?"

She didn't blame his surprise—she had been so upset when Esther had shown up in Pinecraft. "Yes. We, um, decided to make some changes."

He grinned. "Good for you."

"I'm trying. No, Esther and I both are. I'm grateful for that."

"What did you girls do today? Did you go to the beach?"

"We did and we loved it so much. What about you? Did you work on Nancy's molding?"

"I did. I found a hardware store and a carpentry shop."

"I'm sorry you had to work."

"Actually, I'm not. It was a good experience." Looking down at the piece of wood he still held in his hands, he added, "It forced me to think about making some changes. Some changes that I'm starting to think were far overdue."

"Really? Like what?"

His eyes darted to the stairs. "I'll have to tell you about that later."

"Sorry!" Lilly called out as she hurried down the stairs.

Mary smiled at Lilly before turning back to him. "I'd like to hear, whenever you have time." She felt her cheeks heat. Hopefully he didn't think she was being too forward.

But instead of looking like he thought she was being pushy, he said, "I'm going to go to the beach tomorrow morning to watch the sunrise. Would you care to join me?"

By their silence, Mary knew that the three other girls had heard his question and were waiting to hear her reply. She felt self-conscious, but she didn't hesitate. She wanted to spend time with Jayson. "What time is the sunrise?"

"We'd need to leave about a quarter to six."

Oh, that was going to be early, but it would also be so worth it. "All right. Should I meet you here?"

He grinned. "Jah. See you here in about twelve hours." Looking at the others, he added, "If you want pizza, go to Abo's. If you'd like Italian, try Papa's Italian. And Tacos to Go has really gut tacos and the like." He smiled sweetly at her again before heading down the hall.

Unable to help herself, Mary noticed that his room was just three doors down from hers. The other girls' giggling pulled her attention back to them.

She felt her cheeks burn as each looked more amused than the next. "Um, where do you all want to go?"

"I don't care, but it does sound like nowhere is going to be as special as watching tomorrow's sunrise," Lilly said with a knowing smile.

Mary wasn't anxious to tackle that. "How about tacos?"

"I think that sounds great," Esther said.

"Me too. I love tacos," Lilly said.

When Betsy simply giggled, Mary attempted to keep her

composure. She'd thought the toughest thing about this evening's supper was going to be sitting with Esther. She was beginning to realize, however, that the Lord had a sense of humor. Esther wasn't going to be the issue at all.

Instead it was going to be fending off her girlfriends' knowing glances while pretending that she wasn't giddy with excitement about Jayson asking her to go walking.

Especially since that was all she really did want to think about.

18

Esther had a feeling that when she got back home to Trail and reflected on her journey to Florida, she would decide that her trip had been an eye-opening one. As she walked to dinner with the other girls, Esther let her mind drift back to how much had changed in her life already.

Two days ago, when she boarded the Pioneer Trails bus in Berlin, she'd felt discouraged and upset about so many things.

Of course she'd been upset about Xavier. Even though she hadn't been positive that they would eventually get engaged and married, he'd been such a constant that she had assumed that would be the case. When everything between them fell apart, not only did she feel disappointed and hurt, but she also felt as if she'd let her mother down. Her mamm liked everything about Xavier—including the fact that his family was well-respected and successful. It wasn't right, but her mother acted as if Esther would be elevating her social status if she snagged a man from such a well-to-do family.

When they broke up, her mother had said she wondered whom Esther was going to find who would be as good of a catch. That comment had made Esther feel even more upset, as if her mother was hardly taking her heart into account.

Just as upsetting had been her falling-out with Violet and Abbie. They'd been her constants her entire life. When they turned on her, she hardly knew how to take it. She was so hurt—and naively surprised—by how mean they were to her. Some of the things they'd said to her had really hurt.

That was when she realized how much she'd been embedded in that toxic world. She'd become so accustomed to the way she treated so many people—Mary in particular—that she'd fooled herself into believing her words and actions hadn't been that bad.

Now she knew better.

Although she'd been disappointed about Mary's initial reaction to her apology, it had forced her to really think and pray about what she wanted—and how she was feeling. Esther had even begun to understand that it had been shortsighted of her to expect that one simple, heartfelt apology could erase years of hurt. She realized too that she had been selfish to even think such a thing was possible.

All that was why she'd been so startled by Mary's invitation to supper. She wondered what had changed her mind—or had God been speaking to her about everything too?

She was brought away from her thoughts by Betsy stepping to her side as they walked down Bahia Vista Road toward the restaurant.

"Esther, I don't know anything about you other than you are also from Trail," Betsy said. "Do you have any siblings?"

"I do. I have three younger brothers. One is eight, one is twelve, and one is twenty."

"My goodness."

Esther smiled. "I know! Most people are shocked when they discover both the fact that my parents had three boys after me and how spread apart in age we all are."

"Are you close to them?"

"I get along with all of them well enough, but my favorite is Junior. He's the eight-year-old."

"I bet he's fun."

"He is, but he's just a nice person too. He and I have complementary temperaments. We're always looking at each other when one of our parents says something really corny or when Adam, the twelve-year-old, is being especially difficult. What about you, Betsy?"

"I have a brother named Bobby."

"Younger or older?"

"Older. We're close too."

"That's nice."

"It is." Betsy smiled, then grinned more broadly as she pointed out a pair of twin girls. They were wearing matching pink dresses, pink sandals, and white kapps. They looked like angels, especially the way they were holding hands. However, they also looked like they might have a bit of a mischievous streak, given the way they kept ignoring their mother's directions.

"Ach, those little girls are being so naughty!" Betsy exclaimed, though she didn't look shocked. Instead, she seemed to be on the verge of laughter. "Look how they're ignoring their mamm and are trying to pet that cat instead. It's going to serve them right if that cat hisses at them."

"Their mother does have her hands full, but they could be naughtier."

"Well, jah. That is always possible, I suppose."

"Did you and your brother do stuff like that when you were little?"

"Hold hands and ignore our parents?" Betsy grinned. "Nee. My brother wasn't exactly the hand-holding type, and mei mamm really wasn't quite that patient. What about yours?"

"She wasn't patient with me not listening. Not at all. My mother was more of the type to expect me to look and act perfect all the time." Realizing how bitter she sounded, Esther added, "Obviously I didn't measure up."

"Being perfect is for Christ, though, jah?"

"I suppose so, but no one ever told my mother that." She smiled again but felt it falter when she noticed Mary gazing at her intently. Embarrassed, she looked away.

"I think this is the place Jayson told us about," Mary said. "What do you girls think?"

Tacos to Go had a big outside patio with tons of white lights strung in the palm trees and hanging from wooden beams over the seating area. Music played in the background, and there were quite a few people inside as well as sitting at the tables outside. Esther didn't see any patrons who looked Amish.

While that didn't bother her, the scene was another reminder of the tight hold her parents had on her. They supervised everything she did—and those supervised activities usually involved only the "safest" and most acceptable people and places.

Furthermore, when she wasn't being guided by them, she'd followed the leads of Abbie and Violet. Only now did she realize that she'd substituted those girls' wishes for her mother's. So far, she'd lived her life being content to be told what to do.

"I'm good with whatever you three want to do," she said quickly.

"Let's go inside," Lilly said. "If there's a long wait, we can decide what to do next."

The four of them stood in line at the hostess table. Around them were people in the bar drinking and at tables laughing. A lot of the people were their ages, but most of the girls were wearing shorts, tank tops, or skimpy sundresses. Esther didn't find anything wrong with that—she just felt even more like a fish out of water.

However, although a few of the patrons did glance their way, no one acted as if they shouldn't be there. After five minutes, the manager said, "Four, girls?"

"Jah," Mary said.

"It's a little loud inside, but we have a table that's free outside. What do you ladies think?"

"I think that would be s-super," Betsy said.

"Great. Follow me, please."

Moments later, the four of them were sitting in the back corner of the outdoor patio. Esther sat to Mary's left with Betsy and Lilly on the other side. The music was a bit softer in their little corner, and the chatter was definitely far quieter. She felt herself relax at last, especially since it seemed as if the other three girls were happy she was there.

"It sure seems like Jayson knows a lot about this area."

Mary nodded. "He's been to Pinecraft several times before. His best friend, Danny, lives here." Looking at the white lights threaded through the trees around the patio, she smiled. "I'm so glad Jayson told us about this place. I wouldn't have ever gone in here otherwise—it didn't look like an Amish-friendly spot."

"Do you go to a lot of English restaurants back home?" Esther asked.

"Not really. But it's not like there are a lot of places to go out to eat in Trail. It's easier just to make something at home."

"We only go out to restaurants about once a month," Lilly said.

"The same with us. What about you, Betsy?" Esther asked.

Betsy's reply was prevented by the arrival of their server, who brought them two baskets of warm chips and small cups of salsa, then took their drink orders.

When she was gone again, Betsy spoke. "I-I guess I am more comfortable with restaurants than you all are. I was in the hospital a lot when I was young. We were in downtown Cincinnati, so we went to a lot of different types of restaurants. I think it's fun to try new things."

"Why were you in the hospital?" Mary asked.

"I had a bad case of croup when I was a baby, then another bad bout of pneumonia when I was a little girl. That's when I had to go to the Children's Hospital in Cincinnati. Anyway, all that, together with my reoccurring asthma, has done some damage to my lungs." She lifted her chin. "I'm a lot better now."

Esther couldn't help but gape at her. "You don't seem sick at all."

"That's what I tell my family! Unfortunately, they don't always believe that. They kept me close for so many years, everyone in our town thinks of me as only 'Betsy, who is very sick and stutters.'"

"I'm sorry."

She shrugged. "I realize now that the Lord had a plan for me. If I wasn't a wallflower back home, I would've never yearned to get away. If I would've never decided to take this trip, I wouldn't have met Lilly and Mary."

"Your fellow wallflowers," Lilly said with a grin as the server brought their drinks.

"Do you all know what you want to eat?"

"We haven't even looked at the menu yet!" Mary said with a laugh.

"Take your time. I'll be back in a few," the dark-haired woman said before moving to another table.

When they were alone again, Esther said, "You all say that you're wallflowers, but I don't know what that word means. I haven't heard that word before."

"I canna imagine that you would," Mary said. "A wallflower is a girl who isn't popular, who kind of gets left out at parties. I read about them in a novel once."

"Wallflowers are the girls who the boys don't pay attention to," Lilly added.

Betsy continued. "Kind of like the forgotten girls."

"Esther, you're looking at what might be the first Amish Wallflower Club," Mary said with a smile.

Esther felt pretty guilty that she'd had a hand in making Mary feel that way. "If it contains the three of you, I think it would be a nice club to be in," she said lightly.

"Danke, but no worries. I'm sure you won't ever have to join a group like ours," Mary said. "Not that you'd ever want to."

"Oh? Why not?"

"Come on, Esther, you know why," Betsy said. "You're beautiful. I doubt you've ever been ignored in your life. P-plus, you said you always had two best friends, right? That means someone's always had your back."

Esther felt as if she'd been slapped, and tears filled her eyes. Not wanting the others to see how affected she was by Betsy's careless remark, she blinked and took a big sip of water.

To her surprise, it was Mary who came to her rescue. "Even though you might be our group's lone popular girl, I'm still glad you joined us, Esther. I started to learn that I'm not the only one in the world who has had troubles. If I've acted like you've never known disappointments or heartache, I'm sorry."

Esther's mouth went dry. Not trusting herself, she simply nodded.

19

It was rare for Michael to get off early from work. Whenever it did happen, though, it always felt like an answer to a prayer. This was one of those nights.

He was exhausted, not just from working several long shifts in a row but also from having more than his fair share of difficult tables. All he wanted to do was go home, retreat to his attic room, and sleep undisturbed for about ten hours. Hopefully by the time he woke up, the world would be back on its axis again.

Walking toward the door, he paused when he saw his manager standing by the door to the kitchen. Kim looked as tired as he felt. Actually, she looked like she would give back the day's pay if she could leave too. As anxious as he was to get out of there, Michael couldn't pretend he hadn't seen her.

"Hey, is everything all right?" he asked.

"Hmm?" His question seemed to jar her out of her daze. She shook her head as if she was trying to clear it. "Oh yeah, Mike. I'm fine. It's just been a long night." After looking around, she added, "We've had a crazy crew in here, haven't we?"

He knew who she was speaking about. Usually everyone dreaded the big groups of college kids on spring break. They were notorious for needing separate checks and leaving next to no tips. For him, the worst groups to wait on were the big extended families. For some reason, there would be tension from the beginning, and then everyone seemed to get more on edge as the night wore on. He hadn't waited on a big party where someone hadn't complained about the bill—or asked him to refigure the separate checks.

He'd waited on a fifteen-person table that evening where it seemed each family member was determined to behave badly. Two of the men had gotten into such a bad argument, they left before they'd finished eating.

Things had only gone downhill after that. A few of the women had burst into tears, which was followed by a large drink order, arguments about dessert, and then a half dozen questions about the bill. Whether the remaining family members were upset that they had to pay for the two dinners that had been abandoned or they were just being jerks, they'd made Michael miserable. They'd even had the nerve to say they didn't trust his calculations and asked Kim to redo everything.

"At least they paid the bill," he said.

She looked at him sympathetically. "They gave you a tip too. I didn't expect that."

"Me neither." It wasn't a great tip—only 10 percent. But it was better than nothing.

"I am sorry they were so rude to you. Usually I would have told them what I thought about their attitude, but I just wanted them to leave."

"I wanted them to leave too." He shrugged. "It was no fault of yours. It just is how it is, ain't so?"

She nodded. "Have you been thinking about what I asked?"

Kim had asked if he'd like a small promotion. He would

be a shift manager and also help with inventory. With the pay raise came more hours. It was a good opportunity. "I'm still thinking about it."

"Do you have any questions?"

"Nee. It ain't the work that I am worried about."

"It's your aunt and uncle." Her voice was flat, which conveyed everything she thought.

"Jah. They have work for me to do at home."

"Michael, I know you want to honor them, but I can't help but think that they like to take advantage of you."

"They gave me a home."

"They don't let you forget it either."

She was right. Vera and Paul really weren't very nice. Or understanding. Or . . . well, much of anything. Not really. But he was too loyal to come right out and speak badly about them. "I'll let you know what I aim to do soon."

"Thanks. I'm sorry to pressure you."

"I understand. You need to hire someone for that position."

"I do, but it's also that I want to give you the credit you deserve. Michael, you might be young, but you're one of my best employees. You deserve that promotion. I think that's why I got so mad at that family today. I hate when our customers act like you don't know what's what. It's so rude."

He chuckled. "Good night, Kim."

When he finally headed home, Michael continued thinking about his quandary. Kim's offer would bring him not only a slight pay raise per hour but also more tips and more hours.

He could easily increase his take-home by several hundred dollars a month. That would enable him to get an apartment—if someone was willing to rent him a room.

But if he did move out, he knew he'd raise the ire of his aunt and uncle. So much so that if everything did go wrong, they wouldn't allow him to come back.

Slowing his pace, he went back and forth about his choices. He wished the Lord would give him a sign so he wouldn't keep debating what to do all the time.

"Michael?"

Surprised, he turned and then practically froze. Esther was walking toward him and smiling so sweetly. "Jah. Hi, Esther." Looking just beyond her at the other three women she was with, he nodded. "Hello to all of you ladies."

"Hello," Betsy said.

The other two women smiled shyly.

"I couldn't believe it when I looked ahead of me and there you were. What are you doing?"

"I just got off work."

"Where do you work?" Lilly asked.

"Over at On the Boardwalk. It's a seafood restaurant."

"We just ate tacos at Tacos to Go," Esther said.

"That's a good spot."

She smiled at him, all the while searching his expression. "Well, um, I didn't want to not say hello. Have a good night."

He realized that she was thinking he didn't want to talk to her. "Sorry. I had a long night at work. I guess I'm not over it yet."

"Oh no! What happened?"

"Nothing worth complaining about. Just a big table full of people acting as if no one else mattered." Unable to help himself, he smiled. "I'm not gonna lie. I was glad to see them leave."

"Were they rude to you?"

"Of course." He shrugged as he searched for the right words to describe the rowdy group. He wanted to be honest but not to sound like he couldn't handle their shenanigans. "They brought over my manager because they thought since I was Amish I couldn't do simple math."

All four of the women looked upset. "That's horrible," Betsy exclaimed. "And so very unfair."

"That's life, right?" He shrugged again.

"I wish it didn't have to be your life, at least not tonight," Esther said.

Michael felt his mood lighten just by being in her presence. It might be shallow, but in so many ways she was the perfect woman he'd never imagined would give him a second look. "Me too, but danke."

"Have you eaten supper?" Mary asked. "If you're hungry, I bet we could find—"

"He just got off work at a restaurant," Esther interrupted.

"That doesn't mean he ate, though. Did you?" she asked again.

"Nee, but I'll be all right."

"Come back to the inn with us," Betsy said. "W-we'll find you something in the kitchen."

"Is that even allowed?"

"I bet Nancy will be fine with it," Mary said. "She's really nice."

"If you came back with us, you wouldn't have to go directly home," Esther added.

She was right. He could spend a few more minutes with her— and maybe even get something to eat that wasn't grudgingly given. Put that way, there was no decision to make. "Thank you. I'd like that," he said.

Her face lit up. "Really? I'm so glad."

Lilly and Betsy gave each other a high five, which he thought was hysterical but kind of adorable too. He was around so many people all the time who seemed to go through each day as if it were a trial. These women seemed to be the complete opposite.

"Are you ladies always this cheerful, or is it just how you act on vacation?"

As he expected, laughter greeted his question.

"Only on vacation," Lilly said. "But I'm hoping to change that. I would like to be happier all the time."

"We might all just have to stay here in Pinecraft," Betsy quipped.

"What do you think?" he teased Esther. "Do you want to stay here for good too?"

"I don't know," she said lightly. "I guess it depends on whether or not I have a reason to stick around."

Michael smiled, but he couldn't help wishing that there would be a way Esther really could stay in Pinecraft longer. He was fairly sure that seeing her every day would lift his spirits.

But his own life was such a mess. What could he offer her that she couldn't find with another, better man? At the moment, not a single thing.

When they arrived at the inn, he had every intention of telling Esther good night at the door and walking home. He couldn't imagine that the innkeeper would be all right with him coming in for a late-night snack. The girls Esther was with had other plans.

"Come on, Michael," Mary said. "Let's go find you some food."

"It's really not necessary. Plus it's late . . ."

"It's ten o'clock. It ain't that late. Come on," Lilly added with a smile.

When he shared a glance with Esther and she simply nodded, he couldn't refuse.

The living room was lit with candles and a pretty lamp on one of the side tables. It looked peaceful and immaculate. He could only imagine what the kitchen looked like. No doubt it was spick-and-span. Years of living with his aunt and uncle had conditioned him not to want to be a bother.

"I wonder where Nancy is?" Esther murmured. "Oh! I hear her! Come on." She practically pulled him into the kitchen.

They found Nancy working in the office. She turned to them and smiled when they entered. "Hello, Esther. Who is your gentleman friend?"

She giggled. "This is Michael. He's a new friend who's had a verra long night working at a restaurant with rude customers. He's hungry."

Seeing the proprietor's dismayed expression, Michael felt like sinking into the well-oiled floorboards. "Esther is being kind. I am just fine."

Nancy bustled forward. "Tell me the truth, young man. Did you eat supper? Do you have supper waiting for you at home?"

There was something formidable about the woman. He could no more lie directly to her face than he could turn away. "Nee, but I'll be all right."

When he turned, she caught his arm. "Nee. Stay here a moment." Lowering her voice, she said, "How old are you, Michael?"

"Nineteen."

"Do you live at home?"

"With my aunt and uncle."

Her gaze was so piercing, it felt as if she were reading everything in his mind. "Come to the kitchen with me. I'll make you a sandwich." Her voice was firm.

"Danke," he said as he followed.

When all the girls looked as if they were going to keep him company, Nancy shook her head. "Esther, why don't you join us, lamb? But I'd like to keep the party quiet in the kitchen, if you all don't mind. I don't regularly make meals for visitors." She turned and walked into the kitchen, obviously expecting him—and Esther—to follow meekly.

Michael noticed Esther exchange looks with the other girls before smiling up at him. "I think we better hurry, or Nancy will have something to say about that."

"I agree."

Ten minutes later, he was sitting on a stool at the kitchen counter eating a turkey sandwich and drinking a glass of milk. Esther was sitting next to him and chatting with Nancy as she put the lunch meat and bread away.

It was one of the most soothing, relaxed meals he'd had in ages. Esther didn't expect him to entertain her, and Nancy didn't ask him any more questions. Nothing was expected of him.

When he was finished, he insisted on washing his dish. "Danke, Nancy. It was kind of you to open your kitchen for me after you cleaned it."

She shrugged off his thanks. "Who are your aunt and uncle, Michael?"

"Vera and Paul Hershberger."

"Ah. Yes."

There was something in her guarded tone that spoke volumes. "Do you know them?"

"I do. Slightly." She smiled again. "You come over anytime, dear. Don't ever let me find out that you went home hungry again."

"See?" Esther said with a smile. "I told you that coming here was the right thing to do."

An hour later, when he climbed into bed after entering a silent, dark house and taking a quick shower, Michael figured there was a wealth of things that Nancy hadn't said about his aunt and uncle.

When he closed his eyes, he wondered what they were.

20

After much debate, Jayson stopped by his favorite market to pick up two cups of coffee and a bag of freshly made donut holes before meeting Mary. Holmes Market had been in the area for years and was a favorite spot for early risers to buy baked goods and visit with Holmes, the store's gregarious owner.

Danny had told Jayson long ago that Holmes wasn't the owner's real name. He'd adopted it when he left the Ohio county. The idea that the man had not only relocated but also taken on a new name had always intrigued Jayson.

When he walked into the tiny market, Holmes himself was standing behind the counter. He smiled at Jayson. "What brings you in so early?"

"Coffee and donut holes for two. I'm taking someone for a walk to see the sunrise."

Holmes raised his brows as he filled a paper bag with donut holes. "Sounds like an outing with your best girl. True?"

"She's not my girl."

"But you're hopeful, jah?"

"Jah, I'm hopeful." He was also in over his head. His understanding with Ellen's father was still lurking in his mind. He was so torn. He wanted to do the right thing for his sister, but there was also a part of him that wanted to do right by himself. And everything inside of him was shouting that getting married to a woman he didn't love wasn't going to make his life easier . . . it was just going to make everything that much harder. After taking the bag and the two paper cups from Holmes, he handed him a five-dollar bill. "Here ya go. Danke."

"You're welcome. I'll wish you well today, son." He winked. "And hope she set her alarm!"

"Me too. Danke." Jayson grinned as he gathered his items and walked out, just as another three customers walked inside.

Walking down the sidewalk, he hoped Mary would appreciate his efforts. Nancy rarely had a carafe of coffee ready before six, and he knew Mary was a coffee drinker. He wanted to do something to show that he cared but didn't want to be too forward.

His hunch paid off. Just seconds after he walked up the front steps of the inn, Mary met him on the porch. Her eyes lit up when she saw the paper cup.

"You got me kaffi? Thank you! I was wondering how I was going to put two sentences together during our walk."

"Of course. I figured it was the least I could do since you were kind enough to meet me this morning."

"I wanted to go walking with you, Jayson." Looking adorably flustered, she shook her head. "I mean, I thought seeing the sunrise from the beach sounded lovely."

Maybe he wasn't the only one who was beginning to wonder if there could possibly be something more to their friendship. He led the way to the closest SCAT stop, taking care not only to keep pace with her but to give her his attention. She wasn't going to be in Pinecraft for much longer, so chances were slim that she'd be able to devote much more time—if any—to him.

Plus, there was something that was just so winsome about Mary. She acted as if everything around her were shiny and new. He was learning to appreciate this area through her eyes, which was something new.

When he got out the money for her fare, she stopped him. "Don't do that. I have a SCAT card in my purse."

He grinned. "When did you get that?"

"Yesterday. I was so worried about getting on and off the SCAT, I thought this would make things easier."

"I hope it did."

"Indeed. I got off and on just like a local."

"Perhaps I should be asking you for directions and such then," he teased.

Her light brown eyes lit up. "I guess I do sound so silly, don't I? I'm twenty-two years old and acting as if even something as simple as riding the SCAT is a grand adventure."

"You don't sound silly," he said as they boarded the bus and then took seats in the very back. "You sound like the kind of person who appreciates new things. I like it. It's refreshing."

"Do you not find that to be the norm?"

"No." Thinking of his father, he shook his head. "I think a lot of people like doing the same things all the time. It's where they're comfortable."

"I can see that."

"But it's not you?"

She paused, looking like she was thinking about it. "My problem is more like I've always wanted to do new things and meet new people, but until lately I never had the chance."

Looking more reflective, she added, "This trip to Pinecraft has been something I've dreamed about doing for some time. To my surprise, it's surpassed all my expectations. I really don't know what I'm going to do when it's over."

He already hated the thought of never seeing her again. "Hopefully you'll be able to come back here again soon."

She nibbled her bottom lip. "I hope that might happen. I don't know though. It's rather expensive."

"Did you have to save a long time for it?"

"Jah, but not as long as you might imagine. My parents helped me pay for this trip."

"They did? Wow."

"You sound shocked."

"I'm not shocked; I just can't imagine my father paying for my vacation. Your parents must have a lot of money."

"I wouldn't say that." She looked away.

He'd embarrassed her, which shouldn't have been a surprise, since he'd talked so much about money and how she paid for her trip. Like it was any of his business. "I'm sorry. I sounded pretty rude." Right there was his opportunity to share what his life was like. How different his life was in Crittenden County. How bitter his father was—and how financially irresponsible, especially when it came to providing for Joy. Deep inside, he knew that revealing such vulnerabilities would only help his friendship with Mary. He'd known from practically the first moment he met her that she felt self-conscious about her faults.

But as much as he knew his sharing would help her, he couldn't seem to do it. Everything inside him fought against it—like if he was weak around her, he would be letting himself down.

"I don't think you were being rude," she said after a moment. Looking a little flustered, she added, "I mean, you did catch me off guard, but I guess I can see how you would be curious." She swallowed, then seemed to coax herself into being a little braver. "I never really thought about it, but I guess my parents do have some money. I've never heard them worry about paying for something. But I have a job too. I make cards."

"Cards? What, like birthday cards?"

"Yes, but they're special. I stamp designs and draw animals on them. Several stores near Trail sell them."

"You'll have to show some to me one day. Or when you write me a letter."

She smiled. "I'll do that."

Jayson breathed a sigh of relief that their conversation was back on track. Hopefully he hadn't offended her too much. "Would you like to eat that donut? You can eat on the bus, you know."

"Thank you, but I'm going to wait." She motioned to the small paper bag that he was holding. "You go ahead, though."

Since he was hungry, he didn't wait any longer. He pulled out a glazed donut hole and popped it into his mouth. As he'd expected, the treat was still slightly warm and delicious.

While he was chewing, she said, "Are you that type too? Do you like doing new things?"

"Yes and no. As I've told you, I'm from Kentucky, so being here is something new. But on a daily basis?" He thought about it as he popped another donut into his mouth. "I wouldn't say that I'm very adventurous. Once I find something I like to do or meet someone I like to be with, I don't stray. I guess I'm steady."

"Steady is good."

He smiled at her. "I agree."

At Jayson's suggestion, they waited until the third stop in Siesta Key, then he guided her off the bus. As he'd hoped, Mary looked around in amazement. "This doesn't look like anything I saw yesterday."

"This part of the key is where a lot of the locals go. It's not as flashy, but it is a little bit calmer. Since you like to see new things, I thought you might like it."

"I do." She pointed to a group of pink condominiums. "Aren't those buildings cute? I can't imagine living in a pink place like that."

He laughed. "All the buildings do look a bit like sherbet, don't they?" They continued on, Mary finding interesting things about nearly everything: the dogs they passed, someone's surfboard, a goofy-looking lawn ornament in someone's front yard.

"Uh-oh. I bet I'm talking too much, right?"

"Not at all."

A line formed between her brows. "Are you sure? Because I have a bad habit when I get excited to jabber on and on about nothing."

"You weren't. I was just thinking that I need to hang out with you more often."

Just as she was about to say something, Mary seemed to freeze. He turned to see what had caught her by surprise but didn't see anything but a group of girls approaching. They were Amish like them. When they got closer, he realized that he knew one of them. It was Danny's sister, Judith.

She and her girlfriends stopped. "Hiya, Jayson."

"Morning, Judith." He smiled at the other women. "You all are sure up early."

"I could say the same about you." Judith smiled at Mary. "Hiya."

She returned the smile softly. "Hi."

He gestured to Mary. "I told Mary here how pretty the mornings are on the beach. She decided to see for herself. Mary Margaret, this is Judith. You already met her brother, Danny. I played golf with him, remember?"

"I remember. It's nice to meet you. I usually go by Mary."

"Nice to meet you too. Mary, this is Annie and Beth." After another round of hellos, Judith said, "Jayson, I heard you might be moving here permanently. Is the rumor true?"

"I think so." Fully aware that Mary was hearing all about this for the first time, he added, "A man I met hinted that I could maybe do some carpentry work for him in the future. Everything is up in the air, though. I'm, uh, still trying to figure everything out."

"I hope you figure it out fast! We'd all love to see you here year-round."

"I'd like that too. It would be a real blessing."

Still sounding excited, Judith added, "Have you started looking at places to live? You should live near the beach if you can."

"Siesta Key is too far away from most of the jobs I'd be doing. I'll likely be over in Pinecraft."

"Tell Danny when everything is settled. We can all go out to celebrate. It will be fun."

"Will do." Realizing that the conversation had gone on far longer than he'd anticipated, he added, "I better show Mary the beach."

"Oh. Of course." Looking at her kindly, Judith said, "Where are you from, Mary?"

"Trail, Ohio."

Her eyes lit up. "Home of Trail bologna. I bet you really like that, huh?"

"It's all right." Mary looked even more uncomfortable.

When it became obvious that Mary wasn't going to say another word, Judith bit her bottom lip. "Oh, well, since it's supposed to rain at the end of the week, it is gut that you're here. Yes, you should probably look at the ocean while you have the chance." Lowering her voice, she said, "Hope to see you soon, Jayson."

Jayson glanced at Mary. She wasn't smiling. Actually, she didn't look very happy at all. "Sorry about that. Judith likes to talk."

"I noticed."

She still hadn't met his eyes. "Hey, are you all right?"

"Of course." Her voice was an octave higher. She didn't sound all right at all.

"I'm sorry about that. I didn't mean to keep you standing there so long."

"I'm glad I was. I learned a lot."

"What do you mean by that?"

"Well, I learned that you talked to someone about working here and are seriously thinking about moving here."

"That all happened very recently."

"I see."

Trying to backpedal, he added, "Like I told Judith, I'm not sure what I'm going to do. I mean, nothing is finalized. It's a big decision."

"Were you planning on telling me about it this morning?"

"About my job offer? I'm not sure," he said. "I only told Danny. I guess he couldn't help but tell his family."

"So you weren't going to tell me about it."

Now she looked even more irritated, which made him feel more than a little defensive. "Mary, I'm not sure what I did that made you so upset with me. Is it the job offer or the fact that I told one of my best friends before you?"

"I don't know." She shook her head. "I think it's just that it took me off guard. I thought I knew quite a bit about you, but I guess I really don't."

"You know most things that matter." Of course, as soon as he said the words, he knew it was a lie. She didn't know about all the things that kept him up at night. She didn't know about Joy or Ellen.

"Since we just met, I guess that should be enough, shouldn't it?"

Her question hit him hard, especially since he had been keeping his arrangement with Ellen from her. But what could he do? If he told Mary the truth, it would change everything between them, and he desperately wanted their time together to be special.

Besides, it wasn't like anything between them could really last. No matter if he was in Florida or Kentucky, she would be headed back to Ohio. They'd likely never see each other again.

Of course, that made him feel even worse.

"You're going to have to help me out," he said at last. "What can I do to make things better?"

She paused, then said, "Nothing. I'm just being silly."

"We can talk about it if you'd like."

"There's nothing to talk about. You will likely live here soon and already have several friends you are close to. There's nothing wrong with you talking to them."

Jayson felt the same way, but he also felt like there was something going on that she wasn't telling him. But since he couldn't do anything about that, he simply led her through a narrow opening and down a winding path. Five minutes later they were on the beach.

"There's hardly anyone around. I'm amazed."

Pleased that she sounded happier, he relaxed a bit. "This is what I was hoping you'd see. It's peaceful here, right?"

"It is. It's wonderful."

They sat down on the sand, kicked out their feet, and watched the sun finish rising. Rays of light coated the water, making it glow. Sipping his coffee, Jayson peeked at Mary again. As he'd hoped, she looked as awestruck as he always felt.

"Every time I do this, sit on the cool beach and watch the glory of God's creation, I think it's worth waking up for."

"I think so too. If I lived here, I'd try to do this as often as I could."

"I'm glad you like it too."

She reached into the bag and pulled out a couple of donut holes. "I'm sorry if I sounded cross earlier. I guess I hate thinking about you being here and me being in Ohio."

Just thinking about being so far away from her hurt. They were just starting to get to know each other. Just starting to trust each other. He wasn't sure how they'd ever have a real relationship if they could only exchange letters and phone calls.

Determined to keep things upbeat, he made a joke. "Listen, if I am, I'll promise not to write you about the warm weather in the middle of January."

"That's not what I meant," she said softly.

"I know. That's not what I meant either," he admitted.

When she met his gaze again, there was so much hope and longing there, he wished he could say something to make things better. But he couldn't.

Instead, he reached for her hand, linked their fingers, continued watching the sunrise, and fervently wished that things in his life were different.

21

Two days after his early morning walk with Mary, Jayson had received a handwritten note from Larry over at Pinecraft Construction. The note was full of compliments about Jayson's work and about how the other men thought he would be a good fit. At the end of the note was a formal job offer. A very good job offer—at least a third more than the pay Ellen's father, Wood, had promised. Even with the difference in the cost of living, it was better pay.

He'd sat in his room at the inn and debated what to do. He'd prayed that night, then wrote out a list of pros and cons. But in the end, he knew there was no real choice. He could either stay in Crittenden County, continue supporting his father and caring for Joy, work for Wood and marry his daughter—or he could bring Joy to Pinecraft.

Pinecraft won. The job was better, Danny was here, and the opportunity to have a fresh start in life was everything he'd been hoping and praying for. He decided he was willing to do a lot for a lot of people . . . but he wasn't willing to give up everything of himself. At least he'd be living where he wanted to live. He could even mail his father a check once a month to help with his bills if that was needed.

Before he changed his mind, he asked Nancy if he could use her phone and then called Pinecraft Construction. Larry answered on the second ring. "I'd like to accept your offer," Jayson said after they exchanged pleasantries.

"That's terrific. Really terrific," Larry said. "The guys will be happy. Not only were they impressed by your skills, they liked you."

"I liked them."

"I think you're going to fit in with us just fine. Come on in later, fill out some paperwork, and we'll make things official. Sound good?"

"Yes. Thank you very much."

"You might not believe this, but you're the answer to a prayer, Jayson."

"I can believe it. I feel the same way."

After they hung up, Jayson sat in Nancy's kitchen and tried not to panic. This was the right thing to do. He felt it in his heart.

Though he was tempted to go straight over to Pinecraft Construction, he knew he needed to make one more phone call first. Feeling like his heart was in his throat, he dialed his home phone.

"Jah?"

"Hi, Daed. It's me."

His father's gruff voice turned even more defensive than usual. "Why are you calling here yet again? Joy said you called a few days ago."

"I'm calling to check on Joy." It was hard to hold his patience in check. "Where is she? Can you put her on?"

"She ain't home."

"Where is she?"

"I don't know," he snapped. "Your sister left this morning when I was still asleep."

Biting back the criticism that was on the tip of his tongue, Jayson said, "How is she doing?"

"She is fine. Just like always. Is that all you wanted?"

His father's voice was clipped, letting Jayson know he resented Jayson's questioning his ability to look after Joy. Jayson pushed back his annoyance. "Jah. I wanted to tell her some good news."

There was his opening. Maybe his father would be interested, and Jayson could gather his courage and tell him the news too.

"Boy, first you're wasting your money on that fool trip, and now you're wasting your money on phone calls. I thought I taught you better."

His mouth went dry as he realized that he couldn't do it. He couldn't tell his father over the phone that he accepted a job in Pinecraft. He was going to have to go back home and tell him and Joy in person. "You're right," he said. "You're right. I shouldn't have called."

The sound of the click was sharp in his ear.

Feeling worse, he leaned back and pressed his hands over his eyes. His father was going to be furious with him. So was Wood.

And even though nothing had been finalized, he knew these new plans were going to upset Ellen. There was a very good chance that she wouldn't want to leave Kentucky. What would he do then? Would he really be able to neatly break things off with her and move his sister to Florida?

That brought him to Joy herself. Here he'd been making plans for her future, but he wasn't giving her any choices. That wasn't fair either.

The waves of guilt he was feeling were nothing less than he deserved.

Nancy peeked inside. "You all done?"

Realizing she was probably anxious to get her kitchen back, he stood up. "I am. Danke for letting me use the phone."

"No problem. That's what it's there for."

Needing some fresh air, he slipped on his sunglasses and went outside. The front porch was empty, but he watched for a moment as several people strolled along the sidewalk in front of the inn. Everyone looked relaxed. Happy.

"That is going to be your choice," he whispered to himself. "You can decide to be happy . . . or stay where you are."

It might not be right, but he couldn't help thinking that he needed to move to Pinecraft. The Lord had brought about too much for him to ignore. Then, too, was the constant reminder of his father. His father lived with disappointment and bitterness as his constant companions. Jayson couldn't allow that to become his future.

Feeling like he would suffocate if he didn't continue forward, Jayson decided to go sign that paperwork and then look at housing choices. He needed to do something positive instead of continuing to sit and stew and wish that things were different.

An hour later, he'd signed an employment contract and was holding two addresses for housing that one of the guys at the construction office had recommended.

The first option was just two blocks away from the construction company. It was the English-run apartment complex. The manager was a seemingly conservative man. He said that he was formerly Amish and wanted to provide housing for both Plain and formerly Plain men and women.

Sure enough, there were some rather sparse-looking units.

The stoves and refrigerators were run by gas, and there was next to no ornamentation on the walls or woodwork. There were, however, electric lights and a full membership to the apartment complex's fitness club and pool.

Jayson left the area knowing that it wasn't the place for him. He was far from the type of man who kept account of whether someone was obeying the rules set by the Ordnung, but having electricity and a swimming pool seemed to perch precariously on the edge of what was acceptable.

Plus, the few men his age who were obviously former Amish looked to be sowing some wild oats. Even if he had elected not to be baptized, Jayson knew he wouldn't be going down that path. That simply wasn't who he was.

He walked to the next place. It was only four blocks away, but it couldn't have felt more different. The house was pale green, had a variety of lovely, well-maintained bushes and shrubs, and also had a smooth, black roof. It was a sprawling place. Most of it two stories—three stories on one end. There was also a large front patio and an even larger stamped concrete patio off the back porch. The proprietor had planted bright red geraniums, jaunty pansies, daisies, and zinnias in window boxes.

It was the type of place that his mother would have stared at longingly. It really was that pretty.

When he finally entered, a woman was standing in the entryway with a faint smile on her face. "Here ya are. I was wondering when you were of a mind to come in."

He couldn't help but smile at her comment. "Did you see me walking around?"

"Couldn't help it, but I didn't mind. I figure it might save me from giving you a tour." She chuckled at her joke.

"I'm sorry, but I'm still going to have to put you to work.

I'd like to see one of the rooms." He held out his hand. "My name is Jayson Raber."

"Nice to meet ya." She walked to a small room directly off the foyer and picked up a big ring of keys. "My name is May, like the month."

"It's gut to meet you."

"We have two rooms available. They're fairly different from each other, so I'll show you them both."

"Danke."

"Let us go upstairs first. I like to get the steps out of the way." She smiled at him over her shoulder before heading up.

The stairs were covered with a dark green runner. At the top was a large landing with a number of chairs and tables set up and a large bookshelf against the wall. Opposite of the landing was a long hallway reaching out in both directions. He counted at least five doors.

"How many boarders do you keep, May?"

"Eight most times. I've got seven currently." She smiled at him. "Room for one more, but not two."

"I thought you had two unoccupied rooms."

"Oh, I always keep one room empty, don'tcha know. There's always someone Plain traveling whose plans don't work out for one reason or another. I keep the room open for those folks." She winked. "It's my emergency room."

He was both touched and intrigued. "You're looking out for others."

"I try to." She lowered her voice. "It might not seem like much, but I make sure to feed them a meal and don't charge them much for their stay. Every person I've had has such a sad story, it's nice to be the one person who helps them."

"I imagine so."

She stopped at the very end of the hall. "Here's your first choice. It's bigger, a little more expensive, and there's no one on one side of you." She smiled. "Or above you! That can be a gut thing, jah?"

When she opened the door, he stepped inside and knew immediately that he'd found his new home. There were no electric lights, just a gas-run oven and refrigerator. However, the bathroom had a decent-looking shower, and the large space was big enough to have both sleeping and living areas. The floors were all tile, and the woodwork was beautiful. Everything about the room felt comfortable, familiar, and yet like a step up from how he'd been living.

"I like the woodwork," he said. "It's very fine."

"I thought so too." She gave him a closer look. "Sounds like you know something about carpentry."

"I do. I'm a finish carpenter."

She smiled. "So you are a man who can appreciate a nicely turned baseboard."

Chuckling, he pointed above them. "And crown molding."

"Take a look around. When you're done, we'll go see the other room, but I'm telling ya now that it ain't half as special as this."

"I think we both know that this is the room for me." He did as she suggested, though, and peeked around, turning on faucets and looking in the large closets.

When they were finished, May led him back down the stairs and to a room just off the kitchen. It was exactly as she'd said. The room also had its own bathroom but the rest of the space was far smaller than the other and didn't have crown molding. And being between the rest of the house's kitchen, and the main living areas, he knew it would be noisy.

"Have you made up your mind yet, son?"

"Jah. I'd like to rent the room upstairs."

"Do you want to think about it for a spell?"

"Nee." He pulled out his wallet. "I came prepared. I have money for the first two months."

May's smile widened. "I knew we'd get along fine, Jayson. Come into the office and we'll get the paperwork taken care of."

"Thank you so much."

"No need for thanks. I have a feeling you're going to be happy here—and that I'll be glad you came." She tapped her forehead with one finger. "I can tell these things, you know."

"Me too," he said with a smile.

22

P ractically another week had passed by in a flash. Mary knew she shouldn't have been surprised. She and her girlfriends had spent so many amazing days together. Sometimes they rose with the sun and then went to museums. Other days they all slept late and spent the majority of their afternoons lazing on the inn's front porch and reading.

They also went to the beach.

Mary wasn't sure how they'd managed it, but not only had all four of them agreed to go to Siesta Key one last time, but Jayson said he and Danny would try to meet them there . . . and Michael said he'd do the same. When they'd shared their plans with Nancy, the proprietor had helped them put together a picnic—and she wouldn't even let them pay her for the extra meal.

"You girls have been a joy to have here," Nancy had proclaimed. "I'm going to miss your smiling faces when you're gone."

"I'm going to m-miss being here something awful," Betsy had said. "You've been so nice, Nancy."

"That just means that you're going to need to come back

very soon, dear." She handed them an insulated canvas tote bag. "You ladies have a good day. Wear sunscreen!"

Sitting on a bright blue beach towel hours later, Mary said, "I don't think I'm ever going to be able to look at a bottle of sunscreen without thinking of Nancy and the Marigold Inn."

"Same," said Lilly.

"She must say that a dozen times a day," Esther added.

Mary, Lilly, and Esther were lying on the beach while Betsy was in the water with Jayson and Danny. The six of them had been hanging out at the beach together for the last two hours, and it had been so fun. She and Esther were getting along well, and the addition of Jayson and Danny made the group feel like a party. Danny seemed to know half the people on the beach, and a lot of them came over to say hello. After years of only watching from a distance, Mary was in the middle of a big group of friends. She didn't know if she'd ever been so happy.

"I'm going to remember this day for the rest of my life," Lilly declared. "It's not too hot, the sky is perfect, and I've laughed more in one afternoon than I usually do in a week."

Esther laughed. "I'm going to remember the sight of you sitting on the beach in that violet dress and your movie-star sunglasses for the rest of my life. I'd take a picture of you if I could."

Lilly chuckled. "Don't tell my mamm, but I really wish you could. I'd love to have a photo of all of us."

"We'll just have to keep remembering it," Esther said. "And promise to write each other all the time after we get back."

"I agree," Lilly said. "Especially since I can't wait to plan another trip."

"Do you think your parents will allow you to do that?" Mary

asked. Now that she knew more about how strict Lilly's adoptive parents were, she wondered if they would let her travel alone ever again.

Lilly shrugged. "I've decided that I'm going to have to figure out a way to get back here, whether they want me to come or not. I can't go back to just wishing that something would change."

"I'm proud of you, Lilly," Esther said. "That's wonderful."

"Danke. I'll be counting on all of you to help me keep my resolve, though."

Mary squeezed her hand. "Whatever we can do to help, we'll do. All you have to do is ask."

Looking at the water, Lilly lowered her voice. "Hey, have you two noticed how much Betsy and Danny have been talking to each other? I think there might be something going on there."

"Really?" Mary turned to look but didn't notice anything other than Betsy wearing a huge smile. "I have noticed that once Betsy gets comfortable, she talks a lot more and hardly stutters at all."

"I've noticed that too," Esther said. "She's adorable."

Still looking at their three friends in the water, Lilly mused, "Wouldn't it be wonderful if something happened between the two of them? Then the four of you could maybe do something together in the future," Lilly said.

Mary giggled. "Like what?"

"You know. Like go on a double date."

Esther smiled. "I like that idea too. It would be perfect."

"It would only be perfect in my dreams," Mary teased. "I don't think anything is going to happen between Jayson and me."

"Why not?"

"I can't put my finger on it, but something seems off. Like Jayson is trying hard to keep a wall up between us."

"Maybe . . . or maybe not," Esther said. "Oh! Michael is here." She got to her feet. "Uh . . . I'm going to go see him," she said unnecessarily before walking over to his side.

Mary watched Michael's expression light up the minute he saw Esther. Then, right in front of everyone, he kissed her cheek before they turned around and started walking in the opposite direction.

Lilly grinned at Mary. "Esther is smitten."

"She's not the only one."

"They seem so different, don't they? I mean, besides the age difference. Esther looks so perfect, and Michael is slightly rough around the edges. I never imagined that they'd go so well together."

She nodded. "It is a surprise, but I guess a lot of things about this trip have been a surprise."

Lilly chuckled. "You can say that again."

"What can she say again?" Jayson asked as he joined them.

Mary looked up at him and smiled. "That this trip has been full of surprises."

"You're right about that." He sat down next to her and kicked out his legs. "A lot of things have happened that I never imagined would."

"I hope you are referring to good things and not bad," she teased.

"I promise, it's all good."

Everything inside her seemed to heat up as she met his gaze. And for the first time, she actually thought that there was something more between them than just sun and fun. That she wouldn't be saying goodbye to him forever in just a couple of days.

"Um, I think I'll go put my feet in the water," Lilly said as she walked away.

"Okay," Mary said.

At least, she was pretty sure she'd just said something to Lilly. All she seemed to be aware of was the way Jayson was staring at her.

Like she was the most important thing in the world.

23

She was smitten. Infatuated. Borderline obsessed. No—at the very least Mary should be honest with herself—she was falling in love with Jayson. Why, she might already be in love!

The day at the beach had changed everything for her—or maybe it had simply cemented all the feelings that had been hovering around her heart. Whatever was happening, she knew that she wasn't the same. No longer would she be the girl who had never had a relationship, never flirted, never been the focus of a handsome man's attention. She now had those things—and she was grateful for them too.

But like a spoiled girl who wants just one more thing on her birthday, Mary wanted even more. Unfortunately, she didn't want just one more hour or day with Jayson. She didn't want their relationship to end. He seemed to be attracted to her too . . . but he also seemed to have a wall up around him. She wondered if it was because his life was in upheaval or if there was something else going on.

She wished she knew.

"Way to wish for the stars when you've been given the moon," she muttered to herself as she walked down the hall to breakfast.

"Did you ask me something, dear?" Nancy asked.

The innkeeper had obviously caught sight of her talking to herself. "Nee, I was mumbling. I don't think I'm awake yet."

"That's a good sign. It means you're relaxing."

Walking into the dining room, Mary nodded. "I bet you're right. Just when we're about to leave too."

"You get on the bus tomorrow, don't you?"

She nodded. "All four of us are heading out at noon."

"That's a shame. You four ladies have given this place a boost of energy. It's going to be a lot quieter here when you all are gone."

"That might be a good thing," she teased as she sat down.

"Oh no. I enjoy all my guests, but it's rare to get so many young faces here at one time. I've enjoyed watching you girls get your sea legs. Now you relax for a bit. I'm making Dutch babies this morning. I'll bring you out one in just a few," she said as she handed Mary a cup of coffee.

Lilly and Betsy joined her just as Nancy placed a giant puffed pancake covered in powdered sugar in front of Mary.

"W-what is that?" Betsy asked.

"Something called a Dutch baby." Spearing a piece with her fork, she took a bite. "It is really good."

"How am I going to go back to eating oatmeal five days a week? I don't want to leave," Lilly said.

Mary smiled at her. "Me neither. I was just sitting here thinking that I can't believe that this is our last day. It's gone by too fast."

"Maybe we can just happen to m-miss the bus tomorrow," Betsy joked.

"I've thought the same thing," Lilly said as she picked up the carafe Nancy had left on the table and filled their cups. When she spied Esther walking down the stairs, she smiled at her. "Want some kaffi, Esther?"

"Jah, please."

When Esther joined them, Mary noticed that she had faint smudges under her eyes. "How are you?"

"Tired. I didn't sleep a wink—until this morning. All I kept thinking about was how much I am going to miss being here."

"We've just been saying the same thing," Lilly said.

"Oh, good. All four of you are here," Nancy said as she bustled in with two filled plates in her hands. "Your Dutch baby is coming right up, Esther."

She smiled at them. "Are you all as sad as I am?"

"Oh yes," Betsy said. She and Lilly were quiet for a moment while they silently gave thanks. Then they dug in with as much enthusiasm as Mary had.

"What are your plans today?" Mary asked Esther. "I think we're going to go to Yoder's and look at the shops one more time. You're welcome to join us."

"Danke. I might join you, but I think I'm also going to see Michael."

"The two of you have gotten close, haven't you?"

She nodded. After looking around the room, she whispered, "I almost kissed him when we were walking on the beach."

Lilly set her fork down. "Why didn't you?"

"I don't know. Maybe it's because he hesitated—or that he knew I was hesitating." She paused to sip her coffee. "It's funny. When I left Ohio, all I thought about was Violet and Abbie—and of course you, Mary. Now it's like Violet and Abbie don't even matter to me. All I want to do is think about Michael."

"I-I saw the way he looked at you," Betsy said. "When you're around, it's like he doesn't see anything else."

"That's how I feel when I'm with him." She paused as Nancy brought her Dutch baby before being called to the living room by a family who had just arrived. "To be honest, he's nothing like the man I thought I'd want to marry one day. He's younger than me, isn't close to his family, doesn't really have much money, and lives far away."

"But . . ." Mary prodded.

Esther smiled. "But none of that matters to me. When I'm with him, all I feel is hope."

"It's like your heart is in charge instead of your brain," Mary whispered.

Esther blinked. "That's it. That's it exactly. And the sad part of it is that I don't care. I've spent most of my life overthinking every little thing I've done. Now all I want to do is feel."

The girls stayed silent for a moment while Esther prayed. When Esther raised her head again, Mary said, "I was just thinking much of the same thing about Jayson."

"Do you two have plans tonight?"

"We do. What about you and Michael?"

Esther nodded. "He's going to try to get off work early. He offered to call off completely, but I know he's trying to save money to move out of his aunt and uncle's house."

"Betsy, I guess it's just you and me this evening," Lilly said.

"I'm good with that," Betsy said with a smile. "The two of us can be completely relaxed, put on pajamas early, and play cards. You girls can have all the drama. All I want to do tonight is have fun and not worry about anything."

"Just you wait," Esther said. "One day soon, you two will be in our shoes."

"I hope so," Lilly said. "But at least when that happens, you girls will be able to counsel me about what to do!"

Mary lifted her cup. "Cheers to that!"

"Cheers!" the other girls said as they clanked cups.

Walking by them again, Nancy grinned. "I really am going to miss you girls when you're gone."

The four of them smiled at each other. It was obvious that each one of them felt the same exact way.

24

Soon after breakfast, Nancy knocked on Mary's door. "Jayson called and asked me to relay a message."

"Yes?"

She glanced down at the sticky note in her hand. "He asked if you could meet him at noon for lunch instead of tonight. He said something about other obligations?" She shrugged. "Anyway, if you can do that, just wait for him on the porch. But if you can't, you're supposed to call this number and whoever answers will give him the message. Does that make sense?"

"It does." When Nancy held out the note for her to take, Mary shook her head. "Danke, but I won't need it. All I was going to do today was shop and hang out with the girls. I can do that before and after."

Looking relieved, Nancy smiled. "Sounds good."

"Hey, Nancy?"

"Yes, dear?"

"Do you know Jayson well?"

"He's stayed here a couple of times over the years, but I wouldn't say I know him real well." Brightening, she added, "I do know his friend Danny's family well, though. Danny is a good sort, and he's always seemed to get on well with Jayson. Does that help?"

Mary shrugged. "Kind of. I guess I'm looking for some idea about what to do next with him."

"I've been a widow for a while, but I have learned one or two things from observing all my guests."

"What's that?"

"The first is that there's someone for everyone, and the second is that there is no real rhyme or reason to how love works." Looking amused, she folded her arms over her chest. "I've seen some couples who look like they wouldn't have a thing in common be as happy as clams . . . and others who at first glance seemed to be perfect for each other look miserable."

"So I just have to figure things out on my own."

"No, child. You need to realize that you're not on your own at all. There's someone in your life a whole lot brighter and steadier than you—or any of us."

She swallowed. "You're speaking of God, aren't you?"

"Of course. Have you forgotten that He's always there?" She paused, then added, "Forgive me, but I think you need to lean on Him a little more."

Mary had been praying, but she realized that she hadn't actually opened up her heart to Him. Not about her and Jayson. "I do, don't I?"

Nancy nodded. "He'll never let you down."

Feeling better, she smiled. "Thanks for the reminder—and for the message."

"Have a good time." Nancy winked. "You can tell me how it went tomorrow morning," she called out over her shoulder as she hurried down the hall.

When she was alone again, Mary closed her eyes. "Nancy's

right, Lord. I should be leaning on You more, especially since You're the One who's brought me so many blessings this past week. Will You help me find the right words for Jayson today? I have a feeling he and I are about to have one of the most important conversations of our lives."

Two hours later, Mary sat on one of the white wicker rocking chairs on the front porch. It was almost noon. She was excited to see Jayson and wondered what he had planned for their last day together.

After she'd received Nancy's message, she'd told the girls that she'd be able to join them that night but would be out for the rest of the day. Oh, the girls had teased her about that!

"What if he asks you to marry him?" Lilly had asked with a smile.

"Don't be silly. Of course that isn't going to happen."

"B-but it could," Betsy had said. "Just think about how much time you two spent together during these two weeks. Some courting couples only spend an hour or two together once a week—while the girl's parents are watching!"

Betsy hadn't been exaggerating. Mary and Jayson really had spent a lot of time in each other's company. As much time as their schedules allowed. Plus, when they were together, he was so attentive and sweet. There had even been a couple of times when he stared at her so intently and was standing so close . . . well, she was sure he was about to kiss her.

She would've let him too. She'd waited all her life to have a romance. To have her first kiss on the beach in Siesta Key or during a moonlit walk? Well, it would be the pinnacle of their time together.

Not that she would ever admit to such fanciful things.

"Sorry I'm late!" Jayson called out as he approached.

She jerked her head toward his voice and smiled. "No worries. I was having fun watching everyone walk by. I even saw a pair of little bright green hummingbirds flitting around the garden."

"Ah, that explains it," he said as he stopped at the bottom of the steps. "I've been watching you, and you hardly moved. You looked like you were lost in thought."

Walking down to meet him, she giggled. "I guess I was. But I'm ready to go now."

"What do you think about going to the Blue Star Café? It's usually not too crowded for lunch. Most people either head there for breakfast or a late supper."

"That sounds great." And she was not going to let herself dwell on why he wanted to meet in such a private spot. At least, not too much.

"I'm sorry that I had to change our plans," Jayson said as they started walking down the sidewalk.

Looking up into his handsome face, she smiled. "It's fine. I understand that you have other things to do. I don't want to waste a minute with—I mean—of the day before it's time to get on the bus."

"I feel the same way." He glanced at her again.

She noticed he wasn't smiling now. Actually, Jayson looked rather worried—almost nervous. The bundle of nerves that had been churning in her stomach swirled again. Against her better judgment, Mary allowed her mind to jump to conclusions again. No, to dream again.

Maybe Jayson really was going to declare himself! Maybe this lunch together was when they would make plans for the future.

Since he didn't seem inclined to talk, she continued to let

her mind drift. When they were married, they could first live in an apartment until he earned enough for them to get a little house. If necessary, she would help out too. She'd seen more than one fabric, needlework, and quilting shop. She could do something at one of those. Of course, she'd continue to make her greeting cards and stationery too.

She was starting to wonder what else he had planned for the day. It felt like he was being purposely vague. "Do you and Danny have plans for tonight?" she asked as they entered the small café. It was decorated in shades of blue. One of the walls was practically made of windows, splashing beautiful rays of morning sun across the interior.

"I'll tell you all about that in a little while. Where would you like to sit?"

"Anywhere is fine with me." They essentially had their choice of tables too. Only one table was occupied. A lone Amish man was sitting in a corner, sipping coffee, eating a sandwich, and reading the newspaper intently.

Jayson chose a table in the opposite corner. It was far enough away from most of the other tables that likely no one would hear their conversation. She sat down and he took the seat to her left. Each table had paper place mats with the menus typed on the front. "Do you want to order right away?"

"I can wait a little bit. I had a huge breakfast."

"I'm not too hungry yet either." When the server approached—an older lady with curly gray hair—they both ordered lemonade.

Mary smiled at him. "I'm glad we're going to take our time." Not only did she want this time with Jayson to last as long as possible, but she was such a jumble of nerves, she knew she wouldn't be able to eat anything.

"Yeah. Me too."

What in the world was bothering him? He looked so nervous. "Jayson, of course you should get something to eat right now if you'd like. I won't mind."

"Nee, I'm not too hungry at the moment."

She smiled and nodded but kept her silence when the server approached with their drinks.

Jayson took a sip of his. "So, how is the packing going?"

"It's almost done. I was worrying about taking home an extra bag, but one of the ladies who's gone back and forth a lot says that the bus driver makes sure there's extra space for everyone's souvenirs."

"That's good. I've made quite a few purchases myself. Joy gave me a list," he said with a laugh.

She chuckled too, but his comment caught her off guard. "Does that mean you're going back to Kentucky soon? I thought you were going to stay here for a while, right?"

"That's, uh, what I wanted to talk to you about. You see—" He paused when the server walked by and filled his glass.

"Would you like to order now?"

"Not yet," Jayson said.

"You two let me know if you need anything else."

"We will."

The server grinned at them. "You two are such a cute couple."

"Danke," Mary said with a smile. She was pretty sure that her cheeks were bright red, but she didn't care. The compliment was right out of one of her daydreams.

When the server moved on to help an older couple who had just entered, she smiled at Jayson.

But instead of smiling back in amusement, Jayson looked even more uncomfortable. He picked up his drink and drained nearly half the glass. "Mary, there's something I need to tell you. To talk to you about."

"Yes?" She couldn't keep the anticipation out of her voice.

He started to speak, seemed to rethink his words, then started again. "I'm sorry, there's simply no easy way to say this."

He looked stricken. Extremely worried. All her silly dreams about proposals dissipated into a pool of nothingness as she realized he was upset about something—and it somehow affected her.

Even though her heart felt like it was hammering in her chest, Mary clasped her hands in her lap and waited. "Take your time," she said in what she hoped was an encouraging and supportive tone.

He sighed. Braced his hands on his thighs. "I first need to tell you that I didn't mean for any of this to happen."

"This?"

He waved a hand, motioning it in between her and him. "This. You know, you and me." Looking even more flustered, he frowned. "Us."

All right. He was thinking of them as an "us" too. Since he looked rather like he expected her to respond, she said, "I didn't expect for us to grow so close either. It's been a surprise. A wonderful-gut surprise."

But instead of looking reassured, Jayson looked rather sick. "I've been keeping something from you. You see, I am moving here. And I do plan to work here. But my plans took place because of a promise I made back home."

"In Kentucky."

"Jah. You see, my father . . . well, he ain't much of a worker." He swallowed. "Actually, he's selfish by nature. We don't have a lot of money, and so he and Joy have been depending on me to help pay for a lot of the expenses. Especially expenses for Joy."

"I understand." He'd already told her much of this. She didn't understand why he looked so stricken.

"What I haven't shared is that Joy will likely always need some medical help. That means years and years of support from me."

"Has something happened to her? Did you just receive some bad news about her diabetes?" If that was the case, everything would make sense.

"Nee, thank the Lord. Joy is doing fine." He sipped his drink again. "I'm afraid it's nothing like that. What I'm trying to tell you is that before I came here to Pinecraft, I was feeling kind of stuck. All I could see was me living with my father and sister, working odd jobs that didn't always pay a lot, and constantly worrying about how to save enough money in case Joy got real sick."

"I'm so sorry. I didn't realize things were so tough."

Jayson shrugged. "It's not like I would want to tell all that to someone I just met, right?" After she nodded, he continued. "Since I was so worried, I made some promises back home. Nothing is set in stone, but there's an understanding there. That's why I ended up coming down here. It was going to be kind of my last vacation for a while." He rubbed the back of his neck. "I mean, the last time I would be on vacation alone."

Alone? "I'm not sure I'm following you."

"I know, but give me a sec." He cleared his throat. "But then, when I got here, Danny told me that I wasn't looking at the big picture. That I could still take care of, um, everyone, but I could do that from here too."

"Which is why you met with Pinecraft Construction."

"Jah. After talking to them, everything changed."

Trying to keep up, she prodded. "You said they offered you a job, jah?"

"They did." He smiled before looking worried again. "But even then, I wasn't sure . . ."

"About what?"

Looking even more pained, he said, "Mary, before I came down here, I was feeling so desperate and so much pressure, I agreed to something I didn't feel good about. I agreed because I felt as if I had been backed into a corner."

She was now even more confused and verging on irritated. If what he had to say was so important, why couldn't he just say it? Surely Jayson knew her well enough by now to realize that she wasn't going to get upset about anything or cause a scene.

Just as he looked ready to veer off in another direction, she blurted, "Jayson, I think you should just tell me what is on your mind. What are you trying to tell me?"

"I'm trying to tell you that I all but promised a friend of the family that I would marry his daughter if he would give me a job. I came down here to Florida to have one last bit of freedom." Looking even more miserable, he added, "I didn't plan on meeting you. I'm really sorry."

Her ears were practically ringing. Mary figured that was because nothing he was saying made sense. He had an arranged marriage? All to help his family? He hadn't planned on meeting her?

She shook her head. "Nee," she said. It was a silly thing to say, but she felt as if her words were stuck in her throat.

Surely she was misunderstanding him.

Jayson took a deep breath. "I don't know what else to say. I hope one day you'll be able to forgive me."

She gaped at him. Jayson was acting like the conversation was over. What in the world?

Her temper flared. "Oh no. I'm afraid you still have a lot to say because you've essentially told me nothing. What do you mean you agreed to marry this daughter?" She took a deep breath and added, "And what do you mean that this visit to Pinecraft was to be your last bit of freedom?"

"Ellen is twenty-nine and didn't take. She's always liked me. I mean, that's what people have said."

"*She didn't take. You've heard she's always liked you.* That's how you're justifying your actions?"

He winced. "You're right. It's nothing to be proud about. Her parents—and her—are desperate for her to get settled. She wanted me."

Mary was still trying to come to terms with the way Jayson was describing Ellen. Maybe he meant something different than she imagined? "What do you mean when you said Ellen didn't take?" she asked softly.

"You know. None of the men in the area have much interest in her."

This Ellen was a wallflower. Just like her. "Why didn't she take? What was wrong with her?"

He looked surprised that she asked. "Why? Well, I suppose there's some reasons, but I don't want to say. She's going to be my wife one day."

"Now you are being loyal to her? That's a little late, don't you think?"

"I wasn't being disloyal to her. She knew I went to Florida."

"Did she know you intended to spend so much time with another woman?" She could hardly hold back her anger.

"Of course not, but I didn't plan on it either."

196

"So you used me?"

"I didn't. I promise I didn't."

"It feels like it, Jayson."

"Nothing happened between us, right?" His voice sounded almost desperate. "I mean, we've just been friends. Why, we never even kissed."

She blinked at his excuse. "Jayson, have you really convinced yourself that a kiss would have meant something more than all the time we've spent together? Than all the conversations we had?" More than all the things she'd shared with him? When he stared back at her, his face a mask, she knew it was time to leave. "I feel sorry for you. Not because of your family or this deal you made or even because you're willing to marry a woman without loving her. I feel sorry for you because you seem to believe that all that is good enough. That there isn't anything better."

Getting to her feet, she added, "I don't understand you. How could you have kept all this a secret until the very last second? Did you enjoy playing me for a fool?"

"I didn't do that intentionally. I . . . I really do like you."

"Does that make you feel better? Because it sure doesn't help me."

She turned and walked out the door. She felt the older couple watching her. No doubt they would have a lot of fodder to tell their friends later that day. She and Jayson hadn't exactly been whispering.

But as she walked back down the sidewalk, looking at the sun that had risen higher, Mary realized that Jayson had taught her something very important. It was easier to keep one's heart to oneself than to share it.

Now hers felt as if it were broken in two. She didn't know how it was going to be put back into one piece ever again.

25

After Mary told them that she had lunch plans with Jayson, Esther, Lilly, and Betsy had headed to Yoder's. It was almost comical the way each of them had proclaimed that they were too full to eat a thing . . . but then ate a slice of pie.

They'd done the same thing when they entered the stores. Though they told each other they were only going to browse, all three returned to the inn with shopping bags in their hands.

After spending a few hours in their rooms reorganizing their suitcases, they went to sit on the front porch to wait for Mary.

"Do you think she's going to be gone all afternoon?" Esther asked Lilly and Betsy. "It's past four o'clock."

"I hope not," Betsy said. "The suspense is killing me. What if Jayson actually did declare himself?" Her eyes lit up. "Oh my stars, wouldn't that be the most romantic thing in the world?"

Esther thought Betsy's words were sweet but not all that likely. "It would be romantic, but it seems a little fast. Especially for Mary."

Lilly nodded. "I agree. Mary doesn't seem quite as impulsive as you, Betsy," she teased. "But I do think you're on the right track. He had to have told her something wonderful-gut, though, right? Otherwise, why would he have tried so hard to spend time with her today?"

"That's a good point," Esther said. "Now we just have to be patient and wait."

Betsy groaned. "I hate waiting."

Esther chuckled at Betsy's dramatics as Lilly got to her feet. "There she is. She's back!"

Esther stood up, took one look at her expression, and felt her stomach drop. "Something bad happened, though."

"She's crying," Betsy said. "Mary, what happened?"

Mary stared at all of them, her bottom lip trembled, then she began crying even harder.

Esther rushed to her side. "Are you all right?"

"Nee," she said. "I'm really not all right at all."

Aware that the four of them were on the sidewalk and people were walking by, Esther led the way into the house. Nancy, who had been dusting the living room, looked up, started to speak, then abruptly stopped. Their eyes met, and it felt as if the two of them conveyed a wealth of words in just a few seconds.

Mary Margaret could barely stop crying as the other girls helped her get into her room and settled on her bed.

After Lilly handed her a pair of tissues, she sat down by Mary's side. "Mary, you've got to talk to us. What on earth happened?"

After a round of hiccups, Mary caught her breath at last. "It was so horrible." She swiped her wet cheeks with the side of a hand. "All this time, Jayson has been promised to another woman in Kentucky."

"What?"

"I know! It's some kind of arranged marriage. This all happened before he got here too. H-he was here in Pinecraft as his last bit of freedom!"

Lilly grabbed her hand. "But what about you?"

"I was nothing, I guess." Looking at all of them, her light brown eyes filled with tears again. "I can't believe I was so stupid. I was nothing to him. J-just someone to pass the time with. How could I have been so wrong? I must have acted so ridiculous, imagining that he really liked me."

"Surely not," Esther said. "I mean, we all saw how he acted around you. It was obvious that he really liked you."

"That's not what Jayson said. He . . . he told me that it wasn't serious because he'd never kissed me."

"I'm so sorry," Betsy murmured. "If that's what he said, then you're better off without him, right? I mean, what matters is your heart, not his kisses." She winced. "Though I have to say that Jayson always looked like he couldn't wait to kiss you."

Mary raised her chin. "You thought so too, Betsy?"

"Of course."

"I was starting to think I had imagined it all."

"You didn't imagine it," Esther said. "He's such a snake!"

"What's awful is that I would've been happy just to get to know him."

"Of course you would've been," Lilly said. "Jayson should've been honest with you from the beginning."

"Lilly is right," Betsy added. "You weren't looking to fall in love. You could've just made a new friend. He treated you wrong."

Looking at her friends, Mary nodded again, but even knowing that she was right didn't make her feel any better. Curving her hands around her waist, she wished she could simply hide for a few moments. No, for a few hours. She was stunned and she was miserable. Worse, she felt like she'd been made a laughingstock again. And Esther had even been there to witness it!

"Are you going to tell Violet and Abbie?" she asked Esther.

"Tell them what?"

"That I've made a fool of myself once again."

"What? Nee!" Esther reached out for her hand. "Is that really how you think I am? After everything that we've talked about and shared these past ten days, do you really not trust me?"

"I want to."

"Then do."

Mary nodded. "I'll try. I'm sorry for doubting you. It's just that . . ." Her voice drifted off. She hated that she sounded so skeptical, but her heart felt crushed.

"It's just that some things are hard to believe, right?" Esther said. "It's like we've gone through all our lives getting used to the way things were. Now that everything changed between us, we have to get used to that new reality."

"You're right. I didn't expect things to change and I really didn't expect things to change so quickly," she admitted as she gazed at the three women surrounding her.

Betsy frowned. "I don't understand. Do you mean change with Jayson?"

"No, change inside of me. I feel different."

Lilly nodded. "I'm going to go home looking like the same girl I was, but I know I'm different inside. I don't think I'll be happy to expect so little from my family or from my life anymore. In some ways, I almost feel like I've become a different person. I don't know how I'm going to be able to return to being the person that I was."

Betsy murmured, "Who says that we have to be the same?"

"Everyone," Esther said. "Things for the four of us might have changed, but everyone in our lives has been doing the same things. They are going to be taken off guard."

Betsy sighed. "I can't even begin to think of what Bobby is going to say when I start refusing to be coddled any longer."

"I guess on our long bus ride, we're all going to need to figure out our futures," Mary said. "Here, in the Florida sunshine, so much seems possible. Back home, when we're surrounded by family, chores, and even jobs, things are going to be much harder."

"We'll have to be prepared for everyone to try to sway us again," Esther said.

"And they will," Betsy said.

"It might be hard," Lilly warned. "We're going to have to stay tough."

Mary sat up a bit straighter and said, "I can be tough. I mean, after all this with Jayson, it's not like I have a choice. I didn't want my life to continue the same two weeks ago. I sure don't want to go back to it now."

"We'll have to make a pact to help each other," Lilly said.

"Tonight we'll do that," Betsy said.

Just as Esther was about to speak, someone knocked on the door.

"Yes?" Mary called out.

"This is Nancy. Um, girls, I'm sorry to bother you all, but I'm looking for Esther. Is she in there?"

Looking puzzled, Esther got to her feet. "I'm right here."

"Thank goodness. You have a visitor, dear. Michael is at the door."

"I'll be right there," Esther said before turning to all of them. "I have to go. I'm sorry!"

"Don't be sorry," Mary said with a brave smile. "I hope you have a good time."

Esther still looked unsure. "I could cancel . . . Would you like me to do that?"

"Nope. Go out and have a good time." Mary stood up and gave Esther a hug. "I really hope he's wonderful tonight."

As Esther was leaving, Mary flopped down on the bed. "I think I need some pie."

"Whenever you're ready, we'll go get some at Yoder's," Betsy said.

"Wait, did you already get some today?"

"I did, but I think this might be a two-slices-of-pie kind of day."

26

Michael's friend Red had called him a fool, and Michael was fairly sure that he was right. There was no reason to expect that Esther was going to want to see him again after she left Pinecraft. It wasn't like they had a lot in common—or that he was a catch. He was well aware of his faults and Esther's many qualities. He didn't need to be a mathematician to know that they didn't add up.

He could hope, though. And he believed in hoping. That was what had helped him survive his parents' deaths and the life he had with Aunt Vera and Uncle Paul. He sometimes felt like without hope he would have nothing else.

He'd been taken aback when Nancy said she had to go find Esther. He'd hoped that she would've been as anxious to see him as he was to see her.

While Nancy searched for his date, Michael tried not to pace in the entryway. Nothing like feeling forgotten to dive-bomb a man's ego.

"I found her," Nancy said. "She said she'd be along shortly. You might as well have a seat."

"Danke."

"Would you care for something to drink?"

Nancy really was so kind. "Thank you but no. I'll just sit here and wait." And try not to feel like an awkward teenager in over his head.

Her gaze softened. "Just to let you know, one of Esther's friends looked to be having a bit of a crisis. I don't think she meant to keep you waiting."

"Thank you," he murmured. "That does help."

"I bet it won't be too much longer," she said as she walked out of the room.

After sitting on the couch for a few minutes, he paced again. Then he sat back down and tried to be patient. If Esther had been helping someone, then she was likely running late and probably had to go back to her room.

Those things took time, he supposed.

Five minutes passed. Then ten.

Sitting back down, he tried to think about other things. His work schedule. The promotion he'd recently accepted.

When a group of women walked down the stairs, he looked up quickly. He leaned back when he realized that none of them was Esther.

When they paused, each eyeing him with a combination of amusement and concern, he realized he'd met them before. "Hiya," he said.

"Do you need anything, Michael?" one asked.

He belatedly realized the woman's name was Lilly. "Danke, but nee. I'm waiting for Esther."

Betsy's eyes were filled with sympathy. "D-do you want me to go check on her for ya?"

The last thing he wanted was for Esther to discover how anxious he was. "Danke, but I don't mind waiting. I'm good."

"Ah. Well, okay," Betsy replied.

The three girls continued to smile at each other as they walked out the front door. No doubt, they were outside giggling about how nervous he looked.

Hanging his head, he sighed. He didn't blame them one bit for their amusement. After all, he knew what he looked like to the women—like an impatient suitor on a first date. It was surely how he felt.

No, a voice in his head corrected. *You are nervous and young, but you are also determined.*

That was true. As far as he was concerned, he had everything to gain and little to lose by boldly approaching Esther just a few hours before she left for Ohio. If he didn't do something, if he didn't at least try to get her to promise to stay in touch, he knew he'd always regret it.

He didn't want to have any more regrets.

"I'm so sorry, Michael," Esther said as she rushed toward him. "I promise I didn't keep you waiting all this time on purpose."

Walking to her side, he tried not to notice every little thing about her. Her yellow dress, her white canvas Keds, the way she smelled faintly of flowers and lemons. "That's okay. Nancy told me that you had a problem with one of your friends."

Looking upset, she nodded. "Poor Mary Margaret. I'll tell you about it during supper. Where would you like to go?"

"I thought we might go to the restaurant where I work. On the Boardwalk. It's a nice place and the food is really good."

Her eyes lit up. "Really? That would be so fun!"

"I hope so." It would also be the right price, since the meal would be free. When they got outside, he said, "The restaurant is quite a few blocks away. We can walk or take the SCAT."

"Let's walk. I'll be riding on a bus for hours and hours tomorrow."

"I can't believe you're already leaving tomorrow."

"I can't believe it either," she said. "I wish I wasn't leaving until next week."

He wished she'd never leave, but he didn't dare say that. "I bet your family will be glad to see you back."

She nodded. "I'll be glad to see them, and Junior especially."

"Are you bringing him back anything?" he asked as they waited to cross the street.

"Oh, jah. A bunch of seashells. He'll love them."

They shared a smile as they continued to walk.

When they arrived at On the Boardwalk, he introduced Esther to Kim.

"Michael said he might bring you here tonight, Esther. We kept this table open just in case." Kim led them to the best table in the restaurant, which was next to the window and had a view of the entire back garden.

Michael was shocked. Almost every day someone called to reserve this particular table. "You didn't have to do that, Kim."

"Of course we did." Smiling at Esther, she added, "We all think the world of Michael."

"I'm glad," Esther murmured.

Michael felt about ten feet tall—and as embarrassed as he'd ever been in his life. After they sat down, Kim said, "Have a good evening, and relax and enjoy yourselves!"

"Thanks again, Kim."

When they were alone, Esther ran a hand along the starched white tablecloth. "This restaurant is so fancy, Michael. You told me that you worked at a nice restaurant, but I didn't expect this."

It was prideful, but he was glad she was impressed. He felt like he was at such a disadvantage where she was concerned.

At the very least, he'd be able to give her a nice meal before she left. "I like working here."

When Chris, one of the older waiters, took their drink orders, he said, "Glad to see you're finally eating here, buddy. Good for you."

"Thanks."

After he walked away, Esther raised an eyebrow at him. "What did he mean?"

"I've worked here a long time, but I've never brought anyone."

"Not even your friends?"

"Nee."

"Why not?"

"I wanted the person I brought here to be special," he admitted, then felt his cheeks heat up. "And now I've completely embarrassed myself."

"And charmed me," she said softly. "Thank you for making me feel special."

"I'm glad you wanted to come here."

She lowered her voice. "Does this mean we get to eat at a discount, I hope?"

"Jah. It will be free."

Her sweet smile widened. "I'm glad. I would've felt really guilty if this meal had cost you a lot of money."

He was so relieved by her reaction, he laughed. "Thanks. I wasn't sure how you'd feel about me taking you out to a free meal."

"I feel great about it."

Chris returned and encouraged them to order appetizers and salads as well as main entrées, so they did just that.

When they were alone again, Esther looked at him intently.

It was obvious that she was waiting for him to share why he'd brought her out.

It was time. Nerves were starting to get the best of him, but he tamped them down as best he could. "Esther, I not only wanted to take you out to a nice dinner, but I wanted to talk to you about something."

Looking so proper, she folded her hands in her lap. "All right."

He took a deep breath. "I don't know how you feel about me, but I really like you." He inwardly winced. Did he sound like a stupid kid again?

Her eyes warmed. "I like you too, Michael."

"You do? Ah. Well, I'm—"

"Here are your salads," Chris interrupted as he placed a dish in front of each of them. "Would either of you like fresh-ground pepper?"

"None for me," said Esther.

"I'm gut, Chris."

"I'll bring your shrimp and crab cakes out in a minute. We figured you two might enjoy eating them together."

"That sounds good." Michael was glad the staff was helping him navigate this date.

After Chris walked away, everything he'd meant to say bubbled up inside him, but he pushed it away. Instead, he forced himself to do what was right. "Should we pray now?"

She blinked. "All right."

Closing his eyes, he silently gave thanks for the food, his job there at On the Boardwalk, and meeting Esther. He also quickly asked for some help, because he sure needed some at that moment.

When Michael lifted his head, he noticed that Esther was still patiently watching him.

"Ah, Michael, what were you saying before our salads came?"

"I was going to say that I don't want tonight to be the last time I ever see you. I want to write to you. To call you too. But, um, I'm not sure how you feel about that."

She smiled. "I'd be verra glad to receive letters and phone calls from you."

"That's . . . that's great. I'm glad too."

Her eyes warmed again before she looked away and picked up her fork.

Following her lead, he took a bite of salad.

As promised, Chris returned with their appetizers.

"This all looks so good!" Esther said.

"It is," Michael said with a laugh. "I mean, these are the two most popular appetizers."

"I guess you would know, right?"

Her voice was teasing. He felt himself relax as he enjoyed the food.

"Do you eat all of this a lot?"

"Nee. Every so often, Marco, the chef, might make more of something and offer it to the servers, but I don't usually eat any."

"Why not?"

He shrugged. "Most of the time I'm not too hungry. We stay busy here too. I like to do my job, not eat."

"I can understand that."

When they finished both the appetizers and the salads, Esther shifted in her chair. Whether it was an unconscious gesture or a move she'd practiced many times, she smoothed her light yellow dress about her legs as she did so.

Michael realized then that he had no idea if other women did that as well or not. He'd never been as fascinated with another woman as he was with her.

"Ah, you're done," Chris said as he returned. "Was everything all right?"

"Oh yes," Esther said.

"Your main dishes will be out soon."

When they were alone again, Michael said, "I'll have to get your phone number and address tonight. I'll ask Chris to bring out a pen and paper."

"All right." She smiled, then said hesitantly, "Michael, I meant what I said. I do like you . . . but, ah, are you sure that I'm not simply a novelty in your life? That maybe you haven't spent so much time with an older woman before?"

"I'm positive. Besides, you're not that much older than me."

"I'm five years older, Michael."

"That probably means a lot to you, but it doesn't to me."

She still looked a little hesitant. "All right . . . but if you meet someone else, will you promise to let me know?"

"I don't plan on doing that."

"Don't forget, new buses arrive every day."

He was starting to feel like she was talking down to him. "I know that, Esther. Don't you think that I'm aware of how many tourists arrive here all the time?"

"Yes, of course, but—"

"Esther—" He obviously hadn't explained himself well enough.

"Hi, kids," Kim said. "I told Chris that I'd bring out your meals. Did you order the redfish, Esther?"

"I did."

"Michael, I hope you enjoy the pasta."

"Thanks. I know I will." It was fettuccini with a cream sauce, grilled chicken, and broccoli. The dish was his favorite, and on the rare nights when he brought something home to eat, he always chose it. Taking a bite, he couldn't help smiling. The pasta was a whole lot better when it was just out of the kitchen.

Esther looked to be enjoying her meal too. There was so much he still needed to say, but he didn't want to ruin the meal. He elected to keep quiet until they were finished.

Practically the moment their plates were clean, Chris appeared with dessert menus. "I don't know if Michael has told you, but our key lime pie is amazing."

Esther smiled. "He didn't tell me that, but I'm so full. I don't know if I can eat another bite."

"Maybe you can share something? Baked Alaska, perhaps?"

"What do you think, Esther? It's ice cream and cake surrounded with meringue and baked. It's really good."

She nodded. "I think that sounds wonderful. I've never had that before."

When they were alone again, Michael leaned forward. He wished he could take her hand. However, even if she let him, he knew he'd never do that in front of everyone at the restaurant. They'd never let him live it down. So he settled for speaking from his heart. "Esther, what I've been trying to tell you is that I . . . I really like you. I've never done this before."

"Done what?"

"You know, walk up to a woman on the beach. Visit her at her inn . . . see her as much as possible. It's not just because you're someone new or so pretty either. It's how serious you are. It's the way that there seems to be a part of you that's a lot like me. That both of us have experienced some pain before."

She'd gone still. "Michael."

"It's okay if you want to wait to give me your heart. I'll even understand if you change your mind about me when you get home. But, please. Don't discount how I'm feeling. I would never do that to you."

"You're right. I'm so sorry."

"One baked Alaska," Chris said as he put the dessert in between them. "Would you like me to cut it in half for you?"

"Nee. I'll do it," Michael said.

"Here's the knife, buddy," Chris said with a wink.

When he was gone, Michael neatly cut it in half with the large kitchen knife and set half on the plate in front of Esther before doing the same for himself.

"What?" he asked when he noticed she was smiling even more broadly.

She giggled. "I was just thinking that I bet you have your share of admiring diners, Michael. There's something about you that is mesmerizing."

"I just need you to think that," he joked.

She didn't reply, but the warm glance they shared haunted him while they walked back after supper. "Mind if we go back a different way to the Marigold Inn?" he asked. "It doesn't take much longer but it's quieter."

"I'd like that."

Two right turns later, they were walking on the sidewalk near a park. Next to no one was around. The air felt cooler. Unable to help himself, he reached for her hand.

She linked her fingers with his. "Michael, ah, just to let you know, you might be thinking that whatever this is between the two of us is one-sided, but it's not. Everything that you've been talking about this evening are things that I've been feeling too. You're just braver than me."

"More desperate. That's what it is."

"I hope you won't eventually be disappointed with me. I'm really nothing special. Just a girl."

"You are to me." He shrugged. "I don't know a lot about love or relationships. But I do know enough to know that's all that counts."

She stopped. "I forgot to write down my address."

"Hold on. I grabbed this on the way out." He pulled out a pencil and the back of one of his tip sheets from the restaurant and handed it to her.

"Oh my goodness. You came prepared."

"I might have a lot to learn, but I'm determined," he said. When she finished writing all her information down, he folded the paper once and shoved it into his pocket.

They walked another two blocks. "How close are we to the inn?" she asked.

"We're almost there. Three blocks away."

"That's too bad. I don't want tonight to end."

He didn't either. He wanted to walk by Esther's side, hold her hand, talk to her. Gaze at her. He wanted to pile on every memory he could, so he'd have something to hold on to when she was gone.

When they neared a copse of trees, he stopped. "Esther?" he whispered.

She didn't need him to ask. Instead, she stepped closer. He pulled her into his arms. She went without resisting, relaxing against him. He inhaled the slight lemon scent that had been clinging to her hair, reveling in the way she felt so perfect in his arms.

Before he could stop himself, he kissed her cheek, paused, then at last did what he'd been wanting to do since practically the first moment he saw her. He kissed her lips.

214

When Esther wrapped her arms around his neck, he deepened the kiss. Tried to convey every single thing he was feeling as he pulled her even closer with one hand. With his other, he cupped her cheek, loving how soft her skin was.

When they pulled apart at last, he felt out of breath, like he'd just run a mile on the beach. She was breathing harder too but didn't look upset.

No, even in the dim light, it was obvious that she had been just as affected as he was.

"I . . . I better get you home."

"Ah . . . yes."

He took her hand again. When they got close to the inn, he saw that there were several people sitting on the front porch. He dropped her hand and moved a few inches away from her.

She straightened her posture. Lifted her chin a bit. Within seconds, he reckoned they looked like two modest Amish folks simply walking together.

Well aware that the people on the porch were watching them, he stopped a few feet from the front steps. "Thank you for this evening."

"Thank you for supper. I think it was the nicest meal I've ever had."

"I'll let everyone at the restaurant know."

"I'll miss you, Michael."

"I'll miss you too." He forced himself to take a step back. "Safe travels. I'll write you soon."

"I'll look for your letter." She smiled.

He nodded, then before he did anything else that he shouldn't, he turned and walked away. Picked up his pace. Crossed the intersection.

Eventually, the sidewalks filled with more people. More cars were on the road. Children's laughter filled the air. But all he seemed to be aware of was every word they'd exchanged, the paper in his pocket, and the feel of her in his arms.

As far as he was concerned, nothing else mattered. For a few sweet minutes, everything else in the world ceased to exist.

27

Esther hadn't been able to make herself spend time with the girls after she said goodbye to Michael last night. The evening had been so sweet, so romantic, so everything, she couldn't bear to taint it by acting as if it hadn't been special. She would've felt obligated to do that too. Mary's heart was broken, and she needed support. And Esther would do whatever she could to help her. In the morning.

So, instead of talking and consoling, she'd spent the rest of her evening repacking her belongings, writing in her journal, and staring out the window. Most of the time, though, all she'd done was relive every word Michael had said and think about that kiss.

Oh, that kiss!

Xavier had kissed her two times. Both times she'd felt awkward and uncomfortable—the second time, all she'd been able to think about was that his lips felt wet.

It was now obvious that she'd only been waiting for the right person. Her toes literally curled every time she thought about being in Michael's arms.

Luckily, their morning was hectic and frazzled. She'd eaten

breakfast early with Betsy, but beyond saying good morning and Esther filling her in about the basics of her date, they hadn't spoken too much. Betsy still wasn't completely packed, and Esther had needed to pay her bill.

Eventually, they each got their things together, hugged Nancy goodbye, and made their way to the parking lot. The walk felt twice as long, given all the extra things each of them was taking home.

Mary smiled at Esther and waved off her apology for not checking on her the evening before. So while Esther slowly made her way toward the bus, she allowed her mind to drift back to Michael.

In the light of day, she felt a little more clarity. She was pretty sure that everything between her and Michael wasn't supposed to have happened. Actually, Esther knew it. Knew it in the way she knew that the best rosebushes needed careful pruning and that the best pie crusts contained a spoonful of white vinegar. She wasn't supposed to fall in love with a younger man in Florida. In just a little more than a week.

Not a bit of it made sense, and not a bit of it was going to be all right with her mother.

She didn't care, though.

And maybe that was the most concerning part of the entire dilemma. She was through with holding her tongue, biding her time, trying too hard, and pushing away her preferences. She had changed.

Being around Mary, Lilly, and Betsy had inspired her in ways she hadn't even realized she'd needed to be inspired. The other girls, so sweet, so funny, so nice, had made her want to look over her life in a different way.

But even if the other girls hadn't been there, even if Mary

had refused to talk to her, Esther knew that much of her change of heart was due to Michael. His goals, his dreams, and even his story had touched something deep inside her. He might be younger, but as far as she was concerned, she wanted to grow up to be just like him.

Well, the feminine version of him.

"Five minutes, everyone!" Toby called out. "Say your good-byes and load your bags if you haven't already."

"Esther, would you like some help?" Mary asked.

"Hmm? Oh jah. Danke." Pushing thoughts of Michael to the back of her mind, Esther picked up the quilted duffle bag. "Would you mind rolling my suitcase?"

"Not at all."

After checking in her bags and assuring Toby that her other items would fit easily around her bus seat, Esther walked to the side of the parking lot. "I guess it's about time, huh?"

Mary nodded. "The other girls and I went to the market and got a few snacks and some water last night. Did you see the man with the cart over in the shade? I bet you could get some snacks and such from him if you needed to."

"Danke, but I am fine. I picked up everything I might need yesterday."

"Oh. Well, that's gut."

Mary was looking at her intently. It was obvious that she had some questions but didn't want to pry. "Would you like to sit together on the bus?" Esther asked her.

"Sure. I'd like that."

"Me too." Feeling her cheeks heat, Esther added, "Maybe you'll be able to talk some sense into me during our trip back."

"About you and Michael?"

"Of course."

"I don't know if I'm going to be much help there. The two of you look wonderful together."

"It's time to board!" Toby called out. "This bus leaves in five minutes."

Mary wrinkled her nose. "Boy, he seems awfully strict."

"I've forgotten that he wasn't your driver when you came down. He's really nice and not too strict. But he does like to be on time."

They boarded the bus with Betsy and Lilly. By mutual agreement, they elected to be toward the back of the bus but not in the very back next to the bathroom. Betsy and Lilly sat one row in front of them so they could turn around to chat, and so they'd all be able to switch seats and take turns sitting with each other.

For the next few minutes, everyone on the bus was busy getting settled. Esther was amused to see that a few of the older women had already taken out their blankets and pillows and arranged them on their seats. They looked like they were about to fall asleep for the next ten hours.

Since she hadn't brought much with her in the first place, Esther got settled quickly. She looked out the window, only half seeing the activity in the parking lot. Instead, she found herself once again reliving every second of her time with Michael. She wondered if he was doing the same thing.

Had he been just as affected by their kiss? Was he missing her already too?

"Sorry," Mary said when she finally sat down. She had a book on her lap and a water bottle and granola bar in the holder on the back of the seat in front of her. "I thought I was so organized, but I wasn't."

"It doesn't matter to me," Esther said.

"I bet," Mary said with a laugh. "Betsy told me that Michael took you out to a fancy dinner and that you even had baked Alaska. If someone had treated me to a meal like that, I'd be in a happy daze too."

"Doors are closing! Take your seats, boys and girls," Toby said over the bus's intercom. "We're pulling out."

A couple of young children sitting near the front clapped excitedly as Toby moved the bus forward and headed out of the parking lot.

Five minutes later, when they were on the highway, Esther finally responded to Mary's comment. "The dinner was amazing, but it was nothing to how I felt around Michael."

"It went well?"

"Oh yes." Esther was tempted to add more but refrained out of sympathy for her friend. Awkwardly, she added, "I really am sorry about everything."

"Danke." Looking determined, Mary added, "If you don't mind, could we not talk about Jayson just yet? I'd rather hear some good news. Do you think you'll hear from Michael after we're back home?"

"He asked if he could write to me. I told him yes."

"And . . . anything else?"

She couldn't help it. She nodded. "He kissed me last night."

"I knew it!"

Esther giggled. "Shh!"

"So, was it wonderful?"

"It was so wonderful." Realizing that some girls didn't believe in kissing a beau until they were engaged, she added hesitantly, "I hope you don't think less of me."

"Of course not. As far as I'm concerned, you should be counting your blessings instead of worrying about that. I promise. Besides, we all noticed the way Michael looks at you. It's so intense, Lilly said it nearly took her breath away. Anyone can tell that he really likes you, Esther."

"That's what he said. He not only promised to write, he said he'd call . . . and made me promise to write him back."

"Did you?"

"I did. I couldn't help myself."

"Do you think you should have?"

Mary's tone was curious, like she was honestly interested in what Esther thought. It took Esther off guard, not because the question was especially personal but because it forced her to once again figure out what she thought—not what everyone else would think or what her parents had told her was proper. "I don't know," she said at last. "It's hard for me to separate the way I'm feeling with the way I think I'm supposed to be. What do you think?"

"Me? Well, I suppose if I was so blessed to have a man declare his feelings and not care about anything but me, I have to believe that I'd be happy." She bit her bottom lip. "I never even asked, does Michael make you happy?"

"Oh jah."

Mary grinned. "There's your answer then."

"Is it really that easy?" Esther wanted it to be—but she also didn't want to oversimplify everything.

"Did you notice that you didn't hesitate one bit? Your brain might be waffling and going back and forth, but your heart seems certain. I think that should tell you everything you need to know."

"Thank you. I think I'm falling in love with him, Mary." She lowered her voice. "My mamm's going to be so mad, though."

"She might be, but you won't have to worry about that for at least another day."

Esther giggled. "You're right. I'm going to try not to worry anymore about my mother on this bus trip."

"Gut."

Mary's smile didn't reach her eyes, making Esther flush again—this time for a very different reason. "I really am sorry that Jayson treated you so badly."

"I'm sad and disappointed, but I'm not sad about you. Honestly, I think it's good that we've been talking about you and Michael. You've made me remember that not all men are like Jayson. Some are far more honest and trustworthy."

"If it's any consolation, Xavier and I courted for years just to realize that we didn't suit. When we broke up, we disappointed both sets of parents, and it left me feeling like I'd just wasted years on something that wasn't going to go anywhere. I'd been sure that he was the one and that everything between us would get better. At least you found out about Jayson's true colors before things got even more serious."

"You're right. That is gut." Mary smiled but she still looked so sad.

"I really am sorry he was such a snake."

"Me too. I thought I knew better, but I guess I didn't."

"It's his fault, not yours. You didn't do anything wrong."

"Even if that's true, it doesn't make me feel any better right now. Hopefully one day it will."

Esther nodded. She felt so sorry for Mary. That girl was so in need of something good to happen in her life. She hoped the Lord would take care of that soon.

28

Mary's bus had departed for Ohio right on time. Jayson knew that because he hadn't been able to stop himself from joining the crowd in the parking lot to watch the latest group of travelers board and head off on their way north.

Of course, he'd stayed in the background. The last thing he wanted was for Mary to see him there. He felt bad enough without her wondering why he couldn't let her leave Pinecraft in peace.

He should be able to let her do that, at the very least.

After the bus left and the crowd dispersed, he walked down to the Mennonite church just a couple of blocks away. They had a nice seating area on the side of their lot and didn't seem to mind if people rested there from time to time.

There, he made some decisions. It was time to come to terms with his feelings. As much as he loved his little sister, he couldn't always put her before his own needs. As much as he appreciated Wood Schrock's help, he couldn't marry his daughter out of obligation. Ellen deserved so much more. Marriage vows were sacred, and living a good married life was challenging, even for the happiest of couples. Marrying out of obligation without love would be a travesty. He should have known that from the start.

Furthermore, as much as he worried about his father, he couldn't continue to support him when he did so little to support himself.

Even though he'd promised the folks at Pinecraft Construction that he could start working in a few weeks, he knew he was in no position to do anything until he went home and straightened things out with his family.

However, he couldn't bear to sit for hours on that bus. Feeling torn up inside about the way he treated Mary, he'd gone to Danny, told him everything, and asked for help. Danny did him one better. Two hours later, he showed up at the boardinghouse with his cousin Will. Will had elected not to join the church and was now a trucker.

"Danny here told me about some of your problems, lad. I'm real sorry about that."

"Danke."

"I can take you all the way to Marion today if you'd like."

"Today? It's a long drive."

"For most people, it is for sure." He grinned. "For me, it ain't nothing, especially since I'll be going in my Ford Explorer. It's a whole lot easier to drive than a big rig."

"What do you think?" Danny asked.

There was nothing to think about. "I think that you're an answer to a prayer, Will. I can't thank you enough. I'd love to leave today. How much will I owe you?"

"Not a thing. You're in need of a helping hand, and I'm in the position to give that to you."

"That's very kind, but it's too generous. I promise I have quite a bit saved up. I can afford the trip."

Will still shook his head. "Danny told me that you're a carpenter."

"I am."

"Well then, I think we can make a deal of it. I'll drive you to Kentucky this week. One day soon, you can come build some bookshelves for my wife. She's got more books than she can shake a stick at."

Grinning, he shook the trucker's hand. "That's a deal."

"Good. See you in ninety minutes, *jah*?"

"Yes. I'll be ready."

After Will left, Jayson said to Danny, "I can't believe your cousin is taking me all the way to Kentucky for free."

"He likes to drive, plus his wife wants to do some kind of baking marathon with her sisters and cousins at their house. Will told me that he needed to get out of there fast."

"Well, thanks again. I'll contact you when I'm headed back this way. Hopefully it will be sooner than later."

"You won't have to, because I'm coming with you."

"What?"

"I need a break too. Plus, I have a feeling you might need someone there for some moral support. I'm gonna go too."

"Hey, I appreciate it, I really do . . . but that doesn't mean I expect you to do this."

"I'm only going to stay for a couple of days. Will is going to go to Mammoth Cave and hike a bit. He's going to pick me up on his way back."

"You've got it all figured out."

Danny grinned. "I had to, otherwise I knew you'd tell me no."

"Just to warn you, my family doesn't have a lot of money. Our *haus* is small."

"Do you think that matters to me?"

"No, I just wanted to let you know."

"Well, stop overthinking everything. You pack while I head home and do the same. See you in ninety minutes."

"I'll be ready."

As he stuffed a duffle bag with just enough things to see him through a few days, Jayson breathed a sigh of relief. Not only was he glad that he was about to finally have this much-needed conversation, but he was really glad he'd have Danny by his side. The upcoming trip was going to be difficult, but he would survive, especially since he knew at least one person would have his back.

Before he knew it, he was going to be back in Florida and at his new job. He needed to concentrate on that.

When Will and Danny arrived back at the boardinghouse's parking lot a little more than an hour later, Jayson was ready.

"Tell me when you need a break," Will said after tossing Jayson's bag in the back. "Otherwise, settle in for a long ride. We'll stop at a rest stop to sleep."

Will was as good as his word. He was a steady driver. He lingered just about the speed limit and didn't stop for much. He was also good company. Will shared stories with Danny and encouraged Jayson to talk as well. The hours passed like lightning. Other than a few quick stops, they stopped once for six hours to sleep and then arrived midmorning the next day.

Soon, whether Jayson was ready or not, he was back in Crittenden County, Kentucky. It was time to face his past so he could plan for his future.

"Jayson, you're back!" Joy ran toward him. "I missed you so much."

He opened up his arms for a hug and then enfolded her in an embrace. As usual, his little sister smelled faintly of paint, thanks to her fondness for painting with acrylics. "I missed you too, sweetheart." Pulling back, he looked into her eyes. "How are you?"

"Fine."

"You sure? No episodes?"

She rolled her eyes. "Nee. I'm gut." Glancing at Danny, she looked suddenly shy. "Hi."

"Joy, this is Danny. You two met each other years ago."

She blushed. "I remember. Hello again."

"It's gut to see you, Joy. I hope you don't mind me being here. I'm afraid I bullied Jayson into letting me tag along."

"I'm glad you are, though I don't know why you would need to bully your way here. You're always welcome."

"Danke. That is very kind of you."

Jayson noticed that Danny was treating Joy almost formally. As if she was the one in charge of the house and not their father.

Which brought him to wondering why the house was so quiet. "Where is Daed?"

"He went to see Mommi and Dawdi for two days." Their mother's parents lived a few hours away.

"Why didn't he take you?"

Joy shrugged. "I just saw them a couple of weeks ago. I didn't want to go. I think he'll be back tomorrow."

Irritation that their father had left Joy all alone flowed through him. "I see."

Joy grabbed his hand. "Calm down, Jayson. Don't get all mad for no reason."

He gently squeezed her hand. "I'm calm."

"If you're calm, then try to act like it, because I don't think you look real calm at all right now."

He raised his eyebrows. "You sure have a lot to say."

"I am fourteen, remember?"

Danny chuckled. "She's got you good, Jay."

Jayson lowered his voice. "Joy, I know you're not a little child, but your diabetes is a concern. He shouldn't be leaving town like this."

"I think you're forgetting that it's something that I've been living with for a long time." She folded her arms across her chest. "And I've been the one who deals with it too." Before he could interrupt, she lifted her chin. "Jay, I know how to take care of myself. I still prick my fingers every day and still take my shots."

Danny interrupted. "Hey, ah, where's the bathroom?"

"It's down the hall," Joy said. "Would you like me to show you which door?"

"Nah. I can find it. I'm going to wash up, so it might be a minute."

"He wasn't very subtle," Joy said after Danny left the room.

"He didn't need to be. He's a gut friend." Still needing to make sure she was doing all right, he said, "Who's been doing your arms?" She alternated between her arms and legs for her insulin.

"Jill next door."

"Gut." Of course Joy was able to give herself injections, but she sometimes relied on Jayson for her arms.

"You'll help me out today, though, right?"

"Of course. I want to help you with whatever you need."

She smiled brightly before it dimmed. "You always say that."

"I know, and it's because I mean it. You know you always

come first in my life." And she always had—until he decided to accept that job in Pinecraft. "I still canna believe Daed left you home alone."

"It's not like I'm a little girl." She lifted her chin. "I'm out of school and everything." After peeking to make sure Danny wasn't approaching, she added, "It's not like things are easier when our father is here, Jayson. Right?"

"Right." He'd never understood how their father had ended up being so useless in so many ways. Their father insisted on owning two greenhouses but had next to no green thumb. He made ends meet by doing odd jobs around town. That was when he was feeling good. Other times, he simply said that he was too depressed and missing their mamm too much to do much of anything.

Jayson and Joy had grown up knowing that their father loved and cared about them but wasn't exactly dependable. Even their grandparents and aunts and uncles knew it. Jayson couldn't count the number of times that a member of the family had stepped in to help pay bills or assist when Joy had a doctor appointment for her diabetes.

Jayson walked into the kitchen, which was neat as a pin. Though most people would find that a good thing, it sent him warning signals. "Did you eat breakfast?"

"Jah."

"What did you eat?"

"An egg and toast."

"And you cleaned it up?"

"I did."

"What about supper last night?"

"Honestly, Jayson."

He knew he was being a pain, but he couldn't help himself.

He'd been the one to give her juice when her insulin level was off, and he'd been the one to check out books from the library so she'd eat the right foods. "What did you eat?"

"Fine. Jill and Thomas invited me over for supper. They had baked chicken and broccoli and risotto."

"Risotto?"

"It's fancy rice. It was gut. Now stop with the questions and tell me about your trip."

"There's a lot to tell you about," he said. "It might be better to tell you tonight or when we have more time."

"The house is clean, you aren't working, and Daed isn't here. This is the best time for you to talk to me."

"We have a houseguest."

"Does Danny know about your trip . . . and why you look so serious and worried?"

"Of course."

"Then . . ." She drew out her voice.

"Fine. You're right."

Concern filled her eyes. "Oh, Jayson. Something happened, didn't it? Go sit on the couch and I'll bring the three of us some kaffi and rolls."

"I'll hit the bathroom too and meet you there."

He passed Danny in the hall. "Joy wants to hear about the trip. She went to the kitchen to get kaffi and rolls for the three of us."

"You sure you're good with me joining ya?" Written on Danny's face was his new knowledge about how things really were in his father's house. Jayson wasn't sure if Danny was shocked or if things were about how he'd expected after hearing Jayson's stories through the years. He supposed it didn't really matter. The fact of it was that things in his house were

231

difficult, they always had been, and they weren't likely to get much better unless a miracle happened.

"I'm sure. You might even keep me honest. There's a lot I need to share with Joy and a lot I'm not real proud about but needs to be said."

"That's what you want?"

He nodded. "I'm done pretending that things aren't so bad."

"I hope you've also decided that the only way that you're going to make things better is to stop putting everyone else first."

"I have." With one exception, of course. He wanted to one day be able to put Mary first in his life. He wasn't sure how that was going to happen, but he wanted to give it a try.

That is, if she would ever want him back.

29

When the three of them sat down on the couch, Joy shot Jayson a determined look. "Tell me what happened back in Pinecraft that made you look like you've got the weight of the world on your shoulders."

"It's pretty embarrassing. I've done something I'm not proud of." He looked down at his feet and forced himself to be more frank. "Actually, I'm ashamed."

"So?" She countered right back. "I do lots of things that I'm not proud about all the time. You still love me, though, right?"

"Of course. But this is different."

Danny spoke up. "Sorry, Jay, but I think your sister is right. Stop being so hard on yourself and tell her the whole story."

He glanced at his sister, who was staring at him intently. Danny was right. "Fine, but don't say I didn't warn you, Joy."

"Whatever," Joy said. "Start talking, Jayson."

"Fine. It all started back here about three weeks ago," he began. "I was talking to Wood Schrock about work . . . and he brought up Ellen."

Joy's eyes went wide. "Uh-oh."

Feeling like he was falling off the pedestal he'd made for himself, he continued.

Conveying everything wasn't easy. Not only was he not proud of his actions, but he struggled to find a way to tell the reasoning behind them without sounding as if he were blaming Joy.

Within just a few moments, however, Jayson realized that his lofty goal of transforming his story into something that made even a small amount of sense was ridiculous. So was worrying about his pride.

Joy looked incredulous and even Danny appeared uncomfortable.

When she'd muttered, "Wow, Jayson," he'd felt like his face was three shades of red.

Even though her reaction was nothing less than he deserved, he soldiered on. Danny's presence helped, but having his friend hear just how convoluted his entire plan had been was mortifying. Hearing it all out loud made Jayson wonder why he'd ever thought that everything was going to work out.

Joy looked especially disappointed in him. "Bruder, I don't know if breaking that Mary Margaret's heart or agreeing to marry Ellen is worse." She shook her head. "You might think I don't know much at fourteen, but you should've asked me for advice. I would've told you that both ideas were stupid."

"Way to make me feel better, Joy."

"Sorry, but she's right," Danny said. "I know I told you to enjoy your break, but I didn't know *everything* that had gone on before you arrived."

"It's not like I was going to tell you all about my father and our money problems, Danny."

Danny rolled his eyes. "It's not like I wasn't already aware of both of those things."

Thoroughly embarrassed, Jayson leaned back on the couch. "Well, at least you both know what happened."

"Do we know everything?" Danny asked.

"Everything."

"At least there's that," Joy said.

"Sister, watch your mouth. You might be right, but you don't have to be so cheeky about it."

"I'm not being cheeky. All I'm doing is telling you my opinion."

"Which is?"

"Hmm. Well, since you've managed to make this Mary Margaret very sad, I kind of feel like you deserve what you get there." She folded her arms over her chest. "I don't even know what to say about Ellen." She scowled. "I can't believe you actually thought about marrying her!"

"Hey, now. Ellen isn't a bad person."

"Of course she isn't, though we all know that she and I don't get along."

"I know she isn't your favorite person, but I'm sure you two could've learned to be friends."

Joy muttered something under her breath before clearing her throat. "Let's forget about that. How about we all just concentrate on love and marriage." Staring at him boldly, she said, "Don't you think even Ellen Schrock deserves more than a husband who was practically bought for her?"

He winced. "It wasn't like that."

"Sorry, Jayson," Danny interjected, "but I'm afraid it really was."

"Ellen knew about this," he pointed out. Well, she kind of did.

"Even if she knew how you felt—which I doubt—that doesn't

make it better," Joy said. "She was probably pleased because she got what she wanted. You."

He shifted uncomfortably. "That's not fair to her."

"I think it is. Everyone in the county knows that she's always liked you. She's never been shy about sharing that you, Jayson, are her goal."

Danny's eyes lit up. "Did she? I had no idea. You didn't tell me that part, Jayson." Sharing a smile with Joy, he added, "Tell me true, what is it about your brother that women find so appealing? Is it his good looks or his charm?"

"His good looks, of course. But he can't take any credit for that—the Lord is responsible there." She waved a hand. "His other qualities are works in progress. He's still learning how to be charming."

Jayson was now blushing like a kid with his first crush. "Stop. Both of you."

Still grinning, Danny shook his head. "No way. Hearing about someone making you her life's goal is irresistible fodder."

Danny was going to bring this convoluted mess up for the rest of his life. He knew it. "Canna you just forget about that part?"

"Ah, let me think . . . No. Way."

When he saw his sister stifle a giggle, he glared at the pair of them. "Now that you two have had your fun, help me fix things."

"What is stopping you from breaking everything off and going after Mary Margaret? Maybe she'll let you court her if you live in Pinecraft," Joy said. "I mean, if she'd even give you the time of day."

He didn't know how to answer that. He wanted to be honest, but he also hated hurting her feelings. "Something pretty important."

"Just say it, Jayson," Danny urged.

"Fine." He took a deep breath and glanced back at Joy. "You."

Joy inhaled sharply. "What are you talking about?"

"I worry about you, Joy. If I'm together with Ellen I know Wood will look out for you here, just like he looked out for me. If we break up and I court Mary Margaret, he might never forgive me . . . which could ultimately hurt you."

Joy looked stunned. Her eyes darted toward Danny. When he nodded, she looked back at Jayson. "You're serious?"

"Jah."

She jumped to her feet. "Jayson, what is wrong with you?"

"Nothing." He'd expected tears, apologies for making him feel like he always needed to take care of her, maybe even a bit of gratitude that he was willing to sacrifice so much for her. Definitely not this burst of anger.

Still on her feet, she waved a hand. "I am not an invalid."

"I know that."

"I am also not helpless."

"Oh boy," Danny murmured.

"I never said you were helpless, Joy. Come on . . ."

"I am also not going to be fourteen forever." Looking down her nose at him, she said, "I suppose you've forgotten that?"

"I have not."

"What do you think I'm going to be doing when I'm eighteen or twenty or twenty-four?"

"I don't know," he said, losing his patience. "That's a long time from now. We're talking almost ten years."

"You really haven't given it any thought?"

"Come on, sister. I've hardly known what I'm going to do next month."

"Since you're having so much trouble, I'll fill you in." She stepped closer, then to his shock, she crouched in front of him and grabbed his hands. "One day, when I'm older, I'm going to fall in love with a good man. I'm going to get married and have a baby. Maybe two. I'm going to live my life and not be a little girl anymore."

To his chagrin, he realized he'd never actually given much thought to what Joy's life might look like in a decade. He'd certainly never imagined her as a married woman with children. "What is your point?"

"When I'm all those things, I am not going to need you to take care of me. I'll be able to take care of myself—and I'll have a man that I love by my side to help me if I need it."

Still looking at him intently, she added, "I am not going to need my older brother married to a woman he doesn't love, doing odd jobs he doesn't like—all out of some misguided need to be my knight in shining armor." Her expression eased, turning less fierce and far more tender. "Do you understand what I'm saying, Jayson? It's that while I appreciate what you are willing to do, it isn't necessary or needed. Messing up your life is not going to make mine better."

Stunned by her words, Jayson stared as Joy got to her feet.

"She's saying she's going to get her own knight in armor, buddy," Danny said. "She don't need you to become one."

Unable to help himself, he started laughing. "I get it now. Danke."

"Are you sure?" Danny asked.

"Jah." Looking at his sister, he said, "You're right. You're right about so much. I should've talked to you first."

She nodded. "Your life would've been a whole lot easier now. I can promise you that."

"Any chance you want to come with me to talk to Ellen and her father?"

"Nope." She smiled softly. "But I will go with you to Trail, Ohio."

"Really? It's cold there right now, you know."

"I realize that."

"I think I'll skip the trip to Ohio," Danny said. "Southern Kentucky has been cold enough for me."

"It's settled then," Joy said. "After you talk to Ellen, Daed comes home, and Danny heads back to Florida, you and I will head to Trail."

"You've got this all figured out, hmm?"

"I promise, if you still want this woman in your life, there's no time to waste."

"I'd follow her lead, Jayson," Danny said. "I think we've all learned that left to your own devices, you make a real mess of things."

"Thanks for pointing that out."

Danny leaned back and grinned. "Anytime, buddy. That's what friends are for, right?" He winked at Joy. "Friends and family."

30

It had been five days since she'd returned from Florida. It might as well have been five months, it felt so long. Mary could hardly stand being back in Trail. Like a piece of clothing that had grown too small, Trail didn't fit her anymore. The cliques were too settled, the path she'd inadvertently been on since childhood was too defined. She wasn't sure where her future lay. All she did know was that she needed to make a change soon. Otherwise she was apt to whither into nothing.

Unfortunately, she had no idea how to do that. She prayed for help every night, but so far the Lord hadn't sent her any good ideas. Instead, all she kept hearing from Him was that she needed to find peace and patience.

Even her parents didn't seem to understand that she was no longer the same person she was before. They didn't understand why she wasn't content to stay at home by herself anymore. Didn't understand that while she loved her card-making business, she didn't only want to make cards for other people.

They really didn't understand why she was near tears on her way home from church at the Hershbergers' house. When all she could tell them was that she missed the white-washed community church building in Pinecraft, her father lost his temper.

"Mary, Pinecraft is the only place on earth where the Amish worship in a building, you know that. You canna expect things here to ever be like that."

"I don't expect things here to change at all, Daed." Which, of course, was part of the problem.

Her parents were silent until they got home. After her father parked the buggy next to the barn, they all got out.

Just as she started toward the house, her father stopped her. "Mary, it's time you got back to your same old self. Please stop wearing a frown all the time."

"That's all you have to tell me? You want me to start smiling more?" Of course, she was being sarcastic, but if her parents realized it, they didn't let on.

"I fear your father is right, dear," her mother murmured. "While we can understand your end-of-vacation blues, you need to cheer up. Every vacation comes to an end." She smiled. "Besides, I'm sure you'll go back to Pinecraft again one day."

Mary gritted her teeth as she reminded herself that neither of her parents was intentionally trying to be oblivious about her aching heart. The two of them simply were.

Even though they were standing out in the cold and it would be so much easier to simply keep her mouth shut, she couldn't do it. "This isn't about being sad that my vacation is over, Mamm and Daed."

Daed sighed. "Well, I can think of no other reason for your blues."

She attempted to explain herself yet again. "I'm upset because things were different there."

"Of course they were. You were on vacation in a sunny spot. It snowed yesterday, ain't so?"

"I'm not talking about the weather," she fairly shouted. "I'm upset because I was accepted there, and now it's all gone. I had good friends. Best friends. Even Esther was my friend there." Of course, for a time, she'd also even had a special man whom she'd cared about—and who had cared about her.

"I am mighty sorry that you haven't seen Esther since you've returned. But maybe that was to be expected," Mamm said.

"Why?"

"Because vacation friends are different than 'real' friends, dear," she said in an overly patient tone. "Everyone makes friends while they're on vacation because it's so easy to do. There's no worries or jobs then. But they don't always last, ain't so?"

"I know Betsy and Lilly were 'real' friends. We got really close. I was close with Esther too, and it wasn't because we were on vacation."

"I'm sure Esther will come around eventually," Daed said. "But if she doesn't, I don't think you'll be missing much anyway. She made you miserable for most of your life." He paused. "Or have you already forgotten?"

"I haven't forgotten."

Daed smiled as if the matter was finally solved. "See? Cheer up."

As her father went into the barn, Mary followed her mother into the house. She was tempted to argue some more, but she held her tongue. Her parents were simply trying to help her, and she knew that they were doing their best. They always had.

Walking to her room, Mary knew that she was going to have to make some changes. Otherwise nothing would ever be different, and she would likely wither up into nothing. The fact was, now that she'd had the chance to be around real girlfriends, Mary was no longer willing to go back to being the wallflower. The only problem was that she didn't know what she should do. While she loved her little card-making business, it wasn't all she wanted to do with her life.

Actually, even thinking about spending the majority of her day making cards for people to give to each other made her feel ill.

With some dismay, she decided that it was no wonder she'd been so miserable. All she'd ever done was stay home and wonder when things were going to get better.

"Mary Margaret, you have a visitor," her mother called up the stairs.

Confused, she walked downstairs and found Esther sitting in their living room. She was perched on the edge of a chair and looked completely uncomfortable. Mary's mother was standing with her arms folded over her chest near the foyer. She raised her eyebrows when Mary walked by.

Mary pretended not to see.

"Hey, Esther."

Looking relieved, Esther stood up. "Hi. I'm so glad you were home."

She smiled at her. "Me too. How are you?"

"Oh, all right."

Since it was obvious that Esther was just as anxious as she was to catch up privately, Mary said, "Would you like to come upstairs to my room? We can talk up there."

Pure relief lit Esther's expression. "I'd like that verra much."

"We're going to my room, Mamm."

"Oh? Would you like me to bring you girls some snacks?"

Mary almost started laughing. Her mother always complained whenever she carried food into her room. "We're okay."

"Oh. All right."

Feeling like a child again, she led the way upstairs. When they got in her room and closed the door, they started laughing. "Sorry about that," Mary said. "I don't know about you, but I miss my privacy."

"I have three brothers who keep wandering in my room without knocking. I miss living in that inn so much."

"Me too." Mary sat down on her bed and motioned for Esther to join her. "I'm afraid my mother doesn't know what to do with me anymore."

"Mei mamm is the same way. Well, that's not quite true. She keeps telling me that she doesn't like my new attitude. I'm supposed to be glad about my trip and pretend that it never happened."

"I've heard the same thing. I didn't see you at the Hershbergers' house for church."

Getting back on her feet, Esther said, "I begged off, saying I was too tired. Really, I didn't want to face Abbie and Violet."

"Have you seen them since we got back?"

Looking miserable, Esther nodded. "Violet came over on Thursday morning."

"She didn't waste any time, did she?"

"Nope. And to make matters worse, she was just as caustic and hurtful to me as she used to be to you. I'm sorry, but she even asked if I saw you in Pinecraft."

"What did you tell her?" Mary braced herself for Esther saying she lied so she wouldn't have to deal with Violet being mean.

Esther took a deep breath, then blurted, "I told her that I saw you the entire time and that we'd become friends."

"Really?" She was shocked but also felt vindicated. She might have misread everything between her and Jayson, but she hadn't been wrong about her and Esther.

"Of course, really. Oh, I'm not gonna lie and tell you that Violet was nice about it, but I didn't care." Her eyes lit up. "Once she realized that she couldn't bully me around, she left. I didn't even walk her to the door!"

"Esther, you showed her!"

She giggled. "Right?"

"I'm really proud of you."

"Danke. I'm kind of proud of myself too. It wasn't easy to stand up to Violet, but I'm so glad I did."

"What are you going to do now?"

"Do what I always do. Work and save."

"Have you heard from Michael?"

She nodded. "I received two letters from him on Thursday." Looking dreamy, she said, "He was so sweet. And the things he writes! It's like he's been reading my mind."

"He's perfect for you."

"He is. I canna believe he's so young, but I guess the Lord doesn't care about that."

"I don't think anyone would guess that he's not even twenty yet. He seemed really mature."

"He is. He needs to be, though." She lowered her voice. "Mary, I feel so sorry for him. He's so alone in the world. Even though his aunt and uncle have taken him in, they aren't very giving or kind. He's had to rely on the Lord, his friends, and even his coworkers for help and support."

"He seems kind, though. Maybe that was all he needed. Plus, he has you now too."

"I'd like to think that I can make a difference, but like us with Betsy and Lilly, we're far apart." She shrugged her shoulders. "It's like all of us have made connections, but we're stuck living so far away from each other."

"I've been thinking the same exact thing. My parents keep saying that vacation is over, though. Like none of our friendships were real."

"But they were." Esther's voice was firm. "Hey, do you remember the conversation we all had on the bus?"

Mary knew the conversation Esther was referring to. The bus had just crossed the bridge into Ohio, and Toby had announced that they were only twenty minutes from stopping in Cincinnati. "The four of us agreed that anything was possible to do with God's help . . . if we put our minds to it."

"I still believe that. Do you?"

"Yes. I mean, look at us!"

"Right? If the two of us can become good friends, then all sorts of miracles can happen." Looking determined, Esther added, "We'll figure our futures out, Mary. I know we will. We just have to hope and pray and stay positive."

"I'm so glad you came over. I . . . well, I'm afraid I was starting to doubt myself again."

"We need to make plans. Want to come over to my house on Tuesday? I work at the hotel tomorrow."

"I do." She smiled.

"Gut. Come over at ten."

"Now, tell me all about you and Michael. Have you talked to him on the phone yet?"

Cheeks pink, Esther started talking. When she left an hour

later, Mary felt almost as good as when she'd been standing on the beach in Siesta Key. Yes, her heart was still battered by Jayson's duplicity, but she had something else that mattered just as much. She now had a good friend in Trail.

That was a blessing, indeed.

31

Michael had been right. The Lord gave them all gifts . . . and He also gave them hearts and brains and faults and opportunities. Esther decided to use them.

Two weeks after going over to Mary's house and sharing their stories, Esther had made a huge decision. She was going to go back to Pinecraft.

She wasn't going to just go for a visit this time, though. She intended to stay.

After discussing it with Mary several more times, Esther had asked Mary to stand by her side while she called Nancy at the Marigold Inn. Hands shaking, Esther asked for a job. Actually, she asked if she could clean rooms in exchange for room and board. Nancy sounded surprised by the idea but didn't say no right away. She asked Esther for her phone number and said she'd be in touch.

And she had. Three days later, Nancy left her a message that was filled with positive news. Not only was she willing to allow Esther to clean for room and board, but if things worked out, she would be willing to pay her for her services too.

Since she had money saved, Esther bought a one-way bus ticket. She felt terrible about leaving her new friend, but Mary had been the one who had encouraged Esther. Mary had even said that she was going to move somewhere else too. If not Florida, then near Betsy or Lilly.

All that was why Esther was once again standing in the parking lot in Berlin, waiting for the Pioneer Trails bus to arrive.

Her parents weren't happy with her. She didn't blame them and even understood their confusion about her sudden change of plans. Daed had even lost his temper, telling her that gallivanting around the country to find happiness wasn't what the Lord intended for well-brought-up young ladies of the Amish faith.

Esther wasn't so sure about that, however. Actually, she was pretty sure He'd had a big role in her decision. After all, who else could have put Michael in her life when the only reason she'd gone down to Florida had been to apologize to Mary?

Knowing her father would like the idea that she believed God was calling her back to Florida even less than he'd like the idea that she was leaving of her own volition, Esther had held her tongue.

She wasn't wavering. She wasn't a child, and she'd found not only a place to live but also a job. Her heart was proclaiming that she needed to go back to Florida. Needed it as much as she needed sustenance.

Her mother had brought her to the stop in Berlin, which was a large parking lot next to an older building filled with stores that catered to the Amish.

After they learned that the bus would be thirty minutes late, her mamm decided to go shopping. There was a drugstore, a market, a bookstore, and a thrift store. She tried to convince

Esther to visit each place too, but Esther refused. Practically all of her belongings were surrounding her feet. She'd even paid extra to take so much. The last thing she wanted to do was cart even more items—she still had no idea how she was going to get her suitcases to the Marigold Inn.

Besides, she was content to enjoy the relatively temperate day. The April clouds had broken and the sun was shining. It was also in the high forties. Still cold but not unbearable.

"I heard you were leaving today," a familiar voice said. "I guess it's true."

Esther was surprised to see Abbie but supposed she shouldn't have been. She'd heard through the grapevine that her two former friends were still expecting her to beg them to take her back. "Hey, Abbie."

"Hey."

Abbie was standing awkwardly in front of her. Her usually pretty features were pinched. She looked completely uncomfortable. When Abbie didn't say anything more, Esther scanned the parking lot. If she was about to be lectured by the two of them, she might as well be prepared. "Where's Violet?"

"I don't know." Her pale gray eyes looked completely confused. "She and I haven't been getting along all that well of late."

"I'm not surprised." Now that she had the gift of distance, Esther realized just how toxic their relationship had been. It was like they needed someone to hurt in order to be kind to each other. When Mary was out of their lives—along with some of the other men and women from their circle whom they'd kept at a distance—Abbie and Violet had focused on Esther. Now that she was leaving, it made sense that the two of them would turn on each other.

Abbie motioned to the empty side of the metal bench. "May I join you for a spell?"

"Why do you want to do that?" She felt for Abbie, but she sure didn't want to have part of her last hour in Ohio be full of malicious spite.

"I didn't want you to leave without talking with you one last time."

"You can sit, but I'm not sure that we have much to say to each other." No way was she going to sit there while Abbie either talked badly about Mary or attempted to convince Esther to stay.

Looking resigned, Abbie joined her on the bench. Abbie was slight and willowy. Despite her gray eyes, pale complexion, and strawberry-blond hair, she'd always been the most striking of the three of them. Now, however, she just looked washed out, like the light that was inside her had been extinguished.

"I don't know what happened to us, Esther," she said at last. "When we were little girls, we seemed happy. I remember making Valentines for everyone in our school."

"I did the same thing."

Still looking confused, Abbie added, "We played with everyone, right? I mean, I'm not remembering that wrong, am I?"

"Nee. You're not remembering that wrong at all."

A line formed between her brows. "I don't know what happened." She shifted to face Esther. "When did it become okay to be so awful to other people? I don't remember a specific time when everything changed. Do you know?"

"That's the problem. It wasn't okay. It never was . . . and we did it anyway."

Abbie tensed, then nodded. "You're right. Whenever I think

about how much hurt I caused over the years, I'm just as ashamed as my parents said I should be."

"I've been ashamed too."

"Have you made peace with it yet?"

As reluctant as Esther was to discuss their actions with Abbie in the middle of the parking lot, she realized that it might be their last opportunity. Even if she returned to Trail next week, she wasn't going to seek out Abbie to discuss their past.

"Nee," she said at last. "I haven't made peace with my actions. I mean, I've been trying, but I'm not there yet. The Lord and I are working on it." She meant that sincerely too. There was no way she was going to be able to be the person she wanted to be without His help.

"I've learned a lot from Mary Margaret too," she added. "Mary and the other girls I met have taught me much about forgiveness, both about seeking it and about forgiving oneself."

"Is that why you're going back to Pinecraft? Because you have some new friends there?"

There was so much bitterness in Abbie's voice, it almost made Esther want to start laughing. Her former friend's concerns were twisted, and the things she was concerned about were so silly and so narrow. It was obvious that she wasn't looking for a change of heart; she simply wanted things to be how they used to be.

"I'm leaving because I need a change."

"You don't have to leave for things to change." Her voice sounded desperate. "If you and I became close again, Violet would come around—I know she would. And then the three of us would be unstoppable again."

"Abbie, that isn't going to happen. Even if I stayed, I would never want that."

"But if we don't have each other, what do we have?"

252

"That's what you need to figure out."

"It's time you went on home, Abbie," Esther's mother said from over her shoulder. "Esther is moving on, and it's time you did too. Ain't so?"

Abbie jumped to her feet like she'd been caught with her hand in the cookie jar. "I didn't see you there, Mrs. Lapp."

Her mother didn't even smile. "Good day, dear."

"Jah. Good day." After taking three steps forward, she looked back at Esther. "Goodbye."

"Bye."

Her mother joined her on the bench. "You know, I've been so sad thinking about you leaving. But now that I overheard everything you said to Abbie, I completely understand." Reaching out to clasp her hand, she murmured, "It is time for you to look forward, isn't it?"

"I have to, Mamm. Just because I'm going doesn't mean I love you and Daed any less. It's that I want to love myself too. I can't do that here." Plus, there was a certain man in Pinecraft she couldn't stop thinking about.

Her mother folded her other hand over Esther's. "Just this morning, your father realized that it's possible for us to take bus trips to Pinecraft as well. I predict a trip to Florida is in our plans very soon."

"Nothing would make me happier," Esther said as the bus pulled in at long last.

Together they watched the bus stop and none other than Toby hop out. "If you're here for the 11:15 to Pinecraft, come on over. I want to board as quickly as possible. We've got time to make up for."

Feeling a burst of excitement, Esther got to her feet. "I love you, but I've got to go."

Her mother kissed her on the cheek. "Write to me often. Call and leave a message on the phone shanty too. Promise?"

"I promise."

"And be careful."

"I will, Mamm."

"And—"

It seemed like half the bus riders were already either in line or on board. "Mother, I really do have to go."

"Don't forget that we love you and are proud of you."

Esther gave her a hug. "I won't ever forget that. Danke, Mamm." She pulled away and started carting her things to the luggage handlers. She felt her mother move away and mix in with the crowd.

Esther felt a pang of sadness but didn't look back. After all, she had a lot to do. Toby was right, she had a lot of time to make up for. It was time to get started.

32

The customer batted her eyes at him in such a way that Michael couldn't tell if she was actually flirting or simply having a bit of fun making him uncomfortable. He seriously hoped it wasn't the first. If she was having a bit of fun at his expense, he felt like he should give her an award. He didn't know when he'd felt so uneasy.

If only she would pay the bill and leave!

She leaned back in her chair and crossed her legs. "Are you sure you don't want to go out with us? The Beachcomber is only a block away. We'd have a grand time."

"I'm sure. Let me know when you're ready to take care of your check." As he turned around, Michael heard one of the women chastise the flirty lady.

"You're making a spectacle of yourself, Sandra. You need to stop."

"Stop what?"

"Stop flirting with that Amish boy."

Gritting his teeth, he strode past the bar and into the kitchen. Marco, the chef, and three of the other servers and sous-chefs looked up when he leaned against the wall.

"Uh-oh, is she still creeping on you, Michael?" Valerie, the head server, asked.

"I think so." He shrugged. "Or it might be that she's determined to make me feel as uncomfortable as possible."

"And . . . it looks like she succeeded," Marco said.

"She has. I've waited a lot of tables, but I've never had a customer like her before."

Kim strode through the doors. "Have any of you seen Michael?"

"I'm right here," he said. "Is my table ready for me to take their check?"

"They left. I walked over to them after you left and told them that it was time to leave. I wouldn't move until they handed me a credit card."

"You did that?" Valerie asked. "Seriously?"

"Seriously." Still looking annoyed, Kim added, "I don't like them being disrespectful to my staff, and I don't like them disturbing our other guests. We're a fine dining restaurant, not a bar. I told her that too."

"I was trying to encourage them to be on their way," Michael said. "I'm sorry you had to deal with them."

"I'm not. I'd had enough of their antics. Just because someone is dining at our restaurant doesn't mean they get to torture all of you."

Michael pushed away from the wall. "I'll go clear the table." Bussers usually did that, but he didn't mind.

"No need. Joel cleared the table." Walking to his side, she patted his arm. "I'm sorry that woman was being such a pill."

"I could take it."

"I know, but enough was enough! That fool woman was practically propositioning you!"

"She asked him to go to the Beachcomber," Valerie added.

Kim raised one eyebrow. "I hope you said no."

"Of course I said no. One, she's old enough to be my mother, and two, I'm Amish. I don't drink or go to bars." Of course there was a third reason too. He had no interest in any other girls except for Esther.

"I'm sorry, I shouldn't have even joked about that." Still looking upset, Kim added, "Listen, you worked a double shift today. Go find Cutter, settle your tips, and then head on home. You deserve a break."

Michael wouldn't normally agree to leave early, but he really was ready to get out of there. Ever since Esther left, his nerves had been frayed. He missed her something fierce, and simply writing her every day wasn't making him feel better. "Thanks," he said at last. "I'll see if Joel needs any help, then get on my way."

"Are you sure?" Valerie asked. "We can help you out."

"Thank you, but I'm sure." When he walked back into the dining room, only one table was still occupied, and it was in Joel's station. Joel was standing near the bar, wiping down salt and pepper shakers, so Michael joined him. "Thanks for clearing that table."

"It wasn't a problem." Brightening, he added, "Those ladies left you a good tip, buddy. I handed it off to Cutter."

"Thanks."

Cutter, the assistant manager, was in the back room on the computer. When Michael walked in, he grinned. "Here you go, buddy," he said as he handed Michael a thick envelope. "I don't know if this will make you happier, but you've had a good day."

"It will. Danke." He slipped the envelope into his pants pocket.

"No worries, Mike." Just as Michael was taking off his black apron and putting on his regular jacket, Cutter added, "Listen, for what it's worth, you handled that cougar like a pro. Women like that aren't easy."

"It took me a while to figure out what was going on."

Cutter grinned. "That's why we love you, buddy. You might be the best-looking waiter in Sarasota, but there's still something about you that's adorably innocent."

Ten minutes after that, Michael was exiting the front door and more than ready to collapse. He didn't take double shifts very often, but Kim had been in a bind. Plus, since he took the promotion, he only had a little bit more left to save in order to pay the first and last months' rent on the apartment he'd found. He needed to get out of that house. His aunt and uncle had been acting worse and worse. Paul even mentioned raising his rent.

"Michael?"

His body tensed until he realized that his ears weren't deceiving him. "Esther." Her name came out in a whisper—he was having a difficult time even breathing.

There she was, wearing a plum-colored dress, white tennis shoes, and a fleece jacket. So wholesome and pretty.

He was by her side in seconds. "I can't believe you're here. It's like I dreamed you up."

She chuckled. "I'll take that as a good sign?"

"You should take it as the very best sign." Unable to help himself, he kissed her chastely on the cheek. "Why were you out here?"

"When I peeked in, you were still working. I didn't want to bother you."

"You should've come in. They would've remembered you and given you a place to sit." Honestly, Kim, Joel, and anyone else standing nearby would've treated Esther like a queen. Everyone at the restaurant knew how special she was to him.

"I'm glad I sat out here. It was fun to see you in action."

He was just glad she hadn't heard that woman propositioning him. "Esther, tell me why you're here."

"I couldn't stay away," she said. They were standing under a light post. Its beam of light illuminated her skin and allowed him to see her eyes. They looked worried.

Was she honestly worried about how he would react to that?

He had so much to say to her, but there was no way he wanted to say it standing in front of his restaurant. "Let's go someplace else to talk. Where are you staying?"

"The Marigold Inn." She took a deep breath, then added, "Nancy's allowing me to clean rooms in exchange for room and board."

He felt like he was about a mile behind where she was. "Esther, I'm still trying to keep up. What are you saying?"

"I've missed you. I was also ready to leave Trail. It was time . . . so I decided to move to Pinecraft."

She made it sound so simple. "When did you get here?"

"Today."

"Why did you keep it a secret? I would've helped you. At the very least I would've met your bus and helped you get settled."

"I wanted to surprise you." She lowered her voice. "I also wanted to do this for myself. You know, in case maybe I was being too forward."

"Not at all."

Smiling at last, Esther said, "I don't know what to do now."

"I do." Making a decision, he took her hand, opened the restaurant's door, and walked her through the dining room. All the waitstaff looked their way.

"Michael, do you need something?" Kim asked.

"Jah. May I . . . may I take Esther here to the staff room for a moment?"

Kim looked taken aback, but her eyes twinkled. "Of course, Michael. Take your time."

He was sure he heard laughter, but he ignored everything as he led Esther through the back door, turned down a narrow hallway to the right, and eventually ended up in the staff's break room. It was completely empty.

When he closed the door behind them, Esther pulled her hand away. Her face was bright red, and her blue eyes were darker than usual. She was beyond flustered. "Why are we here?"

"Because I couldn't wait another second to do this," he said as he leaned down and kissed her.

Esther stiffened, then melted against him.

When he looked into her eyes again, he said, "I love you dearly, Esther. Seeing you here, having you in my arms again . . . well, it's made me the happiest man in the world."

Esther blinked, then smiled again. "Gut," she said. "Because I love you too."

33

Usually, making cards made Mary happy. She loved creating new designs, using the stamps, adding special touches like glitter and tiny rhinestones, and containing them all in her signature light green satin ribbon.

Today, however, as she was doing her best to finish a big order of twenty-five assorted greeting cards for the Carlisle Inn, Mary couldn't deny the irony of it. She was as down as she'd ever been—and she was spending her day stamping drawings of tiny field mice, chipmunks, and birds and writing positive, whimsical messages.

"How's it going?" Mamm asked.

"Only three more to go after this one." She carefully pushed the "You're a special friend" card in her mother's direction. It had a pair of mice, one holding a tiny teapot, the other holding a little tray of cookies. It was nauseatingly sweet. "What do you think?"

"Look how adorable these little mice are! I tell you, Mary, your cute mice almost make me forget how much I dislike them."

"That's the plan."

"Is this your last order for the week?"

She nodded. "I can't believe how popular they've been lately."

"I saw Suzanna at Walnut Creek Cheese while you were gone. She said that once a few ladies took pictures of your pretty note cards and displayed them on Facebook, everything took off like hotcakes. They had triple the amount of orders in no time at all."

"I'm glad for that."

"It is a blessing." She smiled. "I know you are still blue, dear. I'm proud of you for not letting it get you down too much."

"Danke. I have had many tough days, but things do seem to be getting better." At least she wasn't crying at the drop of a hat anymore.

"Maybe you'll be able to use some of your hard-earned money to see either Lilly or Betsy . . . or maybe even Esther in Pinecraft."

Her mother was being so kind, especially since she still didn't understand how she and Esther had gone from being enemies to good friends so quickly.

She nodded. "I'd like to plan a trip. We'll see." The only problem was that she still wasn't sure where she wanted to go. She kept praying for guidance, but all the Lord ever seemed to do was encourage her to give her worries to Him. She appreciated that, but she would also be grateful for a road map!

Her mother's smile faltered. "Well, now. I'll let you get back to work. I'll make some tea. Come have some whenever you are finished."

"Okay. Danke, Mamm."

"Of course, dear."

Mary stood up. "Hey, Mamm? I just want to thank you for putting up with me these last few weeks. I know I haven't been easy to be around."

"You've been finding your way. There's no need to thank us for that—especially since Daed and I finally decided to get out of your way." Just as she was about to add something else, the doorbell chimed. "Maybe your big order of card stock arrived!"

As her mother darted down the hall, Mary called out, "If it did, call me and I'll put it away." After hearing the door open but not her mother's voice, she sat back down.

After a moment or so, she heard her mother talking about a mile a minute. So it definitely was not a delivery man.

When her mother giggled, Mary smiled. Obviously one of her mother's many friends had come over for a chat. Guessing that it was likely one of the women her mother was working a mud sale with, Mary mentally shrugged. Life really did continue, no matter what.

Pushing thoughts about her mother's friend out of the way, she started on another card. This one said "Your friendship is a bounty of blessings." She added a tiny bird perched on a branch singing. Trying not to roll her eyes at the woodland creatures that were looking up at it with tender smiles, she picked up a fine-tip yellow marker and began carefully coloring the songbird.

"Mary Margaret, look who's here!"

"Just a minute, Mamm. Let me finish this card."

"Nee. You need to come say hello now."

Determined to finish the card, she called out, "Mother, I'm almost done. Just give me two more minutes."

She ignored the quiet chatter in the background, choosing instead to finish drawing the chipmunk and mentally prepare herself to visit nicely with her mother's friend for the next hour.

"I couldn't resist seeing you here."

Everything inside her froze. Surely she was only imagining . . .

"Mary, when you told me that you drew pictures on greeting cards, you sold yourself short. These cards are far more than that. They're amazing."

She turned her head as his voice registered. Met his dark

blue eyes. Her hand slid, making a bold black mark across the entire card. Ruining it.

She couldn't care less.

"Jayson?"

"Jah, it's me." He stood tall and still. Watched her intently. Wariness seemed to electrify the air around him.

Or maybe just her.

Feeling shaky, she got to her feet and turned to face him. "You're here. Here in Trail." Yes, it was obvious, but what could she do? It was as if her brain needed another thirty seconds to catch up with what her eyes were seeing.

"I am. I brought my sister with me too."

"You brought Joy?"

"Oh jah. She refused to stay away. Actually, she said I would need her help." He lifted one shoulder. "I reckon she was probably right."

"So, she's talking with my mamm right now?"

"Jah, though it's doubtful your mother is getting a word in edgewise." His smile broadened. "Prepare yourself, Mary. My sister is a force of nature and she canna wait to meet you. She . . . well, at times, she can be a lot to handle."

"Why?"

"Why?" A line formed between his brows. "She's only exuberant. That's all. She just happens to be especially happy because she knows how important you are to me." Jayson was talking in circles.

"You know that isn't what I meant."

He nodded. "I know. But, Mary, I think you know why I'm here, ain't so? It's because I couldn't stay away."

"But . . . what about Ellen? What about your agreement with her father? And the job? And the money and your promises?"

264

He folded his hands behind his back. "Well now, it seems that it's almost as easy to break things off as it is to put them into motion." He stepped closer. "Mary, from practically the minute I left your side, I knew I had made a mistake. I hated hurting you, but I felt stuck. I didn't know what to do."

"What did you do?"

"I talked to Danny, and he went home to Crittenden County with me. Then we talked to Joy, who wasn't shy about sharing her opinions about the choices I've been making lately."

"And then?"

"And then I spoke with Ellen and her father and my daed. I'm not going to lie. None of those conversations were easy, but there's something to be said about speaking from one's heart. It's freeing."

"Freeing," she repeated. When he held out a hand, she ignored it. "That's what you've been doing all this time?"

Lowering his hand, he nodded. "It takes a while to unravel a mess of bad choices, Mary. It also takes time to get back on track. But that's what I've done."

"I see."

Jayson's expression remained pained but earnest. "I know you have every reason to refuse to give me the time of day, but I'm asking you to do it anyway." After a deep breath, he added, "Mary, will you please come out and speak with me?"

"That's all?"

"That's all."

She knew he'd come a long way to see her. But he'd also broken her heart. What if all he wanted to do was apologize and then be on his way?

Would she be able to survive that?

"Please say yes," a merry voice called out from the doorway.

Mary peeked around Jayson. Standing there was the feminine version of Jayson. A pretty girl with brown hair and dark blue eyes. She was also smiling ear to ear.

Jayson continued to gaze only at her. "Go away, Joy."

His sister looked crestfallen. "But—"

"Give us a minute."

"Fine." Joy turned around and flounced off.

Mary couldn't help but smile. The girl might be the apple of her brother's eye, but she was also fourteen years old.

"I told you she was a lot to handle."

"She might not be the only one in her family who's like that."

His voice lowered. "I reckon you're right." He swallowed. "Mary, please let me explain. I . . . I really need you to do that. Please."

She had been hurt, but she wasn't heartless. She'd also grown up a bit and realized that no one was perfect. Not Esther, not Jayson, and certainly not her. People made mistakes all the time.

But people could also learn from them and make amends.

Feeling like she was in a dream, she finally stepped closer, taking in every detail as she did. Once again, his good looks practically took her breath away. She had definitely not exaggerated that in her mind.

But what caught her heart and made her pulse race was the way he was looking at her. Jayson was staring at her like she was the prettiest thing he'd ever seen. No, maybe the most special thing he'd ever seen. Like she was everything to him.

"I still can't believe you're here," she said. "I never thought I'd see you again."

"I can't believe I waited so long."

It had only been a couple of weeks. He'd been busy too.

Under the circumstances, his comment felt a bit over the top. Or maybe it was the sweetest thing she'd ever heard in her life.

He held out a hand again. "Please, come meet my annoying sister, Joy."

Mary knew she shouldn't take his hand. Nothing had been resolved. Nothing really.

But still feeling as if she were in a dream, she did as he asked. Truly, if she was in a dream, she didn't want to wake up.

The minute their hands touched, she felt a tingling, as if sparks were flying between them. Jayson must have felt it too, because he seemed to falter for a second before curving his palm around hers.

Ten steps down the short hallway brought her face-to-face with her mother and Joy. Her mother was sitting on the sofa.

Joy, on the other hand, was practically bobbing on the balls of her feet. "Hiya. I'm Joy."

She indeed was joy personified. "I'm pleased to meet you. Jayson spoke much about you."

The girl's smile widened. "Jayson's said a whole lot about you too."

"Well, I haven't heard enough," her mother teased. "Mary, why don't you join them, and I'll get everyone something to eat."

"I can do that, Mamm."

"Oh no. You sit down and keep them company. Take their coats!"

"Mei bruder didn't want to do anything besides see you when we got here," Joy explained.

"I think Mary figured that out," Jayson murmured.

She shook her head, hoping to remove the giddy daze she was currently experiencing. "I'll take your coats."

Joy was holding a navy cloak in her arms. She handed it to Mary while Jayson unbuttoned his own black coat. Then, refusing his offer to help, she placed them on the hooks by the front door. When her back was to them, she gave in to temptation and silently screamed. Jayson was here, he was looking at her like she was wonderful, and Ellen was no longer in his life.

They had much to get through, of course, but she couldn't help but give a prayer of thanks. Even if Jayson and she were only meant to be friends, she was so glad to see him again.

She turned around. Jayson and his sister were looking out the windows.

"Is this your patio?" Joy asked.

"Jah. Mei father planted all the bushes around it. In the summer we sit outside a lot."

"It's verra fine."

"Danke."

"Here you all are," her mother announced as she brought in a tray filled with three mugs and a plate of chocolate-orange marble cake.

"Aren't you going to join us, Mamm?"

"Nee, I don't think so. Not yet, anyway." Smiling sweetly at Joy, she said, "Dear, maybe in a little while, you'd like to visit with me in the kitchen?"

"Of course."

"Not yet, though, okay?" Jayson asked her.

"Don't worry. I wouldn't miss this for anything."

Sitting down to join them at last, Mary wondered what he was going to say. Was he coming to make amends . . . or simply to end things in a better manner?

She was afraid to hope.

34

Jayson's entire body was humming. It literally felt as if every nerve ending was frayed. Open-ended. Waiting for Mary to give him a signal so he'd know how to respond.

So far, she hadn't given him much.

After greeting Joy, taking their coats, and joining them in the living room, she'd sat down on the chair next to the fireplace. She smiled at Joy, chatting with his sister about the bus ride and Berlin.

She barely looked at him.

It was evident that she was biding her time until he told her the things she was hoping to hear. Mary was a sweet woman. So very kind. But he had a feeling that if he didn't speak from his heart very soon, he was going to lose the opportunity.

He started to sweat.

How was he going to be able to phrase everything just right? How was he going to be able to convey in a meaningful way how much she meant to him without scaring her half to death?

The task seemed almost insurmountable.

Lord, I know I've been praying and praying, but I really need You right now, he begged silently.

When lightning didn't strike and bells didn't ring in the distance, Jayson knew the Lord was letting him know that He'd already done the hard part. He had put the two of them together.

It was up to Jayson to take it from there. He hoped he could.

Another fifteen seconds passed.

A bit of Joy's smile faded as he continued to fret. After taking a sip of coffee, she lightly kicked his shin. "Jayson, say something."

Whether Mary was enjoying Joy's bossiness or the fact that he was likely going to be sporting a bruise on his shin, Jayson didn't know. But her expression did seem to have lifted when she neatly folded her hands in her lap.

It was time. For better or worse, he could only speak from his heart and hope it was enough.

"Mary, I'm so sorry for everything. I know I already apologized, but I want you to know that I've regretted everything I put you through since we parted."

"He really has. He's been really upset," Joy chimed in. "I told him he was being stupid too."

"That's true. And it was no less than I deserved. Even my father thought my plan was terrible." He sighed. "And so I came clean. I went to Wood's haus and told him that I didn't want to work for him. And then I told Ellen that we would never suit. I told them both that I was going to move to Pinecraft and take the job at Pinecraft Construction."

"How did Ellen take your announcement?"

"Better than I thought, until I realized that I'd been forgetting one important thing—she wanted to be happy too."

"But what about Joy?" Mary asked. "Sorry, Joy, I don't mean to speak about you like you aren't here, but I thought you needed your brother to stay near you in Kentucky."

"I do. I mean, I would like to live near him because he's always been the person I've depended on the most." She smiled. "So that is why I'm going to move to Pinecraft too."

"Your father allowed that?"

"He wasn't real happy, until I reminded him that I am fourteen now." She lifted her chin. "I'm practically an adult."

"There's also the matter of insurance," Jayson said. "My job at Pinecraft Construction offers insurance. Even though we Amish don't usually accept such things, I realize it is a good thing to have if one has diabetes. We made arrangements for me to have her on my insurance." Resting his elbows on his knees, he said, "Joy and I decided to take us living together for six months and see how it goes. It might not work out real well."

"I might not like him telling me what to do all the time," Joy said.

Jayson shrugged. "Our father agreed to that idea."

"I see." Mary smiled. "Well, I'm, ah, pleased for you both."

"You still haven't told her why you're here, Jayson. You need to do that, I think." Standing up, Joy walked toward the kitchen. "I'm going to go find your mother, Mary." After sending one long, meaningful look to her brother, Joy disappeared.

Jayson could hear Mrs. Miller greet Joy in a happy voice. Seconds later, they were giggling like schoolchildren. "I guess your mamm was waiting for her."

"I guess so."

Looking into her pretty brown eyes, feeling their warmth, he knew it was time to stop searching for all the right explanations and just speak from his heart.

At last, everything became easy. "I have fallen in love with you, Mary Margaret Miller. That's why I broke things off with Ellen. That's why I'm here. Yes, I needed to explain everything, apologize again, and beg you to not give up on us. But really, the main reason I came here was to tell you how I felt." Taking a breath, he said, "I really do love you, Mary. I know that I've disappointed you and that I might no longer be the man of your dreams, but I really do care about you. I love you with all my heart."

Her lips parted, but she didn't speak.

He took that as a signal that he should move closer. He moved to her side, reached for her hands, and brought one up to his lips.

Her eyes widened, but still she said nothing.

His insides plummeted. Though his brain seemed to be trying to tell him to take it easy, it was as if the rest of him couldn't do anything but move forward. He couldn't hold his words back if he tried.

"You don't need to love me back," he said in a rush. "I know it's going to take time to trust me. I . . . I'll wait as long as you want for you to feel the same. That is . . . if you think that one day you'll be able to forgive me." Realizing he still didn't know that, he blurted, "Do you think it's possible for you to one day forgive me enough to give us another chance?"

One second passed. Then another. Sweat formed on his neck. The only saving grace was that she still held his hands. Surely that meant something.

"Mary, I know you like to think things through and all, but your silence is killing me. Please, have some mercy on me and tell me what you're thinking. Even if it's bad, I can take it."

She laughed softly. "I'm sorry. I . . . I've been trying to figure out the right words to say. Not because I'm upset about what you said but because I'm not sure how to respond."

That sounded positive. "You don't have to worry about that

with me. Say whatever you want. Stumble over words, I don't care. Just don't keep me in the dark."

"All right then." She swallowed, lifted her chin a bit, then spoke. "Jayson, you know my story. You know you're the first man I've spent much time with. You know that you're the only man I've felt so strongly about. So, I think that means that I don't know a lot about falling in love. I'm not sure about what to say or how I'm even supposed to feel. I'm not even positive about forgiveness or apologies or expectations."

She released his hands and placed one of hers over her heart. "That's why the only thing I have to go by is what is here."

"And?"

She smiled. "And I know that I love you too. I loved you from practically the first moment we met, and it hasn't wavered since."

Love was shining in her eyes. Love, not doubt, not hope. Just a firm commitment. It was so true and so humbling.

Nee, it felt like grace. It felt like his gift for everything that he'd ever done for his family or for his own selfish desires. It was all those things wrapped up in one moment, and it was so perfect, so everything, it fairly took his breath away.

"Joy and I are going to move to Pinecraft. I've got a good job, and I'm going to work hard. I'm going to write you all the time and come up here as often as I can. I'm going to believe in us, continue to love you, and try to do everything I can to prove myself to you. And I'm going to be patient and wait for the day you'll be ready to say that you'll marry me."

Placing her hands back in his, she looked him in the eye. "I'm going to write you every day. I'm going to work on my cards and save my money. I'm going to visit you and Joy in Pinecraft as much as I can. I'm going to believe in us too. I'm going to pray for you and for us. I'm going to be patient and trust in our future. And I'm not going to waver, Jayson. No matter what happens, I will still love you."

Still holding hands, he leaned just close enough to brush his lips against hers. It was sweet. It was a promise.

And it was everything he'd ever hoped for—and so much more than he'd ever dared to dream was possible.

Epilogue

FIVE MONTHS LATER

The day was beautiful. Blue skies and not too hot. Only a faint chance of rain showers was forecasted that afternoon. In a lot of ways, it was just like every other day in Pinecraft. To the three women sharing one end of the pew, however, the day was one to be savored.

"I can't believe we're together again," Lilly said to Betsy and Mary as she watched more people enter the roomy Pinecraft Amish Church on Hines Avenue. "It's been too long."

"Almost four months this time," Mary said. Looking at her two very best friends, she smiled. "Although, thanks to the many letters and phone calls we've shared, in some ways it feels like we just saw each other just a couple of days ago."

"It does, though in other ways, it feels like it's been two years since all three of us have been in the same room for a good chat," Betsy said. "Mei mamm has been teasing me all week, saying that her feelings were going to get hurt if I didn't quit counting the days until I got here."

Mary laughed. "I used to be that way too."

"Until you got married?" Lilly asked slyly.

"Jah. Until then." Not wanting to be apart from each other any longer, she and Jayson had married four months ago in a very small ceremony in her family's barn in Trail. Only about fifty people had attended their wedding, but it had been perfect—especially since she'd had both Betsy and Lilly there as her two maids of honor. They'd worn blue dresses just like hers, of course. Having them both at her side had made her happy day even more special.

"Ach, but you make me jealous," Betsy said. "All you ever do is look content."

"Sorry, but I canna help it." That was the truth too. Most days, she couldn't help but wear a permanent smile. She figured it created a bit of fun for anyone seeing her, but she didn't care. Everything seemed to make her smile these days. When Nancy saw her at Yoder's, she'd proclaimed that Mary wore a perpetual expression of married bliss. Mary didn't know if that was the case or not—all she did know was that she loved Jayson so much and hadn't regretted their quick engagement and quicker marriage for even a second. Life with him was good—better than she'd ever imagined it could be.

"I'd be worried about ya, except that Jayson looks just as happy," Betsy said.

Looking over at her husband, who was sitting on the other side of the aisle with all the men, Mary felt her expression warm even further.

If she appeared to be always happy, Jayson seemed even more so. No longer was he attempting to care for Joy and his father while juggling too many other responsibilities. Joy was living with them, enjoying the warm Florida sunshine, and volunteering at a nearby hospital. She had even talked to Jayson about entering a program to learn how to be a mentor for other children who'd been recently diagnosed with juvenile diabetes.

As if he felt her gaze resting on him, Jayson met her eyes and smiled.

Both girls sitting next to her giggled.

"I'm so happy for ya," Lilly whispered.

"Danke."

"I'm so happy that Joy is living with you two. Otherwise, I would always feel like a third wheel around you both," Betsy joked.

"You wouldn't, I promise. But jah, since Joy is there, you will have plenty of company." Looking over at Lilly, Mary added, "Now all we have to do is figure out how to get you to join us."

"I'm planning to come back for a long visit soon, but I don't think I'll be moving here anytime in the near future."

"I understand," she said. "Like we've been saying, the three of us are now pros at writing letters."

"Oh! Here she is," Betsy said.

As they watched Esther take her seat with Nancy, Mary sighed. "She looks so happy."

"She does. She's as beautiful as ever too."

"Michael canna seem to take his eyes off of her," Lilly pronounced.

"Th-that's as it should be," Betsy said.

When the preacher began speaking, all Mary's attention shifted to the service. For the next three hours, the big crowd listened to the speakers and followed the directives of the preachers, continuing the traditions that began many generations ago.

When it ended and Esther and Michael were man and wife, all three women had tears in their eyes.

"They are such a perfect couple," Lilly said. "Isn't that something? On paper, no one would ever place the two of them together. But in person, it is obvious that the Lord placed them in each other's path."

Mary agreed completely. "God has certainly been with all of us. After all, He put us together, didn't He?"

"The best day of my life was the day an ice storm hit Atlanta," Betsy said.

"I agree," Lilly said.

Reaching out, Mary held both their hands. "We better be careful. If we keep making friends and falling in love, we'll be wallflowers no more."

The other girls' laughter rang through the building, sounding like joy and happiness and everything bright.

The rest of the congregation smiled at the sound. After all, weddings should be filled with happiness and laughter. That's what love was for.

Longing for another escape to Pinecraft?

Turn the page for a sneak
peek at your next vacation with

Her Only Wish

COMING SOON

JUNE

It was a beautiful morning in Pinecraft. Once again, the sun was out, flowers were blooming, and there was the slight undercurrent of salt in the air. It was the kind of morning that made one want to look up into the cloudless sky and give thanks for the chance to experience such beauty.

That's why it was a real shame that Mary Margaret Raber was beginning to get on Betsy's nerves.

No, that wasn't exactly true. Mary had been grating on her nerves for a good fifteen minutes. It was only in the last two or three minutes that Betsy had decided she'd had enough. There was only so much unsolicited advice a girl wanted to get before drinking two cups of coffee.

"Do you hear what I'm saying, Betsy?" Mary asked.

Betsy pasted on a fake smile. "Jah. I've been hearing your words loud and clear."

"Whew. For a moment there, you were looking so confused I thought maybe I was giving you too much advice." Mary brushed a strand of blond hair from her cheek. "Jayson's told me that sometimes I have a tendency to go on and on."

"Don't worry. You were fine." She just wasn't going to take any of her friend's advice.

Relief entered Mary's light brown eyes. "Oh? Well, that's gut. Wonderful-gut."

Betsy smiled as she tapped her foot. Her friend needed to

281

wrap this lecture up real soon or else Betsy was afraid she was going to do that for her. Not that anyone would blame her.

The simple truth was that even though Mary had been married for barely a year, she was already acting as if she had all the answers.

About everything.

If Betsy didn't love her so much, she'd eagerly tell her girlfriend that this absolutely wasn't the case.

However, since Mary and Jayson had invited her to stay in their guest room for a whole month, Betsy did what she usually did with other people. She smiled, looked grateful, and mentally planned to do what she wanted anyway.

When at last Mary took a breath, she studied Betsy with a close eye. "You sure are quiet. Do you understand what I'm trying to tell you?"

"I do. Perfectly."

For the first time in the last hour, Mary looked wary. "Betsy, all I'm trying to say is that you only got here two days ago. I'm sure you're tired. Don't you think you need to get more rest?"

There was good manners and there was being coddled unnecessarily. "I do not. Now that we've had our chat, I'm going to head over to Snow Bird Golf Course and ask them about golf lessons."

Mary Margaret frowned. "Oh, all right. Well, yes. I guess I could rearrange my day. But we should go soon, since it's so warm out."

Mary was four months pregnant. She was still nauseous from time to time, always ready for a nap, and usually wanted to talk about her amazing husband Jayson, Jayson's wonderful-gut job, her pregnancy, or all things baby. Betsy didn't blame her one bit. If their positions were reversed, she'd probably feel the same way.

Perhaps they should have a talk after all. "May we go sit down?"

"Of course. Do you want to sit on the lanai?" Her voice was hopeful.

Their covered screen porch was lovely. "That's perfect. I'll get me another cup of coffee and you a glass of lemonade."

"Oh, you're the guest. I can get them."

"Mary Margaret, I'm going to be here for a month. Don't wait on me."

Betsy went to the kitchen, got more coffee, poured a glass of lemonade, and then joined Mary in the lanai.

The area was big enough to hold a table, four chairs, two cushioned lounge chairs, and a small love seat. Everything was done in greens and teal colors. There were festive, bright-colored pillows on everything, an outside carpet, and about five terra-cotta pots filled with blooming flowers.

"I know I've told you before, but this is my favorite spot in your house. It's so pretty out here," Betsy said as she sat down.

"It's mine too. Jayson built the addition himself a few months after we got married."

"He did a nice job."

"I think the baby is going to like being out here too."

"I'm sure she will."

Mary chuckled. "You are as certain about me having a girl as Jayson is about us having a boy."

"I can't help myself. I'm sure you're going to be rocking a sweet miniature version of yourself in here before you know it."

"Whatever the Lord wants is fine with me."

"I understand." Taking a fortifying sip of coffee, Betsy knew she couldn't delay the inevitable any longer. "I think we need to talk."

"I know. You don't want me trying to mother you, do you?"

Betsy stilled. "You knew what I was going to say?"

"We're good enough friends for me to know what your expression looks like when you've reached the end of your patience. You don't want to rest another two days, do you?"

She shook her head. "I not only don't want to do that, I'm not going to." Looking at her intently, she added, "Mary, I'm grateful to you and Jayson for your hospitality, but I tried to be up-front about what I wanted to do during my visit. I even told you that I didn't mind going to a motel."

"You staying in a motel by yourself was a terrible idea."

Betsy smiled at her. "It probably was. I am glad I'm here instead of a motel—but as much as I like you, I'm not going to give up my list."

"Your bucket list."

Betsy nodded. "I like to think of it as my life list."

Because Mary still looked skeptical, Betsy kept talking. "Don't you understand? All my life I've been standing on the sidelines watching everyone else try new things. I don't want to wait any longer."

"But your lungs . . . Betsy, you know your mother sent me a letter with all your medical history and doctor contact information."

"And you might recall that I was so mad at her for doing that I barely talked to her for a week."

"She wants you to be safe."

"She wants me to be five years old again. Don't you all think it would be strange if I didn't already have all that information? I'm twenty-three years old. Of course I have it!"

Mary Margaret flushed. "I . . . I should've realized that."

"I need you to stop acting like I can't tell when I need to use my inhaler or take breaks or call the doctor."

"You're right." She reached out and clasped Betsy's hand. "I'm so sorry. I'll be better."

"It's okay if you don't want to hold your tongue or you don't feel comfortable letting me do things. But if that's how it is, then let me stay someplace else. We'll still be able to see each other, you know."

"I want you here. I'll stop hovering. I promise."

"I'm going to hold you to that."

"You should." Looking sheepish, Mary added, "Jayson even told me last night that I was sounding too much like a mother hen."

Betsy smiled. "I knew I liked him."

Thirty minutes later, Betsy was walking down Bahia Vista road toward Snow Bird Golf Course. Soon after their talk, Mary Margaret had lain down to take a nap. She hoped she hadn't hurt her friend's feelings, but she was pleased with herself for initiating such an honest conversation. She'd gone through far too much to put her list aside.

The reminder of the many hospital visits and tests she'd had to endure made some of her happy mood fade. Those episodes had been painful and frightening. They'd also been exhausting, because she'd gotten into an unfortunate routine of worrying more about her mother's feelings than her own. She adored her parents and her older brothers, but for once she didn't want to do everything they wanted just to make them happy.

She'd given them an ultimatum a month ago, finally saying that she needed to be gone for a whole month and they needed to accept that fact. Or prepare themselves for her to move out permanently.

Pushing the dark thoughts away, she scanned the busy streets, looking for the golf course's sign.

And there it was. Snow Bird Golf Course, written in plain block letters in blue against a shiny black background. It was attractive and somehow looked very Plain at the same time. Maybe it was because of the utilitarian rectangular sign? She didn't know.

She turned down the narrow lane. And gasped. There, in front of her, was a hidden gem. A bright green golf course with yellow flags at each hole, wide limestone gravel paths, bright white golf carts, a driving range, putting green, and finally, the cutest little pale blue building with shiny black trim.

Picking up her pace, she walked toward it, stepping off of the limestone path and onto the soft green grass. Pleased with herself for not taking the meandering route, she looked around and gasped when she saw a tiny brown bunny.

"Aren't you cute?" she murmured. "Are there bunnies like you all over this place?"

The rabbit froze, then hopped away, vanishing in seconds. Figuring rabbits were rabbits, whether they lived in Kentucky or Florida, Betsy chuckled, then kept walking, scanning the vicinity as she went. There were hydrangea bushes, lovely flowering bougainvillea, and a small pond off to her right. Anxious to take it all in, she slowed her pace.

"Hey!"

She kept walking.

"Hey! Amish lady in the orange dress! Stop!"

She looked down at herself, realized the voice was calling out to her, and stopped—about three feet from where a golf ball zipped across the green. If she hadn't stopped, it would've hit her.

A golf cart zipped forward and stopped next to her. One of the men got out.

By his dress, he was obviously Amish too. Straw hat, short-sleeved shirt, long pants. He also had blond hair so bleached it looked white, blue eyes, and a really great tan.

"Hey, are you all right?" he asked.

"Jah. I d-don't know what h-happened." Hating that her stutter had returned, Betsy tried to calm herself. "D-do people really have to worry about d-dodging golf balls all the time?"

"They do when they're walking in the middle of the fairway," the other guy in the golf cart said. "What were you thinking?"

Stung by his rude tone, she propped one of her hands on her hip. "I-I was thinking that I needed to get to that b-building right there."

"Why didn't you stay on the cart path?"

"I-I didn't know I had to."

"Really?"

The man's voice was so filled with sarcasm, it took the edge off of her nervousness. "S-sorry, but you show me a sign that says stay off the grass and I'll do it. Otherwise, I think you need to mind your own business."

The man in the cart scowled at her. "I'm going ahead, August."

The man who had gotten off the cart—August, she supposed—looked like he was trying not to laugh. "Jah. You do that. I'm gonna help this lady here."

"You want me to wait for you?"

"Better not. There's a foursome two holes behind us."

When the cart drove off, August turned to her. "Come on," he said as he reached for her elbow. "We need to get back on the cart path so we don't get dinged."

Betsy hurried to the path but started to feel like she'd just made a complete fool of herself. "I'm guessing there aren't any signs because everyone knows not to walk on the grass?"

"I'm afraid so. But, um, I agree that a sign or two might be a good idea."

"You know, you really don't need to walk me to the building."

"I think I do."

"No, you don't. I was looking for the person who runs the golf course." She smiled, hoping she sounded far more confident than she felt. "I-I promise, I won't veer off the sidewalk again." She didn't want to offend him, but she wasn't there to be escorted like an errant child.

August looked bemused. "Actually, I was going there myself."

"Because?"

"Because I'm the manager of the course." They stopped in front of the sign mounted to the siding of the building. He pointed to the discreetly written words under Snow Bird Golf Course. August Troyer, Manager.

And then it hit her. "You're August."

"I am. I'm August Troyer, the manager of the golf course. I'm the guy who you came to see." His grin broadened. "What luck, huh?"

"Jah," she muttered as she followed him inside. It looked like they both had some explaining to do.

He was so self-assured. He was also handsome, personable, and very full of himself. And he knew she didn't know enough about golf to stay on the cart paths.

How in the world was she ever going to get up the nerve to ask him to teach her how to play golf?

All of the sudden, all her grand plans about completing all the things on her "life list" were starting to feel very overwhelming. Pretty much impossible.

Shelley Shepard Gray is the *New York Times* and *USA Today* bestselling author of more than one hundred books. Two-time winner of the HOLT Medallion and a Carol Award finalist, Gray lives in Colorado, where she writes full-time, bakes too much, and can often be found walking her dachshunds on her town's bike trail.

Meet Shelley

Find her at **shelleyshepardgray.com**

AND ON SOCIAL MEDIA AT

f ShelleyShepardGray 🐦 ShelleySGray 📷 shelley.s.gray